Death by Chocolate Frosted Doughnut

Death by Chocolate Frosted Doughnut

Sarah Graves

KENSINGTON BOOKS
www.kensingtonbooks.com

KENSINGTON BOOKS are published by

Kensington Publishing Corp.
119 West 40th Street
New York, NY 10018

All Kensington titles, imprints, and distributed lines are available at special quantity discounts for bulk purchases for sales promotion, premiums, fund-raising, educational, or institutional use. Special book excerpts or customized printings can also be created to fit specific needs. For details, write or phone the office of the Kensington Special Sales Manager: Attn.: Special Sales Department. Kensington Publishing Corp, 119 West 40th Street, New York, NY 10018. Phone: 1-800-221-2647.

Library of Congress Card Catalogue Number: 2019951361

ISBN-13: 978-1-4967-1134-2
ISBN-10: 1-4967-1134-3
First Kensington Hardcover Edition: March 2020

ISBN-13: 978-1-4967-1136-6 (ebook)
ISBN-10: 1-4967-1136-X (ebook)

10 9 8 7 6 5 4 3 2 1

Printed in the United States of America

Death by Chocolate Frosted Doughnut

One

"Ahoy, mateys!" yelled the pirates of Eastport, seizing the freshly baked treats we'd set out for them and gobbling them down.

Toll House cookies, chocolate pinwheels, and date-nut brownie bites vanished down their hatches, followed by gulps of milk. Then, brandishing their aluminum-foil cutlasses and pushing aside black construction-paper eye patches, they peered around for more.

One little seagoing villain strode boldly up to the counter in The Chocolate Moose, a small, chocolate-themed bakery on Water Street in the remote island village of Eastport, Maine.

The young scallywag was perhaps six years old, with a wide gap-toothed grin, bright blue eyes, and a mess of blond curls peeping out from beneath the black skull-patterned bandanna tied around his head.

"Rum!" he demanded, so I gave him more milk, and he took it grudgingly.

"A man," he remarked after he'd guzzled it, "can't get a decent drink around here nowadays."

He dragged the back of his hand roughly over his mouth, no doubt imitating the pirates in the movies they'd been showing at the arts center the week before the Eastport Pirate Festival, our little community's last big bash of the summer season.

The first day of the annual festival was here, and on the sidewalks townsfolk and visitors alike paraded in the costumes they'd been assembling all year: leather jerkins and black leather boots worn thigh high over fishnet stockings, tricorn hats with ostrich feather cockades, black eye patches, and gold hoop earrings.

The little pirate shoved his milk glass at me again. I clapped my hand over my mouth to keep from giggling at him.

Then my friend and bakery shop partner Ellie White emerged from the kitchen at the rear of The Chocolate Moose. She seized the pint-sized swashbuckler and eased him toward the door, where his crewmates had already exited.

"You hop along now with the rest of your buccaneer pals," she told the youngster, "before your ship sails without you."

Ellie and I had opened The Chocolate Moose two years earlier, baking and selling chocolate treats to local area residents and to the summer tourists who visited downeast Maine in droves. We didn't often need a bouncer in the shop, but when we did, she was it.

"Nice work," I said, taken aback by the number of used napkins and paper plates the junior pirates had left behind. The shop now looked as if real pirates had rampaged through it.

"Have a kids party, they said." Ellie sighed. "It'll be easy, they said."

For the festivities, she wore a scoop-necked white blouse with puffed sleeves trimmed elaborately in red ribbons, a black satin vest with gold embroidery, and a red satin skirt with a frilly black petticoat peeping from below its hem, the skirt snugly belted with a black silk sash.

The bold little pirate tried stealthily to come in again; she took his shoulders in her hands and turned him firmly.

"Shoo!" she said, scooting him out once more and locking the door.

With her strawberry blond hair curling-ironed into ringlets and a pair of gold studs twinkling in her ears, she was definitely the prettiest pirate queen any of us in Eastport had ever seen. Even rowdy little rapscallions obeyed her, too awestruck to sass back.

Also, this one's mouth had still been full of the chocolate snickerdoodle he'd grabbed on his way out the last time. It was among the sweets we'd baked for the children's cookie-tasting party, an event that had turned out to be more like a plague of locusts descending on a field.

"There," Ellie breathed in relief, leaning her back against the door. "Now we just have to clean up."

"Yes," I agreed weakly, taking in more of the party's aftermath. With its tall bay windows, a vintage glass-fronted display case, and small black cast-iron café tables lined up against the two exposed brick walls, ordinarily the Moose looked neat, sweet, and complete.

Now, though . . . even a glass jar of raspberries in syrup meant for the inside of a filled chocolate sponge cake had somehow managed to get smashed. The pool of sticky red juice spread over the floor made it look as if a bloody pirate battle had happened here.

"Where can I rent a bulldozer?" I added. The whole place looked plundered, including the tipped-over toothpick holder by the cash register and the place mats scattered about.

Under the stamped-tin ceiling, the old paddle-bladed fan turned slowly, stirring the sweet smells of baking and fresh coffee and shifting the paper plates smeared with whipped cream, frosting, and more of those red raspberries from the jar that hadn't gotten broken.

"Or possibly a steam shovel," I said, plucking up a place mat that turned out to have half a chocolate whoopie pie mashed into it.

"Jake," Ellie chided me affectionately, "don't worry. You just run downstairs for the bucket and mop while I tidy up and sweep the floor. We'll have it all put to rights in no time."

And that in a nutshell is my friend Ellie, so optimistic that if the universe should end some early morning in a sudden crashing together of suns and planets, she'll be there eagerly looking forward to whatever comes next while the sky falls all around her.

"And while you're there, grab another carton of napkins and some paper towels. Oh, and lock the door again, please. I opened it to let in the delivery truck driver earlier this morning."

I added paper supplies to my mental cellar list; kids think that napkins grow on trees, naturally, and use them with wild abandon—to hurl at one another, not for their messy faces.

Or their hands. Everything in the shop was sticky, and the glass display case looked as if the FBI had been collecting fingerprints on it. Sighing while resolving never to do this again—but I would, of course, because the Eastport Pirate Festival was an all-hands-on-deck volunteer affair—I put a fresh bottle of spray cleaner on the list, made a mental note to lock that cellar door the way Ellie had asked, and turned to go. But—

"Well?" Ellie inquired brightly. "What are you waiting for?"

"Um," I replied. "Just watching all the people outside."

Peg legs and hooks, fake wounds bloodied with cranberry juice, artificial scars, and teeth blackened with licorice all testified to the many dangers of piracy as a career, but no one seemed to care. Even the babies sported skull-and-crossbones-patterned diaper covers, their strollers wrapped in black bunting and flying the Jolly Roger.

Beyond them, in the air over the fishing pier, small drones swooped and soared while emitting loud snarling noises, their operators onshore working the controls of the devices intently.

"You're, uh, sure the mop and bucket are still in the cellar?" I said.

Across the street, a jester in a belled cap and curly-toed slippers expertly juggled grog bottles, gulping from each one as he caught it, then flinging it up again. Behind him in the early autumn sunshine, the bay spread wide and blue, sailboats skimming like white seabirds across it.

"Because I wouldn't want to go all the way down there just to find out they weren't . . ."

I unlocked the door and opened it, hoping those drones had the sense to stay away from the sailboats' billowing sails. Festival food smells floated deliciously on the brisk sea breeze: pizza, cotton candy, and fried dough, with Italian sausages and hot dogs coming in a close second.

"Or maybe I should go out and buy a new mop bucket," I went on, "seeing as lately we're so popular and profitable. . . ."

We'd done well at the cash register lately. At first a struggling, not-likely-to-survive enterprise, The Chocolate Moose had become a beloved institution on Water Street, soon relied upon to supply everything from massive wedding cakes to a few cookies for an afternoon treat.

"Yes, we can afford new equipment," Ellie agreed, but her violet eyes narrowed knowingly.

"Jake, are you still scared of that cellar?"

"Oh, of course not!" I retorted defensively, and it wasn't a complete lie. I had no problem with the cellar.

What was in it, though: spiders and insects and mice, oh my! Not to mention some mangy wharf rats; we hadn't the heart to trap them—or in my case, the stomach for emptying the traps afterward—so we used an electronic gadget that sent high-pitched sounds into their ears.

Of hungry cats meowing, I supposed, and it worked on the rats. But it had no effect on the dozen or so small brown bats hanging from the old beams down there, high-pitched sounds being their specialty, I supposed.

"I don't care who says those bats don't suck blood," I grumbled. "And even if they haven't before, there's always a first time."

"Hmm," Ellie said skeptically, but before she could ask me if I wanted one of those little boys to come back and protect me with his aluminum-foil sword, the bell over the shop door jingled.

"Ladies," said someone from behind me, and my heart sank. It was well-known food authority and TV personality Henry Hadlyme, his voice at once recognizable from his popular travel and food show, *Eat This!*

Suddenly I wished I was downstairs with the bats. He'd been in town only two days and already he'd made himself unwelcome pretty much everywhere with his oh-so-superior attitude and unpleasant remarks about everything, the restaurants especially. But there was no sense antagonizing him.

"Hello, Henry. What brings you in here this fine pirate-festival morning?"

He'd made sure to come in and introduce himself when he'd first arrived. From his pained tone and wrinkled nose as he'd eyed the place then, I'd thought we'd had ants in the display case, and his attitude hadn't improved.

The opposite, in fact. "*Mmph,*" he replied now, glancing around disdainfully at the mess left by the pirate party. "Keeping the shop in good order as usual, I see."

Hadlyme was in his forties, I estimated, with frizzy yellow hair, pale gray eyes, and a jaw that could've doubled as the Rock of Gibraltar. He wore a black turtleneck, bleached-out jeans, and a blood-red leather jacket that looked as if it cost a mint, plus the sourest expression I'd seen since Ellie forgot to put sugar in the lemonade.

With a moue of distaste, he gingerly plucked a crumpled

napkin from one of the tables and dropped it atop the already overflowing wastebasket.

"Really, ladies, I don't see how my people are going to make a podcast segment here in your shop if you won't bother cleaning up this—"

"Wait, what?" I'd heard nothing about any podcasting in here, and Ellie looked puzzled, too.

But yanking the door open yet again, I spotted his production crew outside, a half-dozen young people in green tee shirts with the phrase *Eat This!* silk screened onto them, waiting on the sidewalk.

"We're putting together an episode of my new *Eat This!* video podcast," Hadlyme explained. "An online version of—"

"No." I yanked the blinds down in the front windows, turned the OPEN sign to CLOSED in the door, and stood in front of it.

"Not a chance, Henry. You're just going to make fun of us the way you did last night at the Happy Crab."

The popular Eastport eatery specialized in deep-fried seafood, which to hear Henry tell it—as everyone in the Crab had, including the owner—was only a slightly better choice than dumpster diving.

Also while he was there, he'd had a few remarks to make about the Moose: that we used carob instead of chocolate when we could get away with it, for instance. And margarine instead of butter. At his words, I hadn't charged up out of my seat in one of the Crab's blue leatherette booths to throttle him, but it was close.

"You're not doing any podcasting or anything else in here," I repeated. "Or in any of the other food places in Eastport, either, I'll bet. We all know what you're up to now, and we're not having any."

At this point, the scornful remarks he'd made were all over town, and I wasn't the only one who'd had it right up to the eyes with him. Actually, considering that there was a pirate festival going on in Eastport, I thought Henry Hadlyme was lucky not to be getting keelhauled right this very minute.

Oblivious to this, or more probably just not caring, he wagged a finger at me. "Now you listen to me, missy . . ."

I just love being called "missy." And finger wagging is a big favorite of mine, too; somehow he apparently thought that because he was a TV personality—and not even a beloved one like that well-known world-traveling fellow—he could do whatever he liked.

"Forget it," I said flatly. "Not a chance in the world." He opened his mouth again to protest.

I put a hand up. "I mean it. And before you pull out your 'I'm a celebrity' card, let me just get it on record for you very clearly that, first, you're not really very famous, you know. Half the folks here in Eastport have never heard of you."

Which was true. That was another thing he exaggerated: his own importance. "And second, I don't give a flying—"

"Jake," Ellie interrupted sweetly, but I knew it was the kind of sweetness that she hoped would put him into a diabetic coma. "Why don't you and Henry step outside so that I can start cleaning up in here?"

Right after I lock him out again, her look added, *and if I have to swat him with this broom to get him going, I'll do it.*

She wouldn't. Ellie was peaceful to a fault. But I'm not, and I wasn't the only one in Eastport who was mad at him. After last night at the Crab, the only place he was welcome to see the inside of around here was a lobster trap, just before it descended into fifty feet of cold salt water.

Still, there was no sense getting hit with an assault charge. "Come on, Henry," I muttered, urging him out ahead of me.

As we emerged, his half-dozen TV crew minions gathered around like vultures. They were young, eager, intelligent-looking vultures dressed in what I thought of as hipster uniforms: plaid shirts, too-short stovepipe trousers, beanies and fedoras, lots of piercings, and fancy tattoos.

They were predatory, and at the moment I was the prey. Feeling their eyes on me, I blinked at the absence of cameras and recorders until I remembered that nowadays they could do it all with their smartphones.

"Now," I told Henry, gesturing at them, "you can tell them to go away, or they can stay and capture footage of famous foodie and TV guy Henry Hadlyme getting his nose flattened by a local shopkeeper."

He looked appalled. "You *wouldn't*," he breathed, while his young crew members glanced expectantly at one another.

Wanting to punch Hadlyme wasn't exactly a rare idea among them, either, I gathered from their expressions. Too bad I was going to disappoint them; I really did need all those cleaning supplies, and I really didn't want to get arrested for clobbering him.

Besides, as I spoke I spotted one of the crew members trying to aim an actual camera at me, and I'm not sure what I dislike more—confronting sourpuss TV guys or having my picture taken sneakily.

Or having it taken at all, for that matter. "Scram!" I told the bunch of them, and they stepped back warily, then gave up and eased away until I was alone facing Hadlyme.

"You," I accused him, "have a motive for being here. And it's not a good motive, whatever it is."

"That's ridiculous." He was defensive, looking over his shoulder for someone to agree with him and finding no one.

All around us, throngs of happy visitors went on enjoying the clear sky, bright sunshine, and tempting food offerings of another successful Eastport Pirate Festival.

A kid on a skateboard went zigzagging by, munching a hot dog. Hadlyme winced, no doubt imagining how much happier and better off that kid would be with a saucer of fresh caviar and a lemon wedge.

I could've told him what to do with his lemon wedge, but instead a new thought struck me.

"What're you doing in Eastport, anyway?" I waved around at the people blocking the sidewalk. Quite a few of them were my friends and neighbors, and they liked deep-fried seafood as much as I did.

More, even. "I mean, what the heck were you expecting," I went on, "some kind of hotbed of cordon bleu?"

In reply he shoved a professionally produced flyer at me. *Eating on the Edge!* was the name of his podcast, it said, and then it listed a half-dozen small New England towns where the first six episodes of the new production would be set.

I frowned at the flyer just as Ellie came hurrying out of the shop looking vexed, locking the door behind her and testing it, and turning to me with her car keys already in her hand.

"Jake, I just got a call from Timmy Franco."

She headed for her car, which was in one of the angled spaces in front of the shop. I followed, pleased to be leaving Henry Hadlyme sputtering on the sidewalk behind me. Whatever he was up to, I figured I'd have time later to put the kibosh on it.

But in this, as in so much else, I was incorrect.

Eastport, Maine (pop. 1,200) is located on Moose Island, three hours from Bangor and light-years from everywhere else, or so it often seems. Reachable from the mainland by a long, curving causeway, the town and its bustling waterfront are also accessible to boats ranging from tiny skiffs and tubby fishing vessels rigged for lobster hauling to the vast, ocean-going freight carriers that visit our deep water cargo port regularly.

"Ellie," I gasped, hustling after her down the steep metal ramp leading to the floating wooden piers in the waterfront's boat basin.

Fortunately, the ramp's surface was serrated, so I didn't just slide down it like a human bobsled. "Ellie, what are we doing?"

Behind us onshore rose the old red-brick storefront buildings of Eastport's downtown, where distant music and laughter indicated that the pirate celebration was still in full swing.

Down here among the fishing boats tied up to the finger piers, though, the creak of rigging and clank of anchor chains mingled with the cries of seagulls overhead, drowning out the festival's din.

Ellie scampered ahead of me; I rushed to keep up with her while trying hard not to fall into the waves slopping the dock pilings. On either side of me, forty-foot fishing vessels floated, neatly slotted into their assigned spaces and secured to nearby pilings by lines as thick as my wrists.

"Ellie?" She was already aboard her own little vessel, a twenty-three-foot fiberglass Bayliner with a black canvas bimini awning, a small cuddy cabin, and a walkaround deck.

From the Bayliner's stern hung a 225-horsepower Mercury outboard engine I'd nicknamed The Beast. "Ellie, d'you by any chance feel like telling me what we're doing here?"

I put one uncertain hand on the bimini's aluminum-tube frame and one foot on the Bayliner's narrow fiberglass rail. Then I pushed with my other foot: up, over, and suddenly I was aboard, and as always I felt absurdly proud of myself that I'd accomplished this.

"Very nice," said Ellie approvingly. "You'll be taking her out on your own before you know it."

It was among her fondest fantasies that she would turn me into a skilled mariner who could get the Bayliner not only out of the boat basin alone but back into it again, too.

Without sinking, I mean. "But never mind that now," she added. She opened the battery hatch next to the engine, reached down into it to snap on the battery switch, slapped the hatch shut, and latched it.

"Tim needs our help," she said, and I noticed that she was still moving along rather briskly.

"Why?" I asked, and in reply she waved at the vacant spot ahead of us in the water, next to the finger pier.

The spot that usually had a familiar boat parked in it. . . . Then I got it. "Wait a minute, wasn't he out of town? You mean he's . . . ?"

Tim and his little motorboat were a familiar sight in the boat basin, where Tim spent his days doing chores and running errands for the fishing crews.

"Uh-huh," Ellie agreed. "I haven't seen him around for a few days. And before he left, I noticed he was wearing new jeans and a new pair of sneakers."

"So he must've gotten work." Tim's clothes were usually thrift shop specials, ragged but serviceable.

"Right. That's what I thought at the time, but he hasn't been around to ask," said Ellie. She switched on the radio, then smacked it sharply with the top of her hand until static blared from it.

"I ordered the new wires for this thing two weeks ago," she complained as she dialed the volume down. "One of these days, it's not going to turn on at all."

But she had better luck with the navigation electronics. On the helm near the steering wheel and the engine gauges, a screen jumped to glowing life at her touch, its display showing among other things that at the moment we were in twenty-three feet of water.

"Anyway, I guess he's back, because right now he's stuck out in Head Harbor Passage and he needs a tow," she said.

"Oh," I said. "That's inconvenient. What's he going to do?"

She pushed a small lever on the throttle, lowering the engine's propeller, then squeezed a rubber bulb on the fuel line a few times to put a dose of gas into the carburetor.

She'd taught me all this just in case I ever fulfilled her hopes by deciding to . . . And then it hit me, what she was saying.

"Wait a minute. Oh no. Don't tell me you mean *we're* going out there to—"

Not that Ellie didn't have plenty of boating experience, and she'd taken so many Coast Guard navigation and boat-handling courses that she probably could've taught one herself. But . . .

She turned the ignition key, starting the engine: *vroom-vroom*, etcetera. "Take the wheel," she said.

"Wait a minute," I repeated, but she didn't. Instead she hopped out onto the dock, untied the lines, tossed them aboard, and hopped back onto the boat again.

So the engine was running, and we were untied, and . . . "Okay, now pull the shift lever backward," she said. "Turn the wheel. Back us out. Come on, Jake, it's just like a car," she advised me kindly.

Sure, but a car wasn't swerving and swaying each time a puff of breeze got caught up in that bimini awning. The canvas was intended to provide us with shade, but at the moment it was acting more like a sail.

"Ellie," I grated out, gripping the boat's wheel nervously as the dock slid rapidly by. We were in reverse, approaching the granite boulders lining the boat basin to our rear.

Or "just off our stern," as these insufferably boaty types like to say. At least I hadn't hit any of the boats around us. Yet.

"You're fine," said Ellie. "Straighten the wheel, put it in forward gear, and give it a little gas."

So I did all that stuff, the alternative being to jump directly overboard, and have I mentioned yet that the water here is very cold?

Even in summer it's only about sixty degrees, which sounds fine but if you're swimming it feels as if ice cubes are floating around with you. And if you're in it for very long, even with your head above water, you'll soon be a floating ice cube, too.

"Get the life jackets out, please," I managed as I cautiously eased the Bayliner out between a crumbling wharf and a barge with a construction crane perched on it, parked just far enough offshore to create a channel.

A *narrow* channel . . . "More throttle." Ellie draped a life jacket over my shoulders. "Remember, if you're not moving, you can't steer."

Against my better judgment I eased the throttle forward, and the boat's handling did improve; Ellie looked satisfied. I snaked one arm and then the other through the life jacket's armholes, meanwhile keeping an eye on our port and starboard sides, our bow, and on the depth gauge displayed on the glowing GPS screen in front of me.

"Now start your turn," said Ellie as we emerged from between the barge and the wharf's dilapidated corner, thankfully without hitting either of them; I attributed this mostly to beginner's luck.

Dead ahead, though, lay the fish pier, where the boats unloaded their catches: scallops, those lobsters I mentioned, and sea urchins, mostly. The fish pier wasn't as big as the concrete breakwater that loomed up to enclose two sides of the boat basin; still, it was solid enough to be daunting.

"Okay," I said, turning the wheel decisively so the boat nosed to port. *There*, I thought, *course change accomplished*; now all I had to do was get out past the—

"Yikes," I blurted, suddenly catching from the corner of my eye the massive fishing vessel *Anne Marie*—all forty feet and who knew how many tons of her—coming up on my left.

I couldn't have seen her until I got out past the barge. But now I sure could. Her huge prow aimed straight at our midsection, and she was way too big to stop for us at this distance. I froze: *Go? Or . . .*

Or what, throw the engine into reverse? Sound the horn? *Get out of the way* was the obvious requirement, but how? And then . . .

Then some deep, primitive part of my brain took over, jamming my hand onto the throttle and shoving it forward.

"Hang on!" I had time to warn Ellie before The Beast took over, the big outboard engine emitting a throaty roar while rocketing us forward as if we'd been shot out of a cannon.

My bag flew off the console and hit the deck behind me, scattering its contents, but I paid no attention; instants later we cleared the *Anne Marie*'s looming bow with mere feet to spare, our wake spraying it liberally, and as we zoomed by I heard the faint congratulatory cheers of the men aboard.

"Whew," I exhaled. Once we got by the fishing boat, I backed off the throttle a little, easing out past the end of the breakwater to the wide blue expanse of the bay itself. And then . . .

"Hey! I did it," I said wonderingly to Ellie.

The sky, vast and cloudless, mirrored the water. A breeze out of the south smelled of salt. A gull cried, sailing on ahead of us like a guide, and the outboard growled pleasantly.

"You surely did," said Ellie, her voice coming not from directly behind me, where I'd believed she'd been standing throughout my little emergency, but from way back in the stern somewhere. "But now," she added, "I need you to do something else."

I glanced over my shoulder at her; we were approaching an area of the bay that was thick with lobster buoys, their brightly painted, wooden lozenge shapes bobbing cheerily on the waves.

My next task was to thread my way through them. She had her back to me, messing about with some ropes—quite a lot of them, it seemed to me.

Gritting my teeth in mingled fright and determination, I steered cautiously toward them. "Ellie! Why're you over there? What if I—"

"You didn't. Also, I knew you wouldn't. Don't bounce us around too much, okay?" She hauled one of the neatly coiled ropes—lines, she'd told me to call them—past me and up onto the foredeck.

Hmph, I thought. Like I was in control of bouncing. But I was too busy to be annoyed for very long, as suddenly those buoys were all around us. Each marked the spot where a lobster trap lay on the bottom, baited and ready for a tasty crustacean to crawl into.

"*Eep*," I said, weaving among them as best I could; it wasn't the buoys themselves that worried me, since our moving prow would simply push them aside without damage to them or us.

It was the line tying each buoy to its trap that would foul our propeller, Ellie had warned me on other voyages—maybe ruining it—and we couldn't assist a disabled vessel if we were dead in the water ourselves.

Ellie stepped nimbly past the boat's windshield and hopped back down onto the deck just as her cell phone jingled.

"Yes," she pronounced into it, pressing the speaker button so I could hear. A tinny voice sounded.

"I seem to be taking on quite a bit o' water," it reported.

"We're coming," Ellie replied. "We'll be there very soon. You're still in Head Harbor Passage?"

With the tide, the currents, the wind, and no engine to steer with . . . well, he could drift, was what he could do, and in these waters full of hidden rocks and ledges, that might be disastrous.

Unless he sank first, which was what that taking-on-water thing could lead to. Also disastrous. I gripped the wheel a little tighter.

"Ayuh," Tim replied. If he was feeling even slightly anxious, his voice didn't betray it. But for a downeast Maine mariner, a second phone call was equivalent to sending up a distress flare.

"Anchor's holdin' a bit better, now the keel's a little lower," he added. "That's the good news."

Not really; it was lower because the boat was heavier, a pint being a pound and all that. What he'd just said about taking on water suddenly felt even more urgent.

Putting the phone away, Ellie took the wheel from me. Her

face wore a look I'd last seen when her eleven-year-old daughter, Lee, got stuck in a treetop; like her mother, the kid just couldn't resist a dare.

"Oh-kay," Ellie pronounced now, which was what she'd said then, too, before dusting her hands together, scrambling up that tree, and bringing the girl down.

Seating herself in the pilot's chair, she gripped the throttle and aimed us east: *vroom*. Across the blue water halfway to the horizon lay Head Harbor Passage, and that little white dot on it, far in the distance, was Tim Franco's boat: disabled and sinking.

"Hang on," she said, shoving the throttle forward yet again. Shoving it *hard*.

I hung on all right, feeling very vulnerable indeed to the briny deep we were racing across, but after a little while it seemed less like we were speeding to a watery doom and more like we were merely speeding. Ellie was good at this, she knew she was good, and her confidence was contagious; also, she'd brought doughnuts.

They were the chocolate frosted ones that we'd made ourselves the night before; I bit in, letting the sweetness flood my taste buds and accepting the thermos of coffee she'd also been smart enough to bring along.

"That twit," she remarked after a little while, skimming us over the foam-topped waves.

"Who, Tim?" But no, she meant my adversary of earlier that day, Henry Hadlyme.

"Who does he think he is, anyway?" She finished her doughnut. "Although after the way you stood up to him, I doubt he'll—"

I hadn't felt like I'd been standing up to him, more like not letting him push me over. But now wasn't the time to discuss it.

"Um, Ellie?" I rose from where I'd crouched to retrieve my bag's contents—wallet and coins and other small items scattered across the deck. A big screwdriver had rolled off the boat's console, too, and this Ellie bent to snatch up, dropping it into her satchel.

The white dot on the waves was a lot closer, and there was a guy standing on it, yelling and waving his arms. "Tim seems to be in some kind of . . ."

Trouble. Oh, definitely. He was anchored securely, we discovered when we pulled alongside him with our engine down to a near idle; too securely, in fact. He'd accidentally hooked his anchor onto something down there under the water, a rocky ledge or whatever it was.

And now the tide was rising fast and he couldn't get the trapped anchor dislodged so he could pull it back up; instead the anchor was pulling his boat down toward it.

"Here," called Ellie, tossing him a big utility knife from our boat's tool locker.

Swiftly, Tim cut the anchor off its line. Instantly his vessel leveled. "Yeah!" he yelled, relief radiating from his face.

He was a deeply tanned, wiry young man, with a shock of rust-red hair flopping over his forehead, wearing red swim trunks, ratty sneakers, and a fraying gray sweatshirt with U MAINE lettered on it.

"Boy, am I ever glad to see you!" he said as Ellie went about the task of lashing his boat to our side; that, I realized, was what all those lines she'd been assembling were meant for.

"Got a buyer for the boat, took 'er out for a last ride before I hand 'er over," he said. "But now I think the fuel pump's history."

That wasn't the only pump he needed. As he spoke, he was bailing like crazy with a blue plastic pail, scooping up water off the deck and dumping it over the side; his bilge pumps had failed, too, apparently.

"Selling? But I thought you loved this boat. You even sleep

in it sometimes," Ellie said as she finished tying the final line, then yanked on it to tighten it down.

It was true; we almost always saw him around the dock or under the tarp he'd rigged for shelter when he stayed overnight. His absence this past week was the rare exception.

At Ellie's words, Tim's grin faded. "Yeah, well, there's a little thing called money, you know? And not much work around here, in case you haven't noticed," he said.

I understood. My grown son, Sam, had the same problem; guys were lined up for the few open spots on the fishing boats, and in a remote area like this one, other jobs were few and far between.

Meanwhile, even among the working fishermen the idea of a living wage was laughable some years. So I doubted Tim got paid much for the errands and chores he did. Still, he got along somehow; too bad about selling the boat, though, I thought.

"Okay!" yelled Ellie, finishing with the last line, and then we were off, back the way we'd come. But this part of our journey ended up being more challenging than the one we'd just completed, since now we were running against the incoming tide instead of with it.

Cold spray slapped my face as we labored through waves shoved by the wind and the powerful currents, slamming us with explosions of white salty foam and then falling away. The boat charged up the wave crests and smacked down again, over and over, one bone-rattling thud after another.

Oh yeah, this was different, all right. "Go put your hand on the lower unit!" Ellie yelled over the engine and the wind.

I must've looked confused.

"The lower part of the engine just above the water!" she yelled. "Lay your hand on it, make sure it's not hot."

"Oh," I said, comprehending finally. Because the engine was big, all right, but now it was hauling two boats. And as Tim's experience was proving, you can never be too careful on the water.

"Barely warm!" I reported when I'd managed to lean out over the stern and flatten my palm to the engine's casing without falling in—and have I mentioned the great big waves all around us?

"Excellent," said Ellie. Then:

"So why d'you suppose Henry Hadlyme wanted to film in our store, particularly?"

I slid onto the other chair at the helm, trying to tell myself that this really wasn't too bad. Owing to her excellent boat-handling skills, we were already two-thirds of the way home.

But now we were approaching the Old Sow. "No idea," I said, eyeing the swirling turbulence on the water ahead. "He seemed upset, though, didn't he?"

I braced myself as alongside us Tim kept bailing like a madman. Now I understood why Ellie had lashed him to our hull instead of towing him behind us: if he started sinking, she wanted to be able to cut him loose efficiently before his boat could drag us down, too.

"And he sure didn't like it when I wanted to know why he'd come here," I added, and then we hit it: the hugest, most boat-devouringly treacherous whirlpool in the Western Hemisphere.

Oh great, I thought, feeling the first tug of the massively powerful whirlpool currents. But Ellie only shrugged, unfazed as the water muscled us around like a giant bully.

"Something fishy about that guy," she said, pushing the throttle again.

To get us through this quicker, I hoped. The Old Sow whirlpool was a no-kidding force of nature, and being in its clutches wasn't fun unless you had a death wish.

"I mean, what did he think, that what he said at the Crab last night wouldn't be all over town by morning?"

Which, of course, it had been; that's how we'd heard about it.

Over on his own boat, Tim had switched from bailing to pumping with a hand pump. Unfortunately, the rough seas hurled water back into his vessel nearly as fast as he could remove it.

"I'm not sinking, though," he cried defiantly, letting out a wild laugh. "So, you know, I've got that going for me!"

Ellie smiled slightly, not taking her eyes off the water ahead. Amidst the whirlpool's swirls, a wide patch of unnaturally calm water stretched before us, small eddies in its surface turning lazily.

Deceptively. The first unsteady lurch of the boat made me grip my chair; the second slid me off it, down onto the deck.

Feet first, luckily. "Whoa!" yelled Tim from his boat, the grin spreading wider on his face. "Ride 'em, cowboy!"

Which was just about what it felt like. "Ellie?" I ventured as the Bayliner chugged through the turbulence, bobbing and weaving.

"Uh-huh," she replied. "I know. We'll be fine, Jake." But then:

"About Hadlyme, though," she said. "What should we do if he does try to come back into the shop, do you think?"

Another lurch delivered yet another shock to my poor nervous system.

"Because we can't have his sourpuss act in The Chocolate Moose," she went on. "He'll scare off the customers."

Personally, I was about a quarter inch from getting scared right off this boat; the only thing stopping me was that the alternative was so much worse. But then suddenly we were getting spat out of the whirlpool, finally, and all the lurching and swerving subsided.

"I really don't want him filming in there," I agreed, climbing back onto my chair as Ellie aimed us across the last half mile of the water toward the Eastport boat basin.

"So we can't let him do it just to shut him up. He could make us look terrible in his podcast, too," I added as we made our way back through the lobster buoys bobbing outside the break-water entrance.

Tim's boat was still tied securely to us, Ellie's ropework holding fine, and to my surprise neither Tim nor his vessel seemed much the worse for wear. On the other hand, we still had to get him to the dock, and with that barge forming such a narrow channel just inside the boat basin it seemed impossible.

But Ellie took it in stride. The barge slid by on one side, so close that I could see the orange paint curls peeling off it, and the wharf with its ancient pilings all blackened and dripping slid by on the other, while beside us Tim sat cross-legged on the deck of his little motorboat, arms folded, lord of all he surveyed.

A hard right turn—starboard, Ellie called it—then a weave-and-a-bobble and . . . *bump*! He was up against his own dock, scampering off his vessel. We backed away, then pulled forward into Ellie's own spot at the finger pier: easy-peasey.

That is, it was easy when she was doing it; despite her urging, I'd never overcome my nervousness about docking the Bay-liner myself. She shut down the engine as I let out a relieved sigh.

Tim stuck out a hand. "Ellie, I thank you kindly."

"Think nothing of it." Her hand vanished in his grip.

"I know you'd do the same for me. That's why Tim and I have each other's cell phone numbers," she added to me. "For just this kind of an emergency."

I thought she deserved much more fanfare after what she'd done. But then I noticed the men on the various fishing boats and on the docks, too, shooting small glances of silent approval her way. And since this from a hard-to-impress downeast Maine mariner is the equivalent of a standing ovation, I felt satisfied.

Ellie shoved her sunglasses up onto her head, going through the Bayliner's shutdown checklist: radio—it took another hand-smack to get it to turn off—battery, GPS, and finally the engine's trim. As the dripping propeller rose up from the water, I ate another chocolate frosted doughnut and watched the pirates competing in the walk-the-plank contest, now going on over at the fish pier.

The narrow plank set up for the contest stuck straight out over the harbor; also, it was greased, to make the whole thing a little more sporting. A splash followed by laughter and applause signaled yet another dunking. Then a fiddle somewhere nearby began rollicking through a jig, with pennywhistle accompaniment.

"Hi, Mom!" My son, Sam, waved from shore at me; tall and dark-haired, physically he was the spitting image of his biological father but utterly unlike him otherwise, I'm delighted to report. With him were his pretty black-haired wife, Mika, and their son, Ephraim, now bouncing happily in his stroller and waving a stuffed toy.

"Hi, kids!" I called back, and then a cannon boomed, making me jump; it was a reproduction weapon without any cannon-balls in it, I happened to know, on account of my husband, Wade Sorenson, being the festival's firearms expert.

Still, it was *loud.* My eardrums were still fluttering from the noise when Ellie's mouth started moving.

"*What?*" I cupped my hands behind my ears and squinted.

She leaned in. "I'm going home! Lee's in the soapbox derby!" Like the greasy-plank contest, it was yet another Eastport festival tradition. "I said I'd watch!" she added.

The idea of the kids in their home-built carts rocketing down Washington Street and around the sharp turn onto Water Street at the bottom filled me with fright: they wore helmets, of course, but their little skulls were still as fragile as eggs. . . .

I was happy to have an excuse not to witness it. "All right!" I shouted before I realized that she could hear me just fine. "I'll go back to the shop, then, and clean up."

And maybe make a few more sales, too, I thought as she departed, since the pirates seemed to like our bakery goodies a great deal.

But by now it was nearly noon, and the pungent aromas of hot dogs, french fries, and onion rings floated from Rosie's Hot Dog Stand, a small red-painted hut located at the breakwater's entrance.

Despite the doughnuts I'd eaten, I felt starved; these watery near-death experiences will do that to you, I guess. So I headed for the hut, brushing between buccaneers and rascals of all shapes and sizes, strolling the breakwater in their costumes.

But my hopes of refreshment were dashed when, as I approached the lunch joint's wooden counter, a familiar voice sounded in my ear.

An *angry* voice. "Jake Tiptree?" it demanded.

A hand gripped my arm, turning me, and of course I didn't wrench it away and shove my elbow into the nose of the voice's owner; why, I just *adore* having my arm grabbed.

"Yes?" I responded instead through gritted teeth. "What is it, Henry?"

Because of course it was him. He knew it was me, too, and from the sound of him he wasn't done with our fight.

"I want a word with you." Still gripping my elbow, he marched me along, past the hot dog stand and up onto Water Street.

"Yes, and when I grow up, I want a pony," I snarled, this time yanking away from him.

By now we were in front of the big old granite post office building on the corner of Water and Washington Streets. "I told you, you're not filming in—"

The Chocolate Moose, I was about to finish, but his bellow of outrage interrupted me.

"Oh, for heaven's sake, don't be so difficult about it. I mean, who do you think you are, anyway, just a couple of foolish women with a silly little—"

People stopped to stare, murmuring in concern as Henry went on. "My production company . . . going to be top-rated . . . I have a right . . . you should be *honored* to be . . ."

A tall bearded pirate in black boots and satin trousers, belted with a jeweled scabbard and topped by a white pirate shirt trimmed in gobs of lace, stepped forward with a rakish bow.

"At your service, ma'am," he said, grinning wickedly.

But the only service I wanted was the kind that would make me disappear, so I waved him away and hurried on across the street.

Henry followed. "You'll be sorry!" he shouted. "You and all the greasy spoons in this backwater burg, you'll all be sorry you didn't cooperate with me when you had the chance!"

I turned sharply, surprising him; he took a startled step back. "All right, now, damn it, you listen to me."

I poked him in the chest with my index finger. It felt good, and his eyes widened satisfyingly at the gesture, so I did it again.

The people staring at us seemed to like it, too, their concern turning to amusement. "You," I pronounced grimly, "aren't going to make anyone sorry, do you hear me?"

Fifteen minutes ago I'd been out on the bounding waves, which as you may have noticed is not by any means a preferred location of mine. Now as a result I was so charged up with adrenaline, I felt as if I could bend steel with my bare etcetera.

I stuck my finger out again, and he backed off some more. "You're going to shut up and leave me alone, that's what you're going to do," I told him, "or you never know. . . ."

Just then, more loud applause and another splash came from the plank-walking contest at the fish pier. The fiddle bounced into yet another rendition of "Sailor's Hornpipe."

The first soapbox derby vehicle came flying down the Washington Street hill and careened around the corner, then swerved into a pile of hay bales amidst the shouts and cheers of the on-lookers.

But a lot of them were still watching Henry and me. "If you don't back off, something bad might happen to you," I finished.

"Are you threatening me?" He turned to the gaggle of onlookers we'd attracted. "You heard it! All of you heard!"

He swung around toward me again. "Fine. I don't need shots of your store's stupid-looking interior. I can get what I need outside."

Waving toward our sign, visible halfway down the block—the silhouette of a grinning googly-eyed moose stuck out nicely from its downtown surroundings, we'd found—he smiled nastily.

"I'll do a whole show on the slop you call food around here," he snarled. "Chocolate bakery," he added dismissively. "In a burg like this one you might as well be selling deep-fried Mars bars. Dip some pork rinds in melted Hershey's while you're at it, why don't you?"

He looked around scornfully at the lunches many of the festival attendees were enjoying: pizza slices, sausage rolls, fries sodden with ketchup. A few of the braver ones were even sampling that ever-popular local delicacy, smoked salmon on a stick.

Or *steek*, as Sam liked to pronounce it. Meanwhile, I'd already been thinking of chocolate-dipping some fried-crisp bacon strips, and now I was determined to do it—this afternoon, even, maybe.

First, though, I had to get rid of Hadlyme. "Look, Henry, you and I don't have anything more to say to each other."

I stepped around him and kept going. But he wasn't finished. "You'll be sorry!" he yelled again. "By the time I roll out of Eastport, I'll have all I need!"

By now he was hopping with fury. "Once people hear my show about you and the junk you sell, you'll be finished, do you hear me?"

I surely did, all the way down the block, ranting about how he was going to destroy The Chocolate Moose while a slowly dispersing audience watched the grown man standing there raging until the veins stood out on his forehead and spittle flew out of his mouth.

I knew this because I turned and peeked. Then, under the moose-head sign, I rummaged in my bag for my keys, which was when I remembered dropping the bag on the boat.

"Drat." They must've been among the things that fell out and I'd missed seeing them when I was retrieving items. Sighing at the idea of going back to hunt for them, I dug out my spare.

Then I unlocked the door and opened it to the bright, familiar jingle of the little bell mounted over the doorframe. Inside I locked it again, not wanting Hadlyme to barge in. The shade was still pulled from earlier, and we could open again once he'd wandered off to torment somebody else, I decided; besides, the whole place was still a mess.

Even amidst the chaos left behind by the youthful pirate crew, though, the shop felt like a refuge. Napkins were scattered everywhere and jelly-smeared plates still covered the café tables, my shoes still stuck to the floor, and that glass-fronted display case really was a disaster. But all of that I could fix.

And now I could do it in peace, just as soon as I got two dozen double-chocolate mint cookies baking, some chocolate-chip nut bread in the mixer, and a batch of chocolate croissants on the rise.

So back in the kitchen I got out the butter, softened it briefly in the microwave, and began creaming it together with the sugar, then beat in two eggs and a teaspoonful of vanilla extract, plus another of mint liqueur. Adding the dry stuff—flour, cocoa powder, baking soda, salt—I felt myself relaxing into the work and especially into the solitude, an unusual luxury for me lately.

I mixed in the chocolate chips; then the cookies got popped into the oven. Next came the banana bread, which I mixed up while the butter for the cookie frosting was softening and the croissant dough was thawing.

Finally I checked the cooler for the semisweet chocolate chunk I thought was in there, since if you're going to dip bacon, it seemed to me you might as well use the good stuff. Shaving it took just moments, and I put the result into a storage bag so it would be ready when I wanted it—that is, after I'd fried the bacon.

By then the croissant dough was ready and the first batch of the cookies had baked. I shaped the croissants and set them out on a parchment-lined pan, then took the cookies out of the oven and put a second batch in.

While I worked, happily oblivious to all but the tasks in front of me—my favorite situation—the radio on the shelf out front played softly. Randy Newman, I think it was, maybe *Little Criminals.*

Something, anyway, that would've sounded ominous if I'd thought about it. But all I did think, safe in the sanctuary of the locked bakery after a wildly eventful boat ride and a loud public shouting match with a hostile near-stranger, was that no matter how angry he was, Henry Hadlyme couldn't do any actual harm to the Moose.

Sure, he was well known to his own audience of food enthusiasts, I thought as I folded the chopped nuts and more chocolate bits into the banana bread batter—I'm pretty sure banana-nut bread can't have too many chocolate bits, aren't you?—but he wasn't *famous* famous; no one on the street just now seemed to recognize him, for instance. So his podcast wouldn't really affect us much, it seemed to me.

Heck, I hardly knew anyone who followed any podcasts, or for that matter even realized that they existed. Way out here at the back edge of beyond the way we were, we were lucky even to have cable TV.

Also, he'd mentioned that he was set to leave Eastport

soon—the flyer he'd shoved at me earlier had said he'd be elsewhere in two days, actually; hallelujah!—and I was pretty sure that I could duck him, meanwhile. So with any luck I'd never see him again.

Sadly, though, I was wrong about almost all of those things, as I would learn only a few minutes later.

When it was too late.

Two

My name is Jacobia Tiptree—Jake to my friends—and when I first came to Maine I thought pie-making, cookie-baking, and the whipping together of the perfect cream-filled chocolate éclair were all subcategories of rocket science.

Where I came from, baked goods arrived in Entenmann's boxes, the ones with the clear plastic windows in the top so you could see inside. *Monkey see, monkey want* was the theory behind this packaging scheme, I suppose, or at any rate it worked that way for me.

But then I found Eastport, soon after leaving behind my serially cheating ex-husband—his name, appropriately enough, was Victor—and hustling my young son, Sam, out of the big city and away from his—oh, all right, *our*—impending doom.

Sam should've been a middle school student. Instead he spent his days playing online video games and his nights riding the tops of subway cars with his equally unhinged young pals while taking drugs so sophisticated that they didn't even have names, just strings of numbers and letters assigned to them in basement chemistry labs.

Amateur labs, and there'd been no way I could stop him; by then he was too big to restrain physically and too defiant to reason with. In the end, I think it was only the sight of my face after I'd walked out on his dad that got him into the car on that last day.

"Mom?" he'd whispered frightenedly from the back seat, all the fight suddenly gone out of him.

Meanwhile, we made our way north through heavy traffic to the 125th Street on-ramp and out of the city.

"Mom, are you okay?" he asked, but he knew. I'd loved Victor so much it'd nearly killed me ever since I'd laid eyes on him fifteen years earlier. The day I left, I couldn't even speak until we were halfway through Massachusetts, and even then I could only manage short blurts, trying hard not to weep in front of my kid.

That night in Freeport we ate, showered, and slept, and the next morning we bought a couple of sweatshirts at the outlet store and some toiletries in town. Sam kept glancing warily at me when he thought I didn't notice. I'd never done anything like this before, and he must have wondered how much worse his mom's freak-out was going to get.

And what it might mean for him. His home life had been terrible, but at least it had been *consistent.* I wondered, too. As we drove north once more on steadily narrower Maine roads, I was terrified that instead of saving my son's life, my impulsive decision might end up being the last straw in the ruining-it department.

But then we reached Eastport, with its quirky old wooden houses perched on steep tree-lined streets angling down to the bay and its harbor crowded with fishing boats. On the water, which was the deep, intense blue of cornflowers, sailboats flew under white sails; bell buoys clanged, and across the waves the long, low Canadian island of Campobello gleamed gold in the slanting rays of late afternoon.

"Wow," Sam said softly as we stood out on the breakwater that surrounded the boat basin on three sides.

People with fishing rods were there casting lines into the bright water, hauling in fish. "Mom," Sam asked seriously after watching for a while, "d'you suppose we could buy a fishing pole?"

This request made of his father would've resulted in not-very-nice laughter. Victor thought the outdoors was perfect for driving his girlfriends through, toward small hotels where nobody he knew would spot him.

But of course we could buy a fishing pole, and the man at Wadsworth's Hardware Store on Water Street helped Sam rig it up, too, with a many-hooked mackerel jig. So while my son took his place with the other anglers on the breakwater, I walked up past the ferry dock onto a stony beach.

The damp air smelled of salt water, wood smoke, and chamomile. Crimson rose hips massed on tall hedges gave off the tangy perfume of crushed fruit, while stick-legged shore birds patrolled the waterline searching for snacks.

I sat on a rock, taking it all in and wishing we could stay. But we couldn't; for one thing, Sam wouldn't tolerate it. Fishing was fun, but for a city kid like him I thought daily life here would be a drag once the novelty wore off.

Anyway, I couldn't afford it. The small, well-kept wooden houses on the tree-lined streets looked like heaven, but they probably cost the earth.

Or so I believed. But when I went back to the breakwater to collect Sam and find a place in town to stay for the night—we could look around a little more, anyway, I'd decided, relax and catch our breaths while we figured out where to go next—I found he'd already made a friend.

"Mom, this is Wooley." The elderly man standing next to him at the edge of the breakwater grinned affably at me, sticking out a work-roughened hand. Ruddy-faced and with a lot of unkempt gray hair poking out from under his Red Sox ball cap, he wore faded denim coveralls over a flannel shirt and sported yellow rubber boots.

"Pleasure," he uttered, and the next thing I knew he'd poured me a mug of coffee out of his red plaid thermos.

His face, furrowed and grooved by age and the outdoors, was like something you might find carved into an old tree trunk, and his grip had felt as tough as bark. I drank the hot, sweet coffee gratefully while he looked on. Then:

"I hear," Wooley drawled, angling his head at Sam, "that you two are looking for a place to live, mebbe."

Hee-yah, the downeast Maine way of pronouncing it. I eyed Sam sternly, but he just bit his lip in silence, staring out at the water.

"And I just happen," Wooley went on, "to be selling one of those places. For the right price, o'course," he added judiciously.

"Can we go see it, Mom?" Sam's face was radiant, suddenly, and right then I'd have put my head into a lion's mouth to keep it that way. But . . .

Wooley waited expectantly, a grin spreading around the cigar stub clenched in his stained teeth.

"The boy," he confided finally to me as I hesitated, "might like having a look."

He lit the cigar again, then went on. "An old sea captain's house, it is, too big for me now, and I've got to go over there, anyway. Why not come along?"

Ovah they-ah. By now Sam was practically hopping with impatient anticipation. "Yeah, why not?" he wanted to know.

Which is how we found the old house on Key Street, not the small, easily kept homestead I'd been envisioning but a vast, many-roomed extravaganza of domestic architecture from the early 1800s: pantries and back stairs and fireplaces, oh my!

While Wooley did whatever it was he'd come to do, I wandered around entranced. The wallpaper was 1940s era, the plumbing likewise. The kitchen was huge, with a tin ceiling, hardwood floor, tall south-facing windows, and beadboard wainscoting; cast-iron hot-water radiators stood sturdily in every room, and there was no sign of rust on any of them.

Sam chose his bedroom, bouncing in the window seats and then running out excitedly to exclaim to me about the view to the harbor. A confirmed landlubber who wouldn't even swim at the Y back home, here he already had his eye on those fishing boats.

"But Mister . . . Wooley," I said when we were out on the porch once more. Up and down Key Street, the elderly maple branches forming a shady tunnel over the pavement, people were mowing lawns and washing windows, planting geraniums and touching up paint.

"It's wonderful," I went on, "it really is, and Sam loves it. But I'm afraid we can't afford such a big house."

Not to mention all the repairs it would need; even I knew that an old house with no one living in it goes downhill fast. Meanwhile, in the fix-it department, I was as useless as a rubber nail. Back in the city, for any job more difficult than changing a lightbulb I'd always just called the building superintendent.

Wooley mentioned a number. "I beg your pardon?" It was less than half what I'd been expecting. "For the down payment, you mean?"

I peered back in through the wooden screen door at the kitchen with the refrigerator and gas stove, which was ancient and equipped with a wood-burning firebox to one side. There was a washer and dryer as well, and a lot of faded rugs, elderly but usable; the floral curtains hanging at the many-paned windows were faded, with their pinch pleats clotted with thick dust, but otherwise in decent shape.

"No," Wooley said around the cigar stub. "That's not for the down payment, it's what I need to get for the whole shootin' match."

He eyed me frankly. "No one wants these drafty old places anymore. I just want to unload it."

"Mom," Sam said quietly from just inside the screen door. "Mom, maybe we should think about—"

I had the money. Not on me, but back in the city I'd had a job, and savings of my own—mad money, I'd called it only half-jokingly.

But now I thought I might really have gone mad, because crazy as this was, I found myself seriously considering the idea: the huge old house with its many antique windows and tall red-brick chimneys, the big backyard with pink peonies and blue hydrangeas blooming in it, and that sky—a cloudless indigo with a few bright stars coming out.

A distant foghorn hooted. A bike with a bell on it rolled down the street in the gathering dusk: *ring!*

All this could be yours, said a soft small voice echoing in my head. *All this and more—if you've got the nerve.*

If you're strong enough. "Mom?" Sam asked tentatively, sounding not at all like the brittle, damaged youngster I'd dragged up here with me, who'd viewed me until only a few hours ago with dismissive contempt.

"Mom, I'm not sure why I think it, but I really, *really* think you should—"

"All right. We'll take it," I heard myself saying, much to my surprise. But I was even more surprised by what Sam did then:

Wordlessly he shoved his way out the screen door past me, sat on the porch steps with his knees drawn up tightly, and dropped his face into his hands, sobbing.

He sounded relieved. Listening, Wooley nodded, seeming to take in if not the specific facts of the situation then at least the general drift.

"We'll just let your young man collect himself, shall we?" said Wooley with surprising delicacy, and I followed the burly old fellow back inside the house again, where we shook hands and agreed on how the money details would go.

Then I wondered aloud where we might find a nearby place with a room we could rent for the night. "A motel," I said, "or maybe they have a vacant cabin at that campgrounds we passed on our way in?"

Outside the kitchen's tall, bare windows, the long afternoon was finally waning, fireflies already flickering in the shady part of the backyard, under the lilac bushes.

"Stay?" Wooley asked puzzledly. "But why would you need that?"

He aimed the cigar out the screen door to where Sam still sat, no longer slumped but instead gazing around wonderingly; he did not, I realized, want to leave this place, not even temporarily. And it *was* being sold furnished. . . .

"Lady," he said, "if there's one thing you *don't* need, it's any more rooms. Why, you just bought yourself a whole house!"

Twenty years later as I stood in The Chocolate Moose, I thought of Wooley, now sadly departed like so many of the first friends I'd made here in Eastport. Funny how a stranger with a cigar stub in his kisser could end up being your guardian angel.

But nostalgia wasn't getting me anywhere, so after dealing with the cookies, the banana bread, the croissants, and the chocolate for the bacon-dipping project, I confronted the job I'd been putting off: cleanup.

The small, ornate cast-iron café tables and chairs, the floor, the glass display case front . . . but especially the floor required thorough attention, still so sticky that the soles of my shoes adhered to it. Now some of the stray napkins were stuck there, too.

All of which meant getting the mop and the mop bucket from the cellar after all, as well as the spray cleaner; if I didn't, I'd just have to go down there again. And as living in an old house had taught me over the years—yes, we'd stayed all this time, and now it was crammed full of my large, complicated family—you might as well do now what you'll have to do later and get it over with.

I checked the shop door again to make sure it was locked, turned off the radio so I'd hear if anyone knocked, then went to the kitchen and pulled up the trap door that was set into the floor there.

And at once noticed something odd: the cellar light was on. The bulb, dangling from an orange extension cord, hung from the rafter by the stairs in all its glowing 40-watt glory.

But not *that* odd, I decided; probably those delivery guys Ellie had mentioned had neglected to turn it off. Its glow didn't extend far, though, and the dark area of the cellar, where the utility closet was, waited silently for me.

Uncertainly I debated putting off this trip until Ellie arrived; then I'd have moral support, and backup, too, in case of emergency. But I knew if I did that, I would have to postpone the shop cleanup.

And she'd know why, wouldn't she? Not that she'd chide me about it, but her understanding silence on the matter would be nearly as bad. The matter, I mean, of my being a complete chicken . . . so in the end I said the heck with it, grabbed a flashlight, and started down.

Stabbing the darkness ahead of me with the flashlight, I crossed toward the utility closet. *Broom, mop, the metal bucket with the mop wringer in it*, I recited to myself, glancing around nervously.

The cellar walls dated from the early nineteenth century when granite, not bricks, was the preferred foundation material. Someone long ago had decided to whitewash the granite blocks, but after many decades the resulting scaly, peeling surface was not an improvement.

Over the stairs, the light bulb swung gently from my brushing against it moments earlier, casting shivery shapes over the cellar's packed-earth floor. Wrinkling my nose, I paused, sniffing curiously as a faint musty smell hit me, but in an old dirt-floored cellar fifty yards from the water, a smell is nothing unusual, so I thought little of it as I yanked open the closet.

Then I stuck one arm through the bucket's handle, wrapped my free arm around the broom and mop sticks and drew them tightly toward me, and began making my way back toward the cellar steps. *So far, so good*, I thought.

Halfway to the stairs, though, I started losing my grip, first on the broomstick and then the mop handle, its rag head already dragging a trail. So I stopped to rearrange them as best I could, and that's how I saw the blood.

Two dark red gleaming drops of it, gleaming wetly as if newly fallen, lay on the earthen floor.

But . . . an icy shiver went through me . . . fallen from where?

As I stared, another drop joined the first two: *plop!* Until now, the silence upstairs had been reassuring, but now it no longer seemed even remotely friendly. Nor did a broom and a mop feel anything like sufficient weaponry for my situation.

Whatever *that* was. . . . Then I spied the metal door leading out to the alley behind the shop and remembered again Ellie asking me to lock it, hours earlier.

Crossing to it, I found that, sure enough, the door's heavy metal bolt was still drawn back. After pulling the door open, I peered up and down the damp, mossy brick pathway leading in from the street.

A palisade fence ran along the opposite side of the alley, and above that an awning of heavy corrugated plastic had been hung, to keep the alley from flooding with the buildings' roof runoff. So the alley was really more like a tunnel, shaded and gloomy.

No one was in it except a cat, placidly washing its face atop a Dumpster; from where I stood I couldn't see anyone on the street, and they couldn't see me.

Unhappily, I closed the alley door and locked it, then realized with a rush of relief: those raspberries from the jar that was broken during the cookie-tasting party—the syrup had run all over the floor. And because the floor was old, over the decades the spaces between the floorboards had widened as the building settled.

I let my breath out. That's all the red stuff was, gleaming in the flashlight's beam: berry juice.

Silly. Scolding myself for being a ninny, I turned toward the steps with the broom and mop sticks hugged clumsily to my side once again and the bucket handle over my wrist. But when I was almost to the top of the stairs, the mop and broomstick shifted, and when I grabbed clumsily for them, the bucket slid up toward my elbow.

The next thing I knew, the broomstick and mop were wedged crossways in the stairwell with me perched just below them, balanced precariously on the narrow step. The sticks' ends had gone between the bucket handle and my arm, with my wrist caught between the handle and the sticks.

Which were also stuck, so I couldn't go up or down. Jammed very firmly, too, as I discovered when I tried dislodging them.

So I was in a pickle. I couldn't let go of the stair rail, since my toes had only the narrowest of purchases on the step. If I let go of the rail I'd fall backward until I was dangling by my other arm—the trapped one, that is. Then my weight would likely free the broomstick and mop and I'd fall the rest of the way; luckily no one was creeping silently up the stairs behind me—

Oh, of course there isn't. But at the thought I jerked my head around nervously because it *was* awfully quiet down there, and the sudden shift in my position loosened the sticks from where they were wedged tightly between the stairwell's walls.

Sadly I'd also been shifting my grip on the stair rail just as this happened; moments later I was sitting with the sticks crossed over my lap and the bucket on my head at the foot of the stairs.

Which I guessed was one way of solving the difficulty. Removing the bucket and making a mental note never to visit the cellar again, I got to my feet. I groaned a little, and swore a little, too, since a tumble down the stairs was yet another thing that hadn't been on my day's to-do list.

After a swift, wincing inventory of my body parts, I determined that nothing was broken but the bucket handle. Still, I was done for a while, I decided; I'd get all the cleanup supplies and paper goods later, when I'd rested and gotten over this.

So with an ill-tempered swing of the mop in the direction of the utility closet I'd been headed for in the first place, I turned to go back upstairs.

But then the mop head thumped the closet door, and the closet door swung open.

And a body fell out.

It was Henry Hadlyme, still wearing the black turtleneck and red leather jacket I'd seen him in earlier—still with his frizzy yellow hair and blocky chin, too.

Now, though, he had a bright red-and-green stuffed parrot perched on his shoulder, fastened there with safety pins stuck first through the parrot's stuffed feet and then into Hadlyme's shirt.

A *familiar*-looking bird . . . but the important thing, I thought through my shock, was the cutlass in Hadlyme's chest, shoved in halfway to the weapon's hilt. So probably the red droplets I'd seen weren't spilled raspberry juice after all. . . .

"Oh, man," I heard myself murmuring. Because this was not good, this was not even a little bit. . . .

"Hello?" A voice from upstairs made me jump. Then Bob Arnold, Eastport's police chief, stuck his head into the stairwell, saw me, and started hurriedly down, frowning in concern.

"Jake! What the—?"

At the bottom he crouched by me where I'd sat down on the floor again without realizing it. Touching my forehead gingerly, he peered at his fingertips and grimaced: red.

"I hit my head," I managed, trying to rise. "That's how . . ."

"Sit." Bob had his phone out. "Stay where you are. I'm calling an ambulance."

"But Bob, he's already . . ." *Okay, now*, I thought. One foot under me. Then the other foot, my hand on the stair rail, and . . .

No problem. Nothing to it at all. Except . . .

Upright, I took some deep breaths, very carefully not looking at Hadlyme lying there with a life-sized stuffed parrot safety-pinned to his shoulder and a blade shoved into its chest. A *familiar* parrot . . .

And a familiar blade. ". . . dead," I finished weakly, and sat down hard again while he spoke brusquely into his radio.

With his round pink-cheeked face, rosebud lips, and thinning blond hair clipped very short around the top of his balding head, Bob Arnold didn't much look like a police officer even when he was in his official blue uniform, as he was today.

But he had a voice that could cut steel when he wanted it to, along with a sort of spin-'em-around-and-swat-'em maneuver that could put an unruly person into his squad car swiftly and efficiently, and Bob wouldn't even be breathing hard afterward.

None of which he needed at the moment. I could've been knocked down by a twitch of his little finger, I felt so shocked by what I'd found.

"Jake, I told you to stay where you were."

Faintly from outside I could already hear a siren approaching, not much to my surprise; as always, the festival was so well policed that you'd think real pirates were invading the town.

He crouched beside me again. "What happened?"

"I'm not sure. I came down here for . . ." I waved at the bucket, the mop, and the broom scattered around me. "And the next thing I knew . . ." I waved at the body. "He fell out of the cabinet at me.

I was on my way upstairs, but I got crosswise in the stairway somehow, and . . ."

Bob squinted puzzledly at me.

"And then I fell," I finished. "It was right before you came in." A different thought struck me. "How'd you *get* in, anyway?" I knew I'd locked the shop door.

Bob shrugged. "Ran into Ellie, and she gave me these."

He held out my keys, the ones I'd dropped on the Bayliner. "I saw the lights on inside and I wanted to give them to you, so . . ."

I sat up. The cellar only spun a little bit, which I regarded as a good sign. But as I sat getting my wind back, it was dawning on me: there was a dead guy lying nearby, and he had a big sword stuck through him. Also, the more I looked at the brightly colored stuffed bird, the more certain I was that I recognized it.

A siren screamed up outside. "You stay here," Bob instructed me, and started back upstairs.

But then he turned. "Jake, you're sure that when you found him, he was just like that. Dead, with the sword run through him. And the parrot . . ." Bob's eyes narrowed. "Say, where have I seen that thing lately?"

It was just what I'd been wondering. At last it came to me. "It's Ephraim's." My grandson's, I meant. "Or he's got one just like it, anyway," I said as something jingled upstairs.

Then footsteps thumped the floor overhead, and two ambulance guys appeared at the top of the stairwell. After hurrying down, they hovered over me intently and began assessing my condition.

It had taken them only a glance to figure out Hadlyme's. "I do not," I began, "need any of your—"

But they were too busy recording my pulse and blood pressure to listen. Once they discovered I had both, they peered into my eyes and examined the wound on my head, pronouncing it superficial.

I clambered to my feet. My surroundings lurched dizzily, but I wasn't about to let them know it.

"I'm fine," I declared, meanwhile determining privately that I would get up those cellar steps and back into the shop or die trying. For one thing, there was coffee up there and I needed some badly.

But for another, I really had begun recognizing that cutlass: unhappily, but pretty darned certainly. It wasn't one of the rubber or plastic imitations that guys in their Blackbeard or Barbarossa costumes were gallivanting around with during the pirate festival.

No, this was the real deal: Damascus steel, a wrapped leather grip, richly engraved at the hilt. It was two hundred years old and valuable, and I knew all this because it belonged to my husband, Wade Sorenson.

I'd last seen it in my own kitchen. The two-foot blade had a few dings in it, but given that the weapon was more a historical item than a useful one, Wade had decided not to fix them.

All these facts came back to me as I stood wavering uncertainly at the foot of the stairs. Instead of saying them aloud, though, I kept my mouth shut and waited for further developments.

For the cellar to stop spinning, for instance. I glanced down at my shirtfront. Blood from my wounded forehead stained it.

"I look," I muttered, "like Lady Macbeth."

By then I could barely put the two words together, I was so—

Dizzy. A sound escaped me. Suddenly six Bob faces whirled like a Ferris wheel in front of me, and my ears rang like gongs.

"Uh-oh," said somebody. An ambulance guy, maybe.

Then I passed out.

"Stay," said my housekeeper-slash-stepmother, Bella Diamond, six hours later.

And yes, I do know that sounds complicated. But the boiled-down version is pretty simple: she'd been my housekeeper, and then she'd married my father. Now they both lived in my big old house with the rest of us: Wade; Sam; his wife, Mika; their little boy, Ephraim; and me.

Plus my headache, which was now so huge I thought it might need to be given a room of its own. Anywhere but in my skull would've been fine with me. In the emergency room they'd determined that I didn't have a concussion, a stroke, a blood clot, or any of the many other serious conditions they were obliged to rule out when a person rolled in through their doors with a headache and a history of passing out.

But oh, did it hurt. "Drink this," said Bella, pushing me gently back down into the recliner where I'd been sitting, then handing me a steaming mug. I sniffed: coffee, heavily spiked with brandy.

Double the fun. Probably forbidden, too. When the docs said fluids, I doubted they'd meant booze. "Bella, maybe I shouldn't—"

We were in the front parlor: high ceilings, ornately carved wooden mantel, tall windows with lace counterpanes and heavy, old brocade draperies.

"Just never you mind," said Bella. In her sixties, hatchet-faced and green-eyed, with frizzy dyed-red hair, big front teeth, and bony wrists like chicken drumstick knobs that were sticking out of her green sweatshirt sleeves, she was my rock, my can't-do-without-her helper, and most of all, my friend.

And right now, apparently, she was my boss. "Don't even start with me," she added in no-nonsense tones. "You've had a shock, and a bad bump, and found a body. And I'm in charge of you."

"Oh," I said, feeling a good deal better suddenly. Bella was bossy all the time, and not always in a welcome manner, but the idea of someone else being in charge seemed particularly attractive at the moment. I took a gulp of my hot drink and felt the brandy molecules percolating through my collapsed brain cells, reviving them.

Or at least making them dance around very happily indeed, which was enough for me at the moment. Leaning back, I regarded my familiar surroundings: beneath the brass chandelier, a small blaze flickered warmly on the tiled hearth and the cranberry-glass lamps under their antique parchment shades cast a reassuring glow over the comfortable old room.

But it was awfully quiet. "Where is everyone?"

It was dark outside the windows, and ordinarily by now Sam and Mika would be upstairs bathing Ephraim, Wade would be (a) out on the water or (b) in his shop fixing whatever rare or valuable weapon somebody wanted expertly repaired, and my dad would be in his studio on the third floor of our massive old dwelling. At age eighty-plus he'd taken up oil painting, a brand-new interest of his, which was why the whole place smelled a little bit like turpentine lately.

"I got them all out of the way," Bella replied. "So you could rest."

"Really? All of them?" I thought about asking her where she'd gotten the bulldozer to do it, but I couldn't muster the energy. For her nursing duties this evening she wore a flower-printed apron over the sweatshirt, plus jeans and a pair of loafers.

No socks. Maybe she'd used a flyswatter, I imagined dreamily. Or a rolling pin. I suspected I wasn't thinking clearly. But never mind.

"Now, you drink that up," she urged. "All of it, mind you, and close your eyes when you feel like it, and—"

"I know, don't move an inch." It was what she always said when anyone in the house was sick, and she gave me a thin, grudging smile in return. She was an overbearing old fussbudget, our Bella, but she would have stepped in front of a freight train for any one of us.

So when she'd gone, I tried to obey: sip, doze, sip some more. I would deal with it all tomorrow, I decided. Until . . .

"*Psst!*"

I lurched up. My head only swam a little bit. The sound,

muffled by the heavy drapes, came from the open-a-crack window behind my chair.

"*Jake!*" It was Ellie, calling to me from outside.

"Ellie, what're you—?"

"Bella won't let me in! Not even a phone call, she says, but I'm afraid if we don't talk before tomorrow—"

I got up and hunkered behind the chair by the window, pulling the curtains apart slightly. The sweet scent of newly mown grass drifted in; since Sam had combated the very real scarcity of local jobs by starting his own independent lawn care business, our whole neighborhood was like a putting green.

Well, except for our lawn, of course. "I'm so glad you're here," I whispered to Ellie through the open window.

From Water Street where the pirate festival was still going on just a few blocks distant, music and laughter drifted.

Ellie's face floated ghostly white in the gleams of lamplight escaping the window. "Me too. That you are, I mean. How are you?"

I touched my forehead: ow. But the dizziness was really fading, I thought. "Fine," I said, stretching the truth a little. "What's going on?"

Plenty, probably. I'd left her with all that baking to finish, plus all the shop cleanup. Not to mention that by now on account of what I'd found, there were probably lots of . . .

"Cops." She finished my thought. "County sheriff's deputies, so far, and a bunch of reporters are showing up, too."

Sure, I thought; Hadlyme really had been a TV personality, even if only a minor one, not as well known as he liked to think. And the pirate cutlass run through him only made his murder more interesting.

I mean, if anything can be more interesting than a corpse with a stuffed parrot pinned to its shoulder. "Do they know—?"

"*Oof.*" A muffled sound drifted up—not a curse, but close. "Darn, I tripped over a root."

The old trees in the yard had roots very near the surface, and they were hazardous in the dark. "And I dropped my . . ."

Then came scuffling noises; I guessed she was retrieving things from her satchel. And while that was happening, Bella came in with a tray in her hands and spied me at the window.

"Who's out there?" she asked suspiciously, but Ellie had already vanished into the darkness among the lilacs at the edge of the yard.

"No one," I told her, "just noise from downtown." Much more of this and my nose would grow longer than my arm. I settled back into the chair and let her put the tray on my lap.

She'd made a slice of toast, homemade and well buttered. I bit in and found that I was hungry. Also it didn't hurt a bit that the tea was Constant Comment steeped in a pot.

"How's Dad?" I took another bite of toast while Bella pulled a clean dust rag from her apron pocket and began running it over the wooden furniture.

"Well, he's no spring chicken, you know," she said, sighing resignedly.

I used to believe her cleaning fetish was part of a personality disorder, but eventually I'd come to realize that it was an aesthetic choice. And living in a house that was always as clean as a surgical suite was not unpleasant, once I'd gotten used to it.

"Thinks he's Michelangelo. He'll be up on a stepladder painting the ceiling before you know it. But it keeps him busy," she went on.

Her voice was like a creaking hinge on account of her being no spring chicken herself. "Out of my hair," she added, sounding put-upon. But she loved him extravagantly, and we all knew it.

She shoved the rag back into her apron pocket. "Now you just go on sitting there, you hear? Let your brains try gathering themselves back together for once. If they can," she finished dryly.

She knew about the body in the shop cellar, of course; by now the news must be all over town. And she was no fan whatsoever of any kind of murder investigation, especially if it involved me.

Which was why she was trying her darnedest to head off this one. "Now, Bella—" I began placatingly.

Over the past few years, Ellie and I had been involved in what even I thought were way too many suspicious deaths in and around our little community. Snooping into them, that is.

"Sam and Mika took the baby downtown to see the torch parade," she interrupted my thought, "to give you some peace and quiet."

So take advantage of it, her tone added sternly as she slipped behind the recliner I sat in and shut the offending window with a decisive thud.

Then she left me to finish my toast, which I did quickly before crumpling my napkin, gulping my tea, and hurrying out the front door into the chilly evening before Bella could come back and catch me.

Ellie was waiting for me just outside the glow of the porch lamp, as I'd known she would be.

"How are you?" she repeated, squinting at the gauze square taped to my forehead.

"Just ducky." I followed her to her car and got in, not slamming the passenger-side door until we'd gotten away from the house.

"I'm still a little dizzy, and I've got a bit of a headache," I said. This last part was putting it mildly. "But don't worry, my brains have gotten stirred harder than this before, without any bad effects."

Ellie glanced skeptically at me as if to say she wasn't so sure. But she was just kidding.

I think. Anyway: "The shop's fine, and the baking for tomorrow is all done. Mika came down to help me finish it while you were at the emergency room," she said.

Besides having produced my excellent grandson, my daughter-in-law was smart, talented, even-tempered, and—most important to me right now—in her life before she met Sam and came here, a prize-winning amateur pastry chef.

"So we're all set to open for business again," Ellie said as she drove us toward downtown.

On Water Street, hilariously drunk pirates hoisted bottles and sang about keelhauling guys just like themselves while dancing around a bonfire in the parking lot by the fish pier.

"Uh, then what are we doing here?" I asked, watching the orange sparks spiral up into the night.

She pulled over in front of the shop and turned to me, her face deadly serious in the glow of the nearby street lamp. "Jake, I'm not entirely sure you understand your situation completely."

"Oh, of course I do. I found the body, and not long before that I had a loud, very public argument with the deceased."

So the homicide detectives who would soon be arriving to look into the murder would be interested in me. But big deal, right?

Or so I thought, which just goes to show how clearly I wasn't thinking, and how right Ellie was to be concerned.

But I didn't realize that, either. "I mean, of course it was murder," I went on.

"People don't just pin toy parrots to their shoulders, fall on sharp cutlasses at exactly the right angle to pierce their hearts, and then shut themselves into basement cabinets so they can bleed to death in peace."

I took a breath. "So yes, I do know the cops will be examining any possible involvement of mine."

But there wasn't any, and they'd figure that out fairly quickly, I still felt certain.

"Right," Ellie agreed, eyeing me closely. "But . . ."

A guy tootling on a flute strolled tipsily by on the sidewalk, only occasionally veering off into the gutter. Behind him Bob

Arnold strolled, unperturbed; a happy drunk was the least of his worries.

"But what?" Once Bob had safely passed without spotting me, I got out of the car and followed Ellie as she went into the shop. Then another thought hit me:

"But never mind being ready for tomorrow, productwise. Can we be open at all? And did Bob say it was okay to mop the floor and—"

It wasn't the first crime ever committed in the Moose, so I knew the police would be touchy on the subject of evidence contamination.

"Yes," Ellie called from out in the kitchen. "The upstairs is okay, anyway, he said. Only the cellar is off-limits."

She returned to the shop front with coffee and a plate of fresh peanut-butter blossoms, each with a chocolate kiss pressed into it.

"All the ambulance people have already tramped in and out up here," she said. "Once for you, and again later for Hadlyme's body. So Bob took a lot of photographs and measurements, yellow-taped the alley door and the trap door in the kitchen, and called it good."

Listening, I devoured one of the peanut-butter blossoms, washing it down with the pure ambrosia Ellie poured from the French press.

Then she sat across from me, still looking more serious than I thought the situation warranted—that is, until I heard what she had to say.

Warranted was the correct word, all right. There'd be one sworn out soon, according to Ellie, who'd heard it from Bob Arnold himself.

A warrant for my arrest. I felt my jaw drop. "But—"

"Motive, method, opportunity," she ticked off on her fingers, the three boxes every murder investigator wants to check.

And all three had my name right next to them. "Well, all right, then, I guess, if they want to be that way about it," I said snidely. But this was serious. "He really thinks so? Bob does, that . . ."

She nodded, biting into a chocolate kiss. "That they'll charge you? Unless some other suspect gets even likelier-looking, yes. Which by the way . . ."

Yeah, yeah. I ran through the likely thought process in my head. There was the argument I'd had with Hadlyme, the fact that during it I'd threatened him, and of course that all the people watching us had heard me do it.

And then there was where the victim had been found, and by whom. "And with all that stuff lined up against me," I said, "I guess maybe you're right, they might not beat the bushes too hard for—"

"For a different suspect," Ellie agreed. "So Bob said to tell you to watch your step, and don't go gabbing any . . . any *things* to any people whatsoever. *Any* things," she emphasized, "even if you're just being sarcastic."

"Who, *moi*?" I tried sounding innocently unfazed, but just then on the street somewhere nearby, a string of firecrackers exploded, and after what Ellie had just said it felt to me as if they'd gone off inside my head.

"Ellie, I came in, I did some baking, I went downstairs for the mop and bucket the way I'd said I would, and then I found him. That's it, that's all there was to it."

She sighed. Since I'd seen her last, she'd changed out of her pirate-queen costume into blue jeans, a dark sweatshirt—in downeast Maine, early autumn evenings were cool—and sneakers.

"Right," she said, "and you just stick to that. Don't add on any gory details. In fact, like I said, just don't talk about it at all."

Black high-top sneakers, to be exact; it was her snooping outfit. I'd seen it before, and I suppose it should have alerted me.

Or maybe somewhere in my heart of hearts I'd already known. I mean, was it a coincidence that when I got home from the hospital earlier, I'd showered and put on a pair of black

Levi's, a dark gray turtleneck, a navy sweatshirt, and my own pair of black Keds? No wonder Bella had been hovering so vigilantly over me.

I got up. Outside, flaming torches and battery-powered lightsabers flared, the evening's carousing now having begun in earnest. But the dark window reflected the room behind me, too, and Ellie's face hovering unhappily.

"What?" I demanded, and then it hit me that there was even more evidence against me. There must be, from the way she looked. And then it came to me.

"The parrot," I said, still gazing out at the happy crowd on the firelit street. "And the cutlass itself. Bob mentioned those things, too?"

She nodded. "He was pretty worried about them, if you want to know the truth. Because it's hard to see how anyone else got their hands on them. Do you have any ideas about it?"

"Nope. Our house is like firearms central what with Wade fixing and restoring them all the time."

His day job was being the harbor pilot for the cargo port, where most days he hopped onto a tugboat, rode it to a waiting freighter, then guided the freighter in through the treacherous tides and tricky currents, over the rocks and granite ledges with which our waters were so plentifully furnished.

But his passion was his weapons collection, along with all the arcana of history, manufacturing, and repair techniques he'd come to know—or in many cases to invent for himself—over the years.

"But it's not like somebody could just walk in and grab one," I said. "All the guns are always locked up securely, and the bladed weapons, too."

Flintlocks, carbines, derringers, pepperboxes, cannons, rapiers, sabers, daggers, and yes, even cutlasses were all represented in my husband's extensive antique weapons collection. In addition, he owned a lot of hunting firearms, plus accessories and ammunition.

Without exception these items were in gun safes and lock-boxes, especially now with baby Ephraim in the house. But I knew where he kept the keys for the gun safes and the blade collections; I could have taken one of the weapons whenever I wished.

And I could've used one of them on Hadlyme, only—"Ellie, how would I have had the time?"

I couldn't even figure out how he'd managed to get killed at all, in the forty minutes or so that had passed between my arguing with him and finding him stabbed to death.

And then there were the parrot and cutlass. "Also," I said, "why would I go to so much trouble to implicate myself?"

"No idea," replied Ellie, shaking her head, "or why someone else would want to frame you, either."

She took our cups to the kitchen, then came back with her jacket on and a dark scarf tied over her bright hair.

"But that's what happened, and that's why we're going to go out right now and find out about a few things," she said, hustling me out of the shop once more and locking the door behind us. "Before somebody who *doesn't* have only your best interests at heart gets to them first," she added.

On the street, happy revelers waved tankards of hot rum punch in tipsy toasts, while across the way in the fish pier parking lot a jolly quartet played Cajun dance tunes on fiddles and an accordion.

"I'd walk the plank to get away from that accordion," I said as Ellie urged me into her car; my poor head felt as if it were splitting. Then she got behind the wheel and pulled out carefully, since by now many of the pirates were past worrying about being run over.

They were in a festive mood, though: they wore eye patches and fake scars, their grins punctuated by painted-on gold teeth. Some of their shirts were even stained with fake . . .

Blood. The sudden memory of Henry Hadlyme's, oozing out around the blade in his chest, made my stomach turn over abruptly. I almost asked to be taken home, but Ellie was determined to see this thing through and I didn't want to make a fuss without at least first finding out where she was going.

At the corner of Water and Washington Streets she turned uphill past the post office building, pausing so a trio of baggy-pantalooned sailors could cross safely, then headed out of town. Minutes later we passed the Bay City Mobil station, a hair salon called the Mousse Island Clipper, the old power plant, and the airport.

Finally, as the village's streets lined with houses gave way to stretches of scrub acreage, we turned onto a narrow lane between towering pines, with a six-hole golf course on one side and a row of older mobile homes with wood-framed additions and pressure-treated decks on the other. Next came a small campgrounds with widely separated campsites, each featuring a concrete pad where an RV could park, a hand pump, and a barbecue grill.

Past those stood a row of cottages overlooking the water. She snapped off her headlights, slowing as we approached the cottages.

"Ellie, what are we doing here?" I looked around puzzledly.

Tents and a few fifth-wheel campers were at the campsites, but no one seemed to be home: no lights, music, or flickering blue TV screens broke the night's dark silence. No campfires, either.

The small rough-hewn wood cottages were set between gnarly old pines on a high bluff looking out over the bay. They each had a red brick chimney, a small gravel parking area with a stone barbecue pit at one corner, and three tiny windows on the driveway side; more windows, I supposed, looked out toward the water.

All the cottages' porch lights were on, but only one of the interiors was lit. "Ellie?" I said. "D'you want to give me a hint, at least, about what we're . . ."

But she still didn't answer—just kept driving until we were up nearly under the big old trees that lined the cottages' clearing, and then up another short, sharp rise in among the low branches until our car was hidden completely.

Three

Under the pines, their massive needled branches a canopy for our car, the first crickets of early autumn chirped tentatively. In the distance, waves crashed endlessly onto rocks.

Everything else was silent. Ellie pulled to a stop on the carpet of pine needles beneath the trees. In the clearing by the cottages overlooking the water stood two cars with New York plates, a van with the familiar crossed-knife-and-fork *Eat This!* logo stenciled on the doors, and a bus-sized recreational vehicle.

A *luxurious*-looking recreational vehicle... Suddenly I knew whose it must be. Had been, rather.

Hadlyme's, of course. Far be it from him to want to rough it in one of the campgrounds' charming but tiny, relatively primitive cottages; slumming with the riffraff, I guessed he'd have called it.

Ellie squinted at the small log-built structures. Shrubbery clustered thickly around them, and I could see her thinking about that.

Planning how to take advantage of it, I suspected. "Please tell me," I began, "that you're not getting ready to . . ."

Her lips clamped together stubbornly. "Break in? What else do you suggest?"

She turned to me in the car's front seat. "Jake, don't you get it yet? We've got to get ahead of this thing. I'm serious, when the state cops get here—which by the way they're going to do any minute—you'll be in real trouble if we don't straighten it out first."

In Maine, only the Bangor and Portland police departments have their own homicide divisions. Murders elsewhere in the state are handled by the Maine State Police.

And she was right, they were going to get here real soon, and then I would be in trouble.

But not for long, surely; how could I be? I mean, obviously I was innocent.

But I could tell that she was thinking very differently about it as she switched off the car's interior lights so they wouldn't go on when the doors were opened.

"For one thing, you'll need a lawyer, and in case you weren't aware of it, good lawyers cost money," she said. "Maybe lots of it."

Well, when I heard that, I got out of the car so fast you'd have thought it was on fire; sure, The Chocolate Moose was doing better financially, lately, but not *that* much better.

Besides, she was right. What we really needed to do was arrange for me not to need a defense lawyer at all. And for that—well, she wasn't dressed in her snooping outfit for nothing, and I wasn't just along for the ride.

Ellie was already hunched over and hustling ahead of me through the shadows under the big pines. Hurrying to catch up, I tripped hard over an exposed tree root, then slammed into a rocky outcropping that suddenly shouldered through the gloom at me.

If Bella had known what I was up to, she'd have murdered

me and eliminated the need for my defense entirely. "So, what exactly are you planning?" I whispered to Ellie.

She turned to me in the shadows, her expression intent. "Look, someone killed him," she told me in low tones. "So probably they had reasons. Let's start by trying to find out what those reasons were, and maybe when we do, the reasons will tell us who. Dunnit, that is."

Huh. Reasonable *and* concise . . . so how could I resist?

"Okay," I replied simply, following her through the underbrush some more, and after fifty yards or so of weeds, brambles, pricker bushes, and a variety of tripping hazards, we were at the bluff's edge.

I peered over, only to confront a straight-down plunge to granite rocks and probable death thirty feet below.

Cringing, I eased along the narrow walkway, glimpsing white foam down there in the darkness where the waves crashed mercilessly. Moments later I slipped in beside Ellie among the bushes growing by the only cottage with interior lights on.

"Maybe Hadlyme's whole podcast crew is in there celebrating the success of their murder plan," I muttered as voices drifted from the open window over our heads.

". . . to Henry Hadlyme! May never an egg like his be fertilized again," pronounced a man's voice from inside, and a restrained but extremely sincere-sounding cheer went up at his words.

A toast, then, I thought, to the not-so-dearly departed. Another voice came through the window, a woman's this time:

"I swear, if that handsy little lech put his arms around me from behind *one more time* . . ."

"You'd have what, killed him dead?" A third voice, sounding only half-joking, piped up.

"I mean, seriously," the voice went on, "where were you when he was getting stabbed to death? You sure you didn't lose that famous temper of yours and—"

"With what, the antique sword I keep in my purse?" The other voice, a young woman's, sounded irritated.

"Anyway, why don't you shut up, Lionel? Because for one thing you're really boring when you're drunk, and come to think of it—"

"Right, you're the one with the motive, Lionel," yet another voice, a man's this time, pointed out. "So I'd watch what I said if I were you."

Whoever Lionel was, he didn't reply. Or maybe couldn't, because someone else, another female-sounding person, spoke first.

"Whatever, he's dead and good riddance," she said in placating tones, sounding as if she might be trying to head off a quarrel. "I don't care if I do end up having to look for another job. It'll be worth it not to see that horrifying little—"

Suddenly I wanted badly to match these voices with faces, so I squinted, looking around for something to stand on to try to peek inside. After spying a wooden lobster crate with geraniums planted in it, I turned it on its side and stepped onto it, balancing precariously to press my face to one of the cottage's little windows.

And there they were, the half-dozen hipsterish-looking young people who'd been following Henry Hadlyme around. Two of the women wore their hair in short bobs with square-cut bangs, one black and one dyed a platinum lime green. The third woman's head held a thick blond braid coiled in a coronet.

"Jake!" Ellie hissed urgently at me. "Come down from—"

"I mean it about the motive, though, Lionel," said the blond-braid woman. Even from a distance I could see she had those cornflower-blue eyes people rave about.

"Wasn't he getting ready to fire you? *And*," she added, "saying he'd make sure you never got work again, too?"

She grimaced at her beer bottle. "I mean, if you want to talk about reasons . . ." she said, letting her voice trail off meaningfully.

Lionel was a wiry young guy wearing a denim jacket over a plaid collar shirt and cargo pants. Leather sandals were on his feet and in his left nostril a tiny gold stud gleamed.

He was the one who'd been trying to photograph me outside The Chocolate Moose, I realized, using that clumsy old-fashioned device called a camera instead of a smartphone.

"Maybe you should try keeping your mouth shut yourself," he retorted to the blond woman. "It'd be a new experience for you, and I know you're big on those, right?"

The blond woman glowered, and the rest of the podcast crew looked uncomfortable. Then one of the other two fellows—one plump and heavily neck-bearded, the other a buff bodybuilder type with a buzz cut and a heavily tattooed scalp—spoke up.

"Listen, we all hated Henry and we all had our reasons, and all of us know it. But what we need is to not let anyone *else* know it."

Okay, now we're getting somewhere, I thought, just as the box I was standing on collapsed under me with a *crack*, toppling me sideways into the bushes beneath the open window.

At once everyone inside rushed out onto the cottage's porch, which was so close to the bluff's edge that it actually stuck out over it a little bit.

Their voices mingled in alarm. "What was that? Did you hear it? Is somebody out there? Who—?"

Sprawled in the darkness with my back hard up against the cottage's rear wall and my head wedged nearly beneath it, I bit back the remarks I felt like making: cursing interspersed with moans of sudden pain, mostly.

Then I looked around frantically for Ellie but didn't see her; probably she had already vamoosed and was somewhere nearby, waiting for me.

I sure hoped so, anyway. Meanwhile, as I lay there, cramped

and thoroughly uncomfortable, I slowly became aware of the sensation of liquid trickling down my neck and into my shirt.

"Hey, has anybody seen Linda around lately?" Lionel called out, but nobody answered. "While we were all talking I think maybe she—"

Warm liquid; blood, probably. *Oh, great . . .*

Now Lionel was stomping around the edge of the gravel parking area near the cottages, aiming a flashlight into the bushes and around the tree trunks. Fortunately he didn't get very far from the clearing, or he'd have come upon our car.

"Linda?" he called. "Hey, Linda, come on, now, you'd better come on back here and—"

Something long and cold moved slitheringly under my hand. Long, cold, and . . . oh, good heavens, the thing was *scaly*.

It was a snake, I recognized with fresh horror as the thing went on wriggling unhappily. And due to the way my cupped hand was trapped atop it in the soft earth around the cabin's foundation, the reptile couldn't escape any more than I could.

So there I was, trapped, bleeding, and about to be snake-bit. It was almost enough to make me wish for a nice, safe prison cell.

Almost. Lionel returned back to the cottage, still searching around with his flashlight beam. "Linda? Linda, are you out here somewhere?"

The snake under my hand *rippled*, trying to get away, which was when I figured it out: Linda. The name of the snake.

The flashlight beam probed suddenly into the bushes around me while Lionel kept calling and the snake squirmed harder. I froze as, at last, the creature slid slickly from under my hand, up and out and swiftly slithering away.

Then came an "Oh!" of discovery from Lionel: "There you are!"

He stepped into the porch light's yellow glow with the snake, passing it familiarly from one hand to the other as it twined between his fingers. Now the whole crew was out there, together on a postage-stamp-sized deck over a thirty-foot drop to the rocks below.

Another pang of anxiety went through me, for their sake instead of my own this time. The deck was fairly sturdy, I imagined, but I wouldn't have wanted to test its weight-bearing capacity myself.

Besides, I was already busy testing my hemorrhage-tolerating capacity; that blood still seemed to be flowing pretty freely. I tried shifting my weight onto my other hand, without success, and both feet were tangled in the demolished box I'd been standing on.

Then: "Jake?" Ellie's voice hissed out of the darkness.

"*Mmph*," I managed. "Hang on, I'll be right with you."

With the snake gone I could at least haul my head out from under the cottage and inch forward slightly. The smells of leaf mold and rotting wooden underpinnings rose up dankly.

"Just another minute or so," I added, which was maybe a little optimistic. But I was very determined. . . .

Hadlyme's podcast crew had gone inside and now they'd begun arguing again—louder now, maybe because they'd been drinking. Through the window I'd seen quite a pile of Sam Adams empties already heaped in the kitchen sink.

And as I struggled to get up, I gathered also that none of them really knew where any of the others were when Hadlyme was murdered.

"But *you* went . . . no, *you* wandered off on your own to . . . wait, *I* never even went near the . . ."

I used their raised voices to cover the sounds of my own hasty scrambling out of the thicket at last, then hurried to Ellie's car.

She was already in it; I hurled myself in as well, taking care to close the door very quietly. Then I squinted into the car's visor mirror to get a look at myself, checking for injuries.

A bloody scratch ran across one of my cheeks, but that was all. It wasn't enough to cause much bleeding, so how . . . ?

"Look," said Ellie, letting the car roll silently downhill and out from under the pines. She took a hand from the wheel to point at my open collar and the skin beneath it, where I'd felt—

Not blood; there was no wound whatsoever, in fact. But something was running there, all right. A *lot* of somethings. . . .

"*Blearrghh!*" I exclaimed, and many other emphatic syllables, too, but none of them quite captured the way I felt about all those caterpillars—small, soft greenish-white ones—spilling from the squirming mass of them that tangled up in my hair while I was stuck halfway underneath the cottage.

"Ellie, stop the . . ." *Car*, I was about to say, but then one of the caterpillars made it into my mouth and got bitten, which kept me very busy and unable to say more while she (a) popped the clutch, (b) got the engine running as quietly as she could, and (c) got us the heck out of there, pronto.

Down the lane, past the campsites where lights were beginning to go on as people returned from the evening pirate festival activities, Ellie drove while I picked little caterpillars off myself and flung them out the window, meanwhile trying not to throw up.

In my mouth. That wiggling larva had been in my *mouth*. . . .

But then she did stop, pulling over onto the gravel at the side of the road, where she snapped on the passenger compartment's overhead light and then inspected me for remaining critters.

"Okay, there's one, and there's another one, and . . . okay, you're clean," she pronounced after picking off the last half-mashed dead insect plus a few more miraculously-still-living ones.

Then she dug out the spray bottle of lavender water that she kept in her bag and handed it over. "Here, use this."

I stepped out of the car and sprayed liberally. "That's better,"

I breathed. It was, too. I wasn't covered with critters anymore. Or cuddled up to a pet snake named Linda.

"Good. Now get back in the car, Jake," Ellie said. "We've got more work to do."

Back on Key Street, my house was lit up like an airport, all the windows illuminated from within and the yard lamps and the porch lights blazing. I threaded my way to the porch between a broken snowblower and a plow blade with a chunk missing from its edge; Sam did winter yard work, too.

"Hello?" I called, climbing the steps and letting myself inside.

Bella had already gone upstairs for the night; I could tell by the spic-and-span kitchen with its porcelain stove top gleaming, the hardwood floor swept and mopped, and the dishes all washed and dried and put neatly away right down to the last curve-handled baby spoon.

Even the sink glowed with recent scouring, and the place smelled as it always did in the evening when she'd finished with it, like a bucket of hot Ivory Snow soapsuds plus about a tablespoon of bleach.

"Anyone?" I called down the dim hall where the old grandfather clock ticked hollowly.

Still no reply, but from upstairs I heard the shower running at one end of the house and a lullaby tinkling out of a music box at the other. So I knew Sam and Mika were putting little Ephraim to bed—he was fussing, and I hoped it wasn't about that missing parrot—and Wade was home and getting himself cleaned up after bringing another cargo freighter safely into port.

That left me alone for once, and ordinarily I might've enjoyed it; around here lately, solitude had become a scarce commodity. But now that I *was* alone, I could feel the soft bodies of little white larvae moving on me again.

Also, I could hear Ellie's words to me on the way here: "Jake, I don't care if they do have motives," she'd said.

I'd been talking about how good it was that Hadlyme's podcast crew hated him, or anyway that they disliked him so very thoroughly. Their reasons might not eliminate all suspicions about me, but they'd have a diluting effect, surely.

But Ellie wasn't convinced. "No one else knows how they all felt about him, or at any rate no one else around here does. And I doubt that they're going to be as forthcoming with the police as they were just now with one another," she'd said.

And she'd been correct, as usual. But there was not much more I could do about any of it tonight, so to distract myself I grabbed a pair of beer bottles from the fridge, then climbed the stairs to the third floor and my dad's painting studio.

Back in the 1800s when the house was built, servants' rooms were up here under the eaves. When I'd first moved in, I'd imagined them in the tiny rooms, warmed by the few sticks of wood they were given for their woodstoves and saying their prayers by gaslight.

Even now the antique gas pipes remained in the walls, their threaded ends exposed and ready for antique lamps to be screwed onto them in places that hadn't been rehabbed yet. But most of the third-floor space was now a modern apartment for Bella and my dad.

That still left another big room up here, though, with four tall south-facing windows where he'd put an easel plus rows of shelves for his other supplies. A fan had been mounted in one of the windows to exhaust fumes of turpentine and other solvents.

"Hey," he said mildly now, looking up from his canvas. Despite the quietly whirring fan, up here the sweet smell of oil paint was intoxicating. "Come on in."

In his eighties, he wore his long, thinning gray hair tied back in a scraggly ponytail. Denim overalls sagged on his thin, stooped frame, and his mottled hands, curved with arthritis, looked way too much like claws for my comfort.

Or for his own; he took a lot of pills nowadays, and some of them were for pain. He'd become a father so late in life—my mother was several decades younger—that most people thought he was my grandfather. But he held his brush steadily enough and managed to get around okay; now he aimed the brush at an orange beanbag chair placed over against the wall.

"Have a seat," he invited; another thing that hadn't faded with his age was that he always knew when I needed to talk.

Other than the shelves and long, wide worktable, the beanbag chair was the only furniture in the room, and I thought its awkwardness was deliberate; this place wasn't for socializing. So I plopped into the thing, adjusted myself until I was at least halfway comfortable, then got right to the point.

"Dad, I've got a problem," I said. "I'm suspected of murder, or about to be."

Those podcast-crew members of Hadlyme's were busy getting their individual stories straight, I felt certain now that I'd had time to think about it. They'd been learning whatever they could from one another while not giving away too much themselves.

That's what all the low-level quarreling had been about out at the campground cottage; everyone feeling the others out as to motives and opportunities, nobody wanting to get blamed. And they were smart to do so; it was in all of their interests to alibi one another if they could.

But if they did it right, that left me holding the murder bag.

I passed my dad one of the beer bottles I carried, then took a long swig from the one I still held.

"Murder, hey?" My dad's tone was unfazed. He'd been accused of a few things in his time, too.

And he'd done a few of them. "You guilty?" he wanted to know.

"Dad! No, I didn't—"

"Just asking." He shrugged, touching his brush to the canvas he was working on, then eyed the result and did it again, glancing from the photograph he was trying to reproduce to the canvas and back.

"Makes a difference, though, you know. In," he added, "the whole getting-out-of-a-pickle department."

"Yes, I'm sure it does," I replied. "But like I say, I didn't."

Back in the old days my dad had been an expert at getting out of pickles, mostly because he'd been so good at getting into them. For a long time, for instance, a great many homicide cops—local, state, and federal, too—thought he'd murdered my mother.

Which he hadn't. He'd loved her the way his lungs loved oxygen. But since he couldn't prove his innocence, he'd spent thirty years avoiding his pursuers.

Avoiding me, too, actually; it's a long, difficult story. But in the end, and after he'd been exonerated, we got over it. Anyway:

"Your son's collection of lawn-care equipment is filling up the whole yard, you know," he told me, changing the subject.

Or seeming to. "Yes, well, he's got his landscaping business going great guns finally, and he needs that stuff to do all the work he's getting."

A sweet little mental picture of the flower-and-vegetable plots I wanted to have out there flitted through my mind and vanished. *Patience, grasshopper*, I told myself.

"Sooner or later he'll be able to afford a separate place for it all, but—"

My dad's bushy eyebrows went up and down skeptically. "Wouldn't count on that. The sooner part, anyway."

He squinted at the canvas, at the photograph, and finally at me.

"Jacobia," he began. That's my whole name; his is Jacob. You do the math. "Jacobia, tell me, when a healthy young woman like Mika starts losing her breakfast every morning *before* breakfast, when she never had any such trouble before, what d'you suppose it means?"

I drew a blank, briefly. Then: "Oh no. You mean she's . . ."

My dad's skinny shoulders moved under his flannel shirt, which was so paint-daubed and faded with washing that its original color was unknowable. His gaze was still on his work in progress, but now it flickered over to me occasionally.

"Your stepmother is sure of it," he said. "And not a bit happy about what it's going to mean."

Me either. Another baby was going to put a serious wrench in our already chaotic household's monkeyworks. Still: "It's not any of our business how many kids they have," I said.

He put his brush down carefully. "Jake, it's not how many, it's where. Bella loves Ephraim, and she'll love a new one, too, you know she will. But it's not about having another one. It's about where to put it."

Correct: if my son and daughter-in-law were expecting, we needed to make a plan, since if we just started trying to shoe-horn another person into this house willy-nilly, the ones who already lived here were going to start popping out the windows.

On the other hand, they hadn't *told* us they were expecting, had they? Not yet, anyway. . . .

"Okay, look," I said, getting up. "Let's give them a little time to break the news to us the way they want. *If* there's news," I added. "I mean, maybe she's just got a stomach bug."

His bushy eyebrows moved up and down once again, silently remarking on what a vain hope this was, but I could see him at least partly coming around to my idea.

"And meanwhile we can be thinking about it," I said.

About Sam and his little family finding their own place to live, I meant, and the very idea nearly made me burst into tears.

Not quite, though; determinedly I bit my feelings back. I'd lived with Sam for a long time and always enjoyed it; despite a few bumps in the road he was the son I'd always hoped he would be.

And I'd miss him terribly. But now as his mother I had to be brave and generous, or try. "What're you painting?" I asked brightly.

My dad stepped back, gesturing me around to the front of the easel.

"Oh," I said, surprised. I'd intended to praise the work even before I got a look at it, or at least to find something positive about it.

But it was much better than I'd expected, and now I did see: it was a painting of my mother, age sixteen or so, done from the old photograph he'd been looking at while he worked.

I hadn't seen the photograph before, either, or at any rate I didn't remember it. "She's beautiful," I said.

His gaze softened. "She surely is. I used to watch her, you know, when she didn't know I was looking at her. Back then, she had no way of knowing I loved her so much."

I'd been three when my mother died in the house explosion that my dad was accused of causing. Now I slung an arm around him.

"That's okay, Dad. She found out."

A smile deepened the wrinkles in his face. "Yes, she did. She's still as beautiful today as she was then, too."

Which surprised me even more. He never talked about the hereafter; I'd never even known that he believed in it. My sense of him was that he felt his proper business was "now," and if he did okay with that, then he'd probably do all right with the "later," too. But I figured I could question him about this some other time.

"Got a lot of work to do on it yet," he said, dipping his brush and wiping it on a rag. "But that's all right. One step at a time. Labor of love, and all that."

His voice trailed off thoughtfully. Time to go, I realized. In a house where space and privacy were at a premium, this was his refuge, and I didn't want to overstay my welcome.

But I couldn't stop gazing at the portrait and wishing I looked exactly like it, not just sort of. The wavy dark hair, dark eyes, and crooked smile of the woman in the picture were the same as mine, and I now wore the ruby studs that had gleamed in her ears back then.

The woman in the painting, though . . . I mean, it's not like I scare small children or anything, but she was *beautiful*.

"Now, this murder you mentioned," he said, still doing something with his brush and the turpentine.

I could almost remember her voice. Like I say, I'd been three. *Hi, Mom*, I thought, and turned from the portrait.

"I did hear something earlier today about a body," my dad added as he turned off the exhaust fan in the window.

Bella thought the turpentine smell in the house was too much for little Ephraim otherwise, and I agreed. "Right," I said. "In our shop's cellar, right after my public fight with him. And . . ."

I was pretty sure Wade hadn't missed the antique cutlass from his weapons collection yet. It could take a whole day to get out to meet a freighter, board it from his smaller boat, and then wait for the tide and the currents to be favorable before guiding them into harbor. When he got back at last, he was always beat.

". . . and there are other problems," I finished, and left my dad locking up his studio, which, like Wade's weapons collection, was off-limits to my grandson.

"Maybe just lay low," my dad offered as I reached the stairs. "Let it blow over a little. After a while other information could come to light, and once the dust settles a bit the cops might just decide to get interested in someone else."

"Maybe," I replied doubtfully, and back downstairs I took the rest of my beer onto the porch and sat in one of the green-painted wooden Adirondack chairs, pondering my options.

I would tell Wade right away about the stolen cutlass, I decided; he'd find out soon enough, anyway, either when he missed it himself or when the cops learned who around here had a lot of old weapons and showed up to ask him about them.

And—inspiration struck me—I could buy a new stuffed parrot for Ephraim, too, just like the old one but without any murder cooties on it. I could do it online right now, in fact, so I fetched my laptop and did.

But the "related products" display on the shopping website led me directly to the other subject my dad had mentioned: babies.

And that raised a question I couldn't answer. We'd find space for another kid somehow, I supposed, but where? Ephraim shared a room with his parents and was getting nearly big enough to need his own. We didn't have another one, though, so if Mika really was expecting. . . .

Well, for that I had no ready solution. But there was still one thing that maybe I could do something about:

Murder. Bloody murder, to be exact. My dad's advice to lay low and see how things developed was probably correct. It had the strong advantage of not risking life and limb, too.

My life and limb, that is. But the disadvantage was that if it was wrong and over time the cops just got more fixated on me, there'd be no second chance, because one of the main things you can't do from inside a jail cell is snoop.

So I decided to resume doing it. Starting right this minute.

Strolling down Key Street in the dark, I passed beneath the branches of the ancient maples, their leaves blocking the streetlamp's glow and making the night seem mysterious. Big old wooden houses like my own loomed on either side, their dark, many-paned antique windows peering down balefully at me.

At the corner between the red-brick Peavey Library and the Motel East, with its parking lot full of out-of-state cars, their owners here for the festival, I turned left onto Water Street, still crowded with clusters of fake pirates and bouncing to the beat of a rock band set up across from the fish pier.

The bay shimmered with moonlight, silvering the fishing boats at their moorings as they moved gently with the waves and tide. But as I passed I spotted another shape out there, too.

Black as night and with its black sails spread against the sky, a boat nosed ponderously into the harbor. A figure on the deck shoved an anchor overboard—it hit the water with a muffled splash—then in a series of efficient movements lowered the sails and furled them until they were wrapped around their masts as tightly as bat's wings.

Beside me, someone let out a low whistle. It was Bob Arnold, his round, pink face looking grim. "Wow, that's some boat," he commented.

"Yeah. Whose is it, do you know?"

He shrugged. "Maybe another pirate wannabe?" His tone said he was not a fan of the celebration at the moment, and since he'd been policing it for the past twenty-four hours, I could understand this.

"Not my problem till they're on land, though," he went on, his eyes still on the dark vessel. "Until then they belong to the Coast Guard and maybe the border patrol." If they'd come over from Canada, he meant. "You heard from the state cops yet?"

I shook my head, still watching the boat. Never mind Canada; with its dark sails and pitch-black cabin windows, the newly arrived vessel looked as if its home territory was the river Styx.

"Yeah, me neither," he replied, glancing at me. "They might be in town by now, but I suppose it's too much trouble for them to let me in on their plans."

It was a common complaint of his. "Jake, I hope you and Ellie aren't sticking your noses into what happened to Hadlyme."

"Who, us?" I attempted to look innocent, and you can probably imagine how well that went. "Now, Bob, you know I'm just—"

He grimaced, shaking his head. "Oh, sure I do. I know you both way too well, actually. Have you forgotten what happened last time?"

I hadn't forgotten. It had involved a poisoned milkshake from the Moose, and without going into too much detail, let's just say it had *also* involved a drowning, an unpleasant amount of bleeding, and some seriously scary near-death experiences.

Too near, and several of them had been my own. "Bob, I promise you, I just came down to check the shop one last time this evening."

Which was not strictly true, but it made sense, as I saw when at that moment a crowd of young men dressed like eighteenth-century deckhands—blouses, pantaloons, laced leather jerkins—poured out of the Waco Diner, singing loudly if not very harmoniously about drunken sailors and what to do with them.

Then from the other direction came an equally rowdy posse of laughing young ladies in low-cut blouses, high-heeled boots, and long black skirts with red petticoats peeping from beneath their hems.

Nobody looked worrisome, just happy and sozzled. The revelers met and greeted one another, clearly pleased to be finding themselves in opposite-gender company.

"Seems like some mingling is about to occur," I remarked, and Bob shot me a look.

"But they don't look exactly sober, do they?"

Yeah, no, they didn't. Not enough to get behind the wheel, anyway, and they were headed for their cars, which to Bob was the equivalent of lighting a book of matches while you're carrying a bunch of dynamite. He *despised* buzzed driving.

Me too, actually. "Good luck," I told him.

Then I quickstepped the rest of the way down Water Street

to The Chocolate Moose. But when I got there I hurried past, since to my unhappy surprise the lights were on inside and some guys with plastic ID badges on lanyards around their necks were moving around in there in a very well-organized-looking way.

And a white van with state police plates was parked outside, too; so Bob had been right. They were evidence technicians, probably. The landlord must've let them in; Ellie and I were in talks to buy the building, but the deal hadn't gone through yet.

Yikes. I strode on toward the post office building, all the while expecting to feel a hand dropping onto my shoulder. They were going to catch up with me sooner or later, after all, and when they did they might even have a warrant ready.

On the other hand, they must've arrived fairly recently, or Bob would've seen them and mentioned it to me. That meant they'd probably be working for a while, and *that* meant they probably wouldn't show up where I'd actually been headed all along.

Crossing the street by the post office building, I passed the hot dog stand, the Port Authority building, and the red-roofed Coast Guard headquarters. Two blocks later, uphill past the lobster pound, I reached the Oyster House, a bar and restaurant spread out along a little inlet at the water's edge.

The parking lot was crowded with cars, of course; the pirate festival tide floated every business in town. Inside, I slipped between crowded tables and made a beeline for the bar.

"Hey, Weasel." I slid up next to the guy on the end barstool. He looked like he'd been there a while. "I was hoping I'd find you here."

Another fib: I'd known. In his thirties, Weasel Bodine was small and long-snouted with two fanglike yellow front teeth protruding from between liver-colored lips. He wore a faded black KISS T-shirt, denim jacket, and dungarees, and this was his usual haunt.

"What's shakin'?" he asked with a grin, and I relaxed inwardly. Weasel was in a good mood.

"I heard you had trouble," he said, only slurring a little bit. Generally Weasel seemed sober right up until the moment when he fell down. "Guy got himself killed in the cellar of your place, I heard."

I signaled the bartender for another beer. But none for me; I'd had one at home already, enough anyway to wash the caterpillar taste out of my mouth, and with my head still aching after the fall I'd taken earlier, I needed to keep my wits about me.

Such as they were. "Saw the guy," Weasel said, reaching without looking to catch the bottle sliding toward him.

"You did?" This didn't surprise me as much as it might have; Eastport was a small place, and Weasel Bodine knew everyone, heard everything, and showed up wherever anything was happening in it.

He'd talk to anyone who asked him about it, too, if the beers kept coming. Now he tipped the bottle back, his skinny throat moving rhythmically as he swallowed.

"He went around back of your place," Weasel went on after putting down the beer. "Not long after you two were yelling at each other."

Into the narrow canopied alley behind our building, he meant, where our exterior cellar doors was.

"Really? And you followed him?" *Oh, tell me that you did.*

"Ayuh," he said. "Partway. It was like somebody was beckonin' him from in there. And the guy kept glancin' over his shoulder."

Another long swallow. "Sneaky-like," Weasel went on after wiping his lips with the back of his hand, "like he didn't want anyone to know what he was doin'."

He set the empty bottle down and dragged his hand over his mouth once more. "So naturally I *did* want to know. You know?"

Yeah, I did. Weasel and I were very different in a lot of ways, but we shared one affliction. Around us the general hilarity cranked up a notch. I raised my voice in the din.

"So then what happened?" The bartender raised his eyebrows at Weasel's empty bottle; I shook my head.

Weasel shrugged. "Dunno. He didn't come back out of the alley, I know that much."

A laugh escaped me. Trust Weasel to put his skinny nicotine-stained finger on it. "No, he sure didn't."

Weasel managed a smile, too, though by now he was pretty loaded. That last beer was one of a long line of them this evening, I gathered.

"I stood there a while 'cause the race was still going on and I didn't wanna get run over by them little monsters on wheels."

Right, the soapbox derby. "And nobody else came out?"

Because that was the problem, or one of them. I'd come in from the street and was working upstairs, so nobody could escape that way. And if whoever it was hadn't gone out the cellar door, either . . .

But here his helpfulness ended. "Dunno. Not for a couple of minutes, anyway, but after that I got out of there," he said.

Catching the bartender's eye I laid a five next to Weasel's empties. Leaving the bar, I slid between folks dressed in everything from jeans and T-shirts like Weasel's to elaborate pirate apparel, all laughing and dancing; it was a happy bunch around here tonight.

Well, except for one guy who was coming across the parking lot toward me when I got outside. Tall and skinny in a gray fleece vest, black turtleneck, dark pants, and sneakers.

It was Lionel, the snake-owning snapshot-stealing member of Hadlyme's podcast crew. He got a look at me, turned on his sneakered heel, and scampered back up to the top of the Oyster House's steeply sloping driveway.

When I got there, he was running away down the street.

*   *   *

Luckily for me, the sneakers had red LED lights in their heels. Every step he took signaled, *Here I am!*

So I followed him easily as he hustled back downtown. I sauntered casually behind him as if wringing his neck was the furthest, etcetera.

At the breakwater he slowed, sliding in among a crowd gathered to watch something happening in the harbor. I slowed, too, still keeping track of the red shoe-flashes moving steadily away from me, out onto the dock.

Past Rosie's Hot Dog Stand, the boat ramp, and the Coast Guard building, the flashes slowed and stopped. Then Ellie was beside me suddenly.

"Him," she uttered, her eyes narrowing as they followed my gaze.

"I thought you were hanging out with Lee tonight?" I said. At eleven, Ellie's daughter wasn't quite old enough to stay home alone.

Ellie shook her head. "George wanted the evening with her."

A devoted father, Ellie's husband treasured what he called his "dad time." Ellie eased forward into the crowds of people all still staring toward the water.

"What're they looking at, anyway?"

I shrugged, squinting around. Somehow Lionel had vanished again. Ellie grabbed my arm. "This way."

No LED flashes . . . maybe he'd taken the shoes off. "Hurry," Ellie said, but I couldn't, distracted by what I now saw happening.

"Look," I breathed. It was the black sailboat, coming around in the harbor. By the dock lights' glow, the gold lettering on her stern was visible:

Jenny, it read. "The schooner's named Jenny," I said stupidly, unable to stop looking.

"She'll be a fast one, then," said a man's voice nearby. "Lookit the foredeck on her, jabbin' out like an arrow."

"Long and low," somebody else agreed. "All rebuilt, though. You wanta bet somebody's remodeled that whole cabin area?"

"Betcha she's smooth underneath," another fellow commented. "They slide like silk, them new low-friction marine surfaces."

And more such talk, all of which went a good deal deeper into twenty-first-century boat design than I felt like getting, now or ever. Still, I couldn't take my eyes off the vessel.

"You know, though," a third voice chimed in, "it was more'n a cabin remodel, you ask me. Got a whole new topside structure on 'er, that cabin stickin' up an' so on."

It was true; what I could see of the *Jenny* didn't look quite standard even to my inexpert eye. Like someone took a sailing vessel and turned it into more of a—

"Diesel engine's on 'er, see the exhaust ports? An' those other apertures down there on the stern, they look like . . ."

But I couldn't see them, and the voice faded as its owner walked away along the breakwater. "Whose d'you think she is, then?" someone nearby wondered aloud, but no one seemed to know.

And somehow that seemed right: black as night, without a single light on deck or in any portholes . . . the mysterious *Jenny* seemed like a boat that was meant to be sailed—or motored, according to the guy who'd been talking about it—by persons unknown.

In the moonlight. Or in the dark. . . . A shiver went through me. The *Jenny* just didn't seem right somehow.

"Jake, let's go." Ellie's voice came from beside me.

"What?" I said, more sharply than I'd intended, tearing my gaze from the dark unknown vessel; boy, that thing gave me the creeps.

"Jake, he's right over there. . . ."

Sure enough, our fleece-vested skinny-legged quarry stood five feet away, staring at the *Jenny* like everyone else.

He hadn't noticed us. "All right, dammit," I began irritably.

"Wait!" Ellie caught my sleeve. "Maybe we should follow him some more and see where he goes."

The notion had its charms; we already knew he had reason to run from us, or thought he did. So why wouldn't he lie to us, too, if we demanded answers out of him? But if we tailed him, we might learn things he'd never say.

"What're those holes down below the rail on the stern?" someone in the crowd said again. "Are those . . . I mean could they be gun ports? Because they sure do look like . . ."

Oh, of course they weren't, I answered silently. Because what in the world would a privately owned vessel here in East-port, Maine, be doing with—

I didn't finish the thought, though, because just then Lionel glanced around and spotted me again, and I saw him preparing to beat feet, as my son Sam would've put it.

Oh, no, you don't. . . . He'd already turned away, so he didn't see me coming when I hurled myself at him.

"*Oof,*" he said as we hit the pavement together. But he didn't struggle; I had my right knee jammed too hard into the small of his back and his left arm bent up too far behind him.

"Lionel," I said quietly, "I'm going to let you up in a minute."

He wiggled unhappily in reply. "But," I went on, "if you try to run, or you yell and make a fuss, or you do one single thing other than exactly what I say, when I say it—well, if that happens, I'm going to do something very unpleasant to you in return. Got it?"

What the unpleasant thing might be I didn't know. It was just the only threat I could think of on short notice to make him obey me, which for a wonder he did as Ellie and I marched him between us back up Water Street toward the Moose.

"I'm calling the cops," he kept saying. "You can't just—"

"Oh, shut up, Lionel," I told him tiredly. I could have been nicer about it, I suppose, but what with an impromptu boat rescue in the morning, a murder in the afternoon, and snooping at night—

Hey, it had been a long day.

"That's right," Ellie put in exasperatedly. "Just keep quiet." Between us, poor Lionel's feet barely touched the ground.

"I mean what're you going to tell cops, anyway, Lionel, that Henry Hadlyme meant to fire you and get you blackballed from other jobs but instead somebody killed him before he could?" she asked.

He sagged in our grip. "So," he said sulkily, "I was right. There was somebody out there by the cottages earlier. You—"

We reached the shop. The white state-cop van was gone and the lights were out, so I guessed the evidence techs had departed for now, anyway, and no yellow tape barred the door. I let us in while Ellie kept hold of Lionel.

"Sit," she snapped at him, giving him a gentle shove. By now he was so unnerved that he didn't even protest, merely stumbling a few steps to one of the small tables and collapsing into a chair.

Outside, the pirate fest went on: bagpipes, a flute-and-fiddle duo, clog dancers. A string of firecrackers exploded *pop!pop!pop!* and Lionel winced as Ellie returned from the kitchen.

"Here, you look like your blood sugar needs boosting," she said, setting hot coffee and a chocolate frosted doughnut in front of him.

"I don't understand," he whispered, eyeing the doughnut hungrily but with caution.

I grabbed it and took a bite, then handed the rest back to him. "See? Not poisoned."

Ellie stood in front of him, hands on hips. "Eat. Drink," she commanded. "Go on, do it."

Slowly he complied, picking up speed as the deliciousness of the doughnut hit him; also, as a mood elevator there is nothing like a solid dose of chocolate plus plenty of butter, sugar, flour, and vanilla.

And in the case of the doughnuts, some nutmeg and cream of tartar as well, but never mind; after his snack he looked noticeably fresher.

Feistier, too; he actually started to get up. Or anyway, he did until Ellie stuck a finger in his chest.

"Sit," she said, and Lionel sat once more, his fingers twiddling nervously with the zipper on his vest.

"Talk," she said, and when he hesitated, she went on.

"Lionel, would you like to see the cellar where Henry died?" she inquired conversationally.

His recently improved color paled again suddenly. "N-no, I—"

"Of course, once you're down there, you can't get out again," she added, still mildly. "Not unless we let you out."

"I think we could get him down there, though, Ellie, don't you?" I said, catching her drift. "The two of us could, I mean. Whether or not he wants to go."

"All right!" He jumped up. "I give in. I don't understand why you two think I'm the one to pick on, but whatever you think you know about me, you're wrong."

We hadn't known anything, really. He was just the one who'd showed up tonight, acting as if he might have something to hide. And boy, did he ever:

"Yeah, I hated him," Lionel blurted. "Hadlyme, I mean, I hated his guts. But he was my father, all right?"

I could just hear Wade remarking on this: *Kid went down like a ton of bricks.*

"Henry Hadlyme was my dad, only he didn't know it," Lionel went on. Skinny fists clenched, he gazed bleakly around our little shop. "I was going to tell him. I meant to, I wanted to tell him. But he . . . he was so . . ."

"Yeah, he sure was," I agreed, and Lionel glanced up at me in surprise, as if other people might've liked Hadlyme.

"Oh, give me a break," I said. "The guy practically had a poisonous cloud hovering around him, he was such a jerk."

Lionel sank back down into the chair at the café table. "Yeah. Yeah, he definitely was."

I sat across from him. Maybe we were getting somewhere. "Okay, let's cut to the chase," I said. "To start with, where were you earlier this afternoon?"

He knew what I meant. "I split from the others and walked out onto the breakwater alone," he said. "I was thinking that maybe I'd just quit, go back to New York before Henry had a chance to fire me."

Outside, a gaggle of little kids who were up way past their bedtime galloped by, waving toy lightsabers. "Then what?" I said.

Lionel watched them wistfully. "On the dock? Stood there and talked to a guy. He was telling me about the boats. Nice guy."

"Uh-huh," I said skeptically. "And for how long did you talk to this guy? Did he have a name?"

Lionel looked regretful. "Half an hour, maybe. I got a hot dog. He saw it and decided to get one, too, and we sat."

At one of the picnic tables overlooking the boat basin behind Rosie's, I guessed. When I suggested this, Lionel nodded.

"Didn't ask the guy's name, though," he added. "I just know he was driving a—"

Just then the little bell over the shop door jingled brightly, and Sam came in.

"Hi, Mom." He looked around curiously. "What's going on?"

Lionel looked astonished. "Hey, this is him!" he said.

Four

Sam's rangy build, dark curly hair, and lantern jaw are like his dad's, but fortunately his temperament isn't. Mostly he's as cheerful and outgoing as a pup; that he'd befriended Lionel didn't surprise me at all.

Now he grinned in pleased recognition at his new acquaintance. "Hey, man, how're you doing?"

I cut in. "Wait a minute, you're telling me you two know each other? Sam, you met Lionel on the breakwater and spent what, half an hour with him, like he says?"

Sam shrugged. "Yeah, we were there. Had lunch. Why?" He looked inquisitively from me to Lionel and back again.

"Nothing. Never mind," I said. This put a whole new complexion on things. I shooed both young men toward the door.

"Lionel, you and the others will be staying at the cottages for a while, is that right?" Ellie asked, and he nodded resignedly.

"Yeah. That police chief, Bob Arnold, came and told us that we'd better. Until we get, like, *questioned.*"

He put an unhappy emphasis on the word. "So I guess I'll, like, see you around," he finished, turning to go.

But before they both left, my son dropped his own bomb-shell:

"Hey, Mom, did you know somebody stole one of Wade's swords from his weapons demonstration?"

I felt my jaw drop. So that's where it had come from.

"No," I said. "I mean, I knew one of them was . . ."

Wade had set up a Weapons of the Caribbean display on the breakwater the day before, but only for a few hours because he'd had to go to work; until now it hadn't occurred to me that the vintage knife might've been snatched right out from under his . . .

"Wade says he was breaking down the weapons display and he just turned his back for a minute, and—"

Well, at least I didn't have to be the one to break the news that it was missing. Meanwhile:

"Darn," I said to Ellie when both young men had departed. We'd clearly gotten all we were going to out of Lionel, at least for now; on his way out the door he'd looked so haggard and shell-shocked, I could've pushed him over with a finger.

But our interview with him hadn't done us much good. "Here we have someone with a wonderful motive, but where's his opportunity?" I went on.

"Right, an estranged son who's about to be fired and black-listed sure seems like prime suspect material to me," she agreed.

By now we were in the shop's kitchen, where Ellie was creaming butter and sugar together in a large bowl, because the cellar was still off-limits as far as we knew, but the upstairs wasn't.

Which meant we needed even more freshly baked goodies so we could open The Chocolate Moose tomorrow. Ellie beat in four eggs and some vanilla.

"Too bad he's got an alibi," she finished. "Lionel, that is. Here, beat this while I put the dry ingredients together, will you?"

I obliged, wielding the wooden spoon with what energy I could muster. By now, Lionel wasn't the only one who was practically dead on his feet, but the batch wasn't big enough to bother with the electric stand mixer.

"So now we need *another* suspect," I complained.

Outside, a fake pirate with a fake knife in his chest staggered by the shop's front window.

"And you know there won't be another one even half as good as Lionel," I went on. "The guy's actual *son.*"

"Yes, there's a reason they call them *blood* relatives, I guess," Ellie replied, looking up from measuring out chocolate morsels.

"I mean, who has better motives than the nearest and dearest," she added as more fake-wounded pirates streamed past outside; one of the fake stabbing victims even wore a fake parrot on his shoulder.

"Somebody," I grumbled, "has got a big mouth."

No one was supposed to gab about anything regarding a fresh murder scene—not the EMTs, the evidence techs, or anyone else professionally involved with the crime or its aftermath.

But human nature being what it is, and the details of the crime being what they were—parrot! cutlass!—not to mention Hadlyme himself being so very unlikely to complain about anything not being done strictly by the book . . .

Not like he was in life, I thought uncharitably, and then it hit me. "Ellie."

But she was already staring out the front window, too. "Knives," she said softly. "I mean, why *that* knife?"

Precisely. Because you could get a decent hunting knife at the hardware store, with your choice of bone, plastic, or carbonite handle, and the people who turned their freshly killed deer, moose, and other game animals into freezer portions could buy a variety of specialized blades locally, too, for dismantling the carcass.

But a cutlass was different, especially one that could be traced back to . . .

I turned to Ellie, who'd begun chopping cherries to bits.

Cherry juice flowed down the groove around the cutting board's edges.

Suddenly that juice looked entirely too much like blood. "You know what?" I said faintly.

Ellie got a look at me and brought me a glass of sweet lemonade. Other than a piece of toast, I had not, I realized, had any dinner.

Or lunch. "No, what?" She put a chunk of bittersweet chocolate into the top of the double boiler and turned the burner on.

"Somebody had to go to a lot of trouble to get that blade." I sipped lemonade. "I mean, how'd they even *know*?"

She'd put a chocolate biscotti in front of me, and I bit into it even though I knew it would make the lemonade taste sour.

Everything tasted sour suddenly. "Right," said Ellie, "I was wondering when you'd get around to that part."

That it was deliberate, she meant; not just the murder itself but the setting up of one particular suspect. Getting that cutlass out of Wade's collection, then using it to murder Hadlyme . . .

"So," I said slowly, feeling my heart sink at how much bigger and more difficult this whole snooping project had suddenly become.

Because it wasn't just the murder. Once the cops learned that I'd had all three of the things a proper murder suspect requires— motive, method, opportunity—they were going to pounce.

But the killing—and who knew how much more, I thought with a sudden burst of darkly ominous premonition—had been planned not only to finish off Henry Hadlyme.

But also—and possibly even more important; who knew?— to implicate me.

"Wade, I'm so sorry about this."

My husband is tall and broad-shouldered, with blond brush-cut hair, blue-gray eyes, and the kind of solidly muscular build that comes from a lifetime of physical work done mostly outdoors.

Also, he is devoted to me; minutes after I went home and told him about everything that had been happening lately, we were in his old pickup truck backing out of the driveway.

"Hey, not your fault." He slung an arm around me.

I didn't know where we were headed, only that when I'd gone over the whole story, Wade had been raring to go.

Now in the truck's dashboard glow, his look was deceptively mild. Deceptive to anyone but me, that is. Oh, he was ripping mad.

"I took a musket, a blunderbuss, a flintlock, and that cutlass—the one that went missing," he said. "And while my back was turned, somebody must've . . ."

Relief touched me, but only briefly. "I was at the shop then," I said. "We were getting ready for the kids' cookie party, and we had a sale going on, too, under the tent by the fisherman statue."

Before the party, I meant, because I don't care how bloodthirsty the pirate, he or she will always want a chocolate-dipped chocolate cookie with skull and crossbones piped onto the top in vanilla icing.

"And in the crowds, nobody would've noticed if I'd slipped over to your display table on the breakwater and snagged the thing, would they?"

No, they probably wouldn't, and that was how the cops were going to be thinking about it, too—that I still could've done it.

He turned onto the campgrounds road, with the Hadlyme crew's cottages perched on the bluff at the very end of it. The big pines lining both sides of the road blocked the moonlit sky, creating a long, gloomy avenue, and the air coming in through the truck's open window smelled like evergreens and cold salt water.

"Wade, what're we doing back here again?" I looked around in puzzlement, wondering what he had in mind and wasn't talking about.

But he just grinned in the half-darkness. In the past, he'd been lukewarm about my snooping habits; gradually, though, he'd realized that I never nagged him about his own ridiculously dangerous boat trips, during which he had to *climb an open ladder* dangling from an *ocean-going freighter* without any *ropes or other safety equipment . . .*

Bottom line, nowadays we didn't stop each other from doing what we had to. Or felt that we had to. I leaned against him as the pickup truck pulled into the clearing near where Ellie had parked before, up under the trees.

No one was around, not even in the cottage that had been lit up earlier. I looked questioningly again at Wade. "Your cutlass won't be here, you know."

I'd thought I'd made it clear that the police had it.

"Yeah, I do know that." He turned the truck's engine off. He'd already doused the lights as we were driving in. "That's not what you'll be looking for."

He scanned the clearing some more. The moonlight still didn't pierce the tree canopy, but it bounced off the bay and reflected onto everything in the clearing with a sideways-slanting silvery gleam.

"I was in the Happy Crab for a little while tonight just before I came home," he remarked conversationally.

Although the cottages were dark inside, all the porch lights were still on, late-season bugs bouncing in their yellowish glow.

He squeezed my shoulder companionably. "And if I'm not mistaken, it was Hadlyme's crew on the stools down the bar from me."

"Really. Young big-city types, they look like the cool kids on the block?"

"Yup. Had little bits of electronic gear in their pockets, and so on." For somebody who was so new to the whole snooping thing, he was good at it.

"And?" I asked. No wonder he'd wanted to come out here right now. He knew that the cottages' occupants were elsewhere.

"And they didn't look grief-stricken," Wade replied.

He gazed out into the clearing thoughtfully. "Ordered food and another pitcher of beer. They were playing pool on the table out back and a couple of 'em were dancing."

"Huh. So they probably won't be back soon." I eyed the distance between us and the cottages, thinking that I would very much prefer staying there in the dim-lit truck's cab with the heater running and my husband's arm securely around me.

Still, he'd brought me out here, and the cottages *were* empty . . .

"Not unless they crawl back," Wade agreed. "They were getting cheerful, and Bob Arnold was right outside, waiting for prospective drunk drivers. Like he does, you know."

Right, I did. So if they were tipsy when they emerged, they'd be even more delayed until Bob found time to give them a ride back here.

I slipped out from under Wade's arm. "So I could go in here, dig around, see what I can find out that might be useful in, uh, saving my bacon?"

He nodded firmly. "And not only that. I know you're not going to find it here, but somebody stole a weapon, a pretty valuable one."

Genuine pirate weaponry could go for many thousands of dollars depending upon provenance and condition. And this cutlass, I happened to be aware, was nearly perfect and so authentic that it practically had Captain Hook's fingerprints on it.

Or, you know, his hook marks. "But that's not the main thing," Wade went on, turning from his scrutiny of the cottages.

"Somebody not only killed a guy with my cutlass but *framed my wife* for it. Jake, this could be a disaster for the whole family."

He was right, I knew, as the seriousness of all this struck me again. Between paying an attorney and sitting in custody until trial—there's no bail on a murder charge in Maine—all our lives would be in tatters, even Ellie's.

"Not to mention . . ." he began.

I was already unbuckling my lap belt. No shoulder strap; what with the elderliness of the work vehicles Wade bought and then drove until they were disintegrating into rust flakes, we were lucky the old truck didn't need to be started with a crank.

"Not to mention what?" I asked when I'd finally freed myself. But in reply he just wrapped his arms around me.

"That anyone who tries hurting you," he murmured into my hair, "is on my list. My you-know-what list."

Hearing this, I relaxed into his embrace. Back when I first found Eastport and met Wade, I was snarky, sarcastic, and unlikely to cut even the pleasantest new acquaintance an ounce of slack.

Then there was the fact that on account of my ex-husband, I'd given up men; this seemed reasonable at the time, like swearing off arsenic or not huffing methane out of a plastic bag.

But Wade just kept showing up: moonlight boat rides, long walks by the bay . . . the guy had a bag of tricks, and he brought all of them to the party—the whole shebang, as Bella would've put it.

And there were only so many times that his fingers could brush the back of my hand before even I had to admit it: I was up to my eyes—and other portions of my anatomy—in love. So we got married, and now here we were, but:

"Wade? Why're we really out here?" Because sure, he was on my side, and he was mad about that cutlass. Worried that I might end up in the clink for Hadlyme's murder, too, just as he should be. But none of that should've made him dive right into the deep end of the snooping pool; tolerant as he was, it just wasn't his style.

His lips pursed. "George Valentine and Lee were in the Crab when I was there," he said. Ellie's husband and their daughter, he meant.

"Getting burgers," Wade went on. "And George saw that bunch of podcast crew members just like I did."

"Ohh," I breathed. "And . . . you mean he recognized them?"

Wade nodded. "They were talking about it pretty loud, how now that Henry Hadlyme was dead they'd all have to be looking for jobs."

He turned to me. "So, yeah, I think he knew who they were."

And when he went home, he'd tell Ellie, and—

"Wade. You knew that if Ellie found out that these cottages are empty, she'd want to come back here and—"

"And do just what we're doing now," he agreed. "Only instead of Ellie, you've got me as backup. Okay?"

In other words, Wade knew that when she *did* find out, she'd be eager for the opportunity to take advantage of the cottages' vacancy, to snoop around in them and find out what cooked.

He knew I'd go with her, too, if she asked me to, which she would. But instead he'd gotten the jump on her.

"Okay," I said. It wouldn't be okay with Ellie when she found out; she'd have wanted to be in on this. But what the heck. Wade was big, he was strong, and have I mentioned he was a weapons expert?

Which of course meant he'd have brought a gun. Sliding my hand under the old denim jacket he was wearing, I felt bulking in it: the rig he had strapped over his left shoulder.

"So here you go," he said, handing me a flashlight and a key fob with no keys on it.

"Alarm," he explained, pointing out the small red button on the fob. "In case of emergency. See the horn icon? You push it, a siren blares."

"Oh," I said. "Right." Personally I felt that a siren should already be blaring, and big letters in the sky should be spelling out *DANGER* in neon red. Where, for instance, was Lionel's snake, Linda, right now?

Also, in an emergency a siren that betrayed my location might not be . . . but never mind, it was too late to worry about any of that.

"I'll tap the horn if anyone shows up," Wade assured me. "If I do, you make a beeline for the truck. Or if you hit trouble, press that button and *I'll* come running."

"Deal," I agreed, making a mental note to amend it if need be. Then, gripping the flashlight and pocketing the alarm fob, I hustled across the clearing.

The cottages were black cutout shapes, dark angles against the silvery bay. Beyond them, the Cherry Island lighthouse strobed the waves, flaring and fading.

A foghorn whonked. Waves crashed on the rocks just below where the cottages perched. Salt and evergreens, new-mown grass, and the faint acid tang of the first fallen leaves perfumed the night.

As I paused by the clearing's edge, the hairs on my neck rose, then settled uneasily. Okay, so maybe I *wasn't* being watched, I told myself, and then, *Of course you're not. No one knows you're here.*

Which was convincing enough for me to turn my attention back to the cottages: dark, lonesome-looking, poised at the top of a sharp drop overlooking the cold salt water . . .

Stop that, I scolded myself, and chose to begin my search in the first cottage, the one the whole crew had gathered in earlier, and leave the other two cabins that they were using for my second and third snooping destinations.

After making my way around the two white wicker chairs and table tightly grouped on the porch, I found that door was locked, but the key was under the doormat. This, I thought, was suspiciously convenient. Because why would you make it so easy for an intruder to . . . ?

But then, Hadlyme's crew was young; maybe they didn't realize that all burglars knew about doormats. Thinking this, I opened the door and went in, then hesitated in the darkness.

"Hello?" I called. Heaven forbid one of them had stayed behind and was asleep in here. "Anybody home?"

No answer. No snake, either, I hoped. I snapped the flashlight on, aimed it at the light switch on the wall beside me, and reached out for that, just as—

From the doorframe above me, Linda dropped down companionably onto my neck.

"Gah!" After dropping the flashlight, I grabbed the reptile with both hands and flung it across the room onto the plaid-upholstered couch. By the time I hit the light switch, the animal had slithered away.

Where? I wondered frantically, glancing around. But the snake was nowhere in sight.

Through the cottage's rear window I saw Wade's headlights flash on and off once. The message was plain: *What the heck are you doing?*

Right, I thought, and shut the light off hurriedly, plunging my scaly new pal and myself into the darkness once more. Wouldn't do to have somebody come home unexpectedly and see a lamp burning.

By the yellow glow of the flashlight I got myself across the cottage's cramped living area—chairs, that couch, a tiny TV, coffee table—into the even smaller bedroom.

And immediately hit pay dirt: spread out on one of the twin beds were a lot of papers. I scanned the flashlight beam across them.

A birth certificate lay there, along with copies of cancelled checks with dates of twenty years ago. A handwritten letter, also a quarter-century old, began with the words "Dear Henry."

I sat on the other narrow bed, reading as fast as I could. But when I got to the end . . .

"Drat," I whispered into the silence. Because the letter didn't really end; instead it simply broke off in the middle of a sentence asking—no, begging—that Henry return to Eastport, marry the letter's author, and acknowledge his son, Lionel. The *unidentified* author. . . .

The page with the signature line on it was missing, but the words on the last page that remained said that if Henry refused to do any of these things, the letter's author would be forced to—

To do what? The letter didn't say, but it seemed pretty clear that whatever it was wouldn't be good. Aiming the flashlight around while trying to keep an eye peeled for Linda the Friendly Snake, I rummaged among the remaining papers on the bed in case the final page of the letter was there somewhere.

It wasn't. And now I was starting to feel pressed for time; it was getting late, and I had three more cottages to nose around in, as well as that big tour bus that Hadlyme had apparently been living in.

Scanning the room for anything else that might be interesting, I got up, feeling suddenly even more anxious. Then I heard someone out on the porch.

Yikes. The porch light went out. And the switch for it was on the inside wall, I remembered, which meant either the bulb in the porch fixture had coincidentally chosen that moment to fizzle out or somebody had *unscrewed* the bulb.

Slowly the cottage door opened with a stealthy creak of hinges. I shrank back on the bed, discovering too late that Linda the snake had the same idea. She didn't like unknown intruders any better than I did, apparently.

What she did like, though, was me. By the moonlight slanting in through the window, I watched her uncoil from a nest-like depression in the pillow and wriggle across the bedspread at me. Her pointy tongue flickered, reminding me that her fangs were probably sharp, too.

At the same time, I was increasingly aware that whoever had

come into the cottage was *still* in it, coming toward me right now just as steadily and relentlessly as the snake.

Just not with quite as much horrifyingly hypnotic bobbing and weaving; she had her head up in the air as if sniffing it and was regarding me steadily with her small, black impossibly intelligent eyes.

Meanwhile, soft footfalls in the cottage's main room were nearly at the bedroom door, which luckily had swung closed by itself when I came in. Linda kept coming, too, and as I shifted nervously to get away from the persistent reptile, the footsteps outside halted.

And then Linda *sprang*. Or that's the only way I can describe it: one moment she was on the bedspread, and in the next she'd drawn back and hurled herself suddenly, and ended up draped loosely around my neck once more.

"*Eep!*" I exhaled softly, jumping up. Linda fell off me, back onto the bed again. And that would've been that in the whole dealing-with-a-snake department except for the part about snake *food.* . . .

When I jumped, I'd knocked a big glass jar of something off the bedside table. The lid fell off, rolling across the floor, the jar's contents boiling out in a dark tide. And then they were on me:

Crickets, hundreds of them, dark shapes skittering and hopping across the bedspread's white chenille. They were what Linda the snake ate, I guessed, not that I had much time for speculation about the diets of pet reptiles, because just then the bedroom doorknob began turning.

So there I was, being attacked by crickets while a snake lurked somewhere in the shadows—where *had* Linda gone, anyway?—and while some unknown but most likely very unfriendly person was about to burst in and catch me.

And what they might do then, I didn't want to think about. There had been a murder around here lately, after all, and there was also a reason that someone had disabled that porch light just now.

On top of which, the crickets were all over me, and if any went down my shirt I would not be responsible for my reaction; at least those caterpillars hadn't felt *skritchy*.

Meanwhile, the doorknob kept turning and the moment lengthened.

And the panic button Wade gave me wouldn't do me much good if somebody burst in here with another cutlass or, heaven forbid, a gun.

But then I had it: I could slide under the bed. Maybe whoever it was would think I'd gone out the window.

Hey, it was worth a try. Swiftly I dropped and rolled. No snake was down there, I was pleased to discover, and it seemed that most of the crickets had stayed on the bedspread.

A couple of stray socks, a paperback book, an eyeglasses case, some dust kittens . . .

I had time for a quick inventory before the door opened the rest of the way and a flashlight beam strobed the room. I shrank back farther toward the cottage's wall as a pair of sneakers crossed the braided rug.

The intruder's flashlight beam poked everywhere: walls, dresser, bedside table, bed . . .

Floor. I held my breath. The sneakers looked familiar, but I was too scared to think much about them.

They moved away. I let a breath out. But then they stopped as if someone had second thoughts. Turned toward me where I huddled. And—

The beam glared under the bed, blinding me. I cringed away sharply, bracing my feet hard against the wall, thinking that if I *shot* out from under the bed very fast and then *flung* myself at the window, maybe I could—

"Jake." The voice was even more familiar than the sneakers had been. "Jake, come on out of there, it's me."

Ellie. Relief flooded me as I scrambled up, brushing madly at any stray insects that might be lurking. Shadows leapt on the walls as she aimed the flashlight around, scrutinizing everything.

"Look out," I warned, "there's crickets, and a snake, and—"

"I don't care." If a snake wanted to cause her any difficulties tonight, it had better be a really *big* snake, her tone suggested. "What're you doing here, anyway?"

I explained quickly. She did the same; George got home, told her about the crew hanging out in the Crab, and here she was.

"I called, but you didn't answer," she said, looking around some more. "Stopped by the house, too, but it's all dark."

I dug in my bag. Fortunately, I'd hauled it along when I got out of the truck, earlier. But I found no phone in it. "I must've dropped it on your boat when I lost my keys," I said. Usually I'd have noticed, but this time I just hadn't happened to. And everyone at home was already in bed.

Which was where I wished *I* was. "Anyway, let's go. It's that motor home of Hadlyme's that we really need to look through," she said, hurrying me out of the tiny bedroom.

It not only was in disarray but also looked like the Great Cricket Massacre had happened in it.

"Wait." I ran back to shut Linda inside the bedroom, figuring it was the least I could do for a snake who hadn't bitten me. Glancing around, I spied an envelope on the floor, where I must've knocked it.

Crouching, I reached for it, then froze as the reptile's small scaly head darted out from under the bed.

Beady little eyes, flickering tongue . . . "Nice snake," I said to it, hoping it would retreat.

But Linda didn't budge. "Jake!" Ellie whispered urgently.

"Go on, now, nice snake. Good snake, go on back under the . . ."

Linda's head shot out past my hand, her fanged mouth opening so wide that I could practically see her tonsils.

Or whatever snakes have for tonsils; in the next instant,

those needle-like choppers chomped onto a cricket I hadn't noticed.

No doubt the cricket had been hoping Linda wouldn't notice it, either, but no such luck; down the snake hatch it went, still kicking its rear legs as Linda withdrew to finish her meal.

"Bon appétit," I whispered, then grabbed the envelope, skedaddled back out of the bedroom, and took off out of the cottage right behind my hurriedly exiting friend.

After relocking the door, I stuck the key back under the mat. Lionel—this was his cottage, obviously—would know someone had been inside, but there was no sense drawing a picture for him of exactly how that had happened.

"Come on, Jake," said Ellie, "we don't have all night."

From across the clearing I could make out the shape of Wade's truck still hunkered under the trees; he must've seen me, too, his headlights flickering briefly again before going dark once more.

"Okay," I said, sticking the envelope into the back of my pants to keep my hands free, "now what?"

Ellie hustled ahead of me along the edge of the clearing toward Hadlyme's big motor home.

"We don't know how long they'll be out," she replied over her shoulder, then scampered up the metal steps and tried the door handle.

Locked. "Rats," she said.

Across the clearing, a shape flickered through the trees . . . or had it? In the darkness I wasn't sure. "Ellie?"

Ignoring me, she clenched her fist, drew her arm back, and gave that door a solid thump like the kind she'd given her boat's radio. In the clearing's chilly silence, the impact sounded like a bomb had gone off.

"Ellie! Come on, now, we should really try to be more—"

The door swung open. I stared. "How . . . how'd you do that?"

"It wasn't locked," she explained simply. "Just stuck shut." She stepped into the gloom inside the RV.

"What do you mean it wasn't locked? That doesn't make . . ."

But then I stopped, because "gloomy" wasn't even the half of it. Suddenly Henry Hadlyme's luxurious recreational vehicle was the last thing I wanted to be inside of; staring into its depths from the relative safety of the entrance, I felt like that cricket confronting Linda's fanged mouth.

"Ellie?" I glanced nervously back to where moonbeams lit the clearing in silvery gray tones, like a stage set for a ghost story.

But in answer only silence yawned darkly from the motor home's interior. Cautiously edging forward, I suddenly recalled reading in a magazine at the dentist's office about Hadlyme's quirks—"Ten Things You Didn't Know about Henry the Foodie (And Why You Should Care)!"—one of which was that he slept in complete darkness.

Meanwhile, the eleventh thing I didn't know about him was who'd killed him, and boy, did I ever want to find out so I could go home. Suddenly all the lights in the living area snapped on.

"Ew," I said, squeezing my eyelids shut.

"Sorry, I didn't know they were all on this one switch," Ellie apologized. "But the windows in these things are tinted, so I don't think you can see the lights on from outside." And then, "Oh dear."

I forced my eyes open again and wished I hadn't. The large luxuriously appointed vehicle could've been home to a family of five, or even more if you counted the cramped slot over the driver's seat that someone was apparently supposed to sleep in.

And all of it had been ransacked. Abandoning my caution, I rushed through the rooms: drawers yanked open, cubbies emptied, wastebaskets overturned. Even the contents of the clever hidden storage spaces in the bedrooms had all been dumped and rummaged through.

But either what someone was looking for hadn't been here, or they'd found it and taken it. After our own search, Ellie and I met in the kitchen area.

"We could go through it all again," I said halfheartedly.

But I didn't begin the task, and she didn't, either. "Nice kitchen," was her bleak comment.

Even the sugar bowl had been dumped out onto the dinette table, and the upholstered bench seats on either side had been slit, their stuffing yanked out.

"Yeah," I replied, feeling as if my own stuffing had gotten the same rude treatment; heavens, this was disappointing.

But then Ellie brightened. "You know, if they'd found something, it wouldn't be such a mess in here, would it? They'd have stopped as soon as they—"

"Huh." I thought about it a minute. "You're right, they kept searching, didn't they? In fact, it looks as if they did everything but take a hammer and bash open the—"

We looked at each other. If we'd been in a cartoon, a thought balloon would've formed over our heads. Then:

"Walls!" we said jubilantly together, because here's the thing: in my old house, if you wanted to shut off the water to fix a leak—a big leak, the kind that is gushing down through the floor into the electrical wiring—you had to bash your way through the plaster with a sledgehammer to reach the valve.

Afterward you covered the hole with a neat plywood patch and painted it to match the wallpaper. Now Ellie smiled, remembering the episode that taught me this just as well as I did.

"Modern places like this have access panels, though," she said, and at this we jumped up and rushed to the motor home's bathroom. It was small but it held all the usual fixtures plus some that I hadn't expected—a jetted tub, for instance, and a walk-in shower with a standard shower head instead of one of those ghastly nozzle-on-a-plastic-hose gadgets.

But even the most luxurious motor homes can have leaks; in this one, the access panel for the pipes was in the rear wall of the sink cabinet.

Ellie pulled out her Swiss Army knife, equipped with every possible gadget including a screwdriver. The big one was still in her bag, too, but its blade was too large for these screws; moments later when the wall panel fell off, a cigar box tumbled out into my hands.

The box was taped shut. Curiosity pierced me. But we could open it later; we'd been in here too long already, so with the box tucked firmly under my arm I turned, intending to vamoose, and Ellie was close behind me.

But we couldn't vamoose because just then a soft warning *toot* from Wade's truck horn stopped us.

"*Oof,*" said Ellie, who'd run into me from behind when I stopped suddenly.

"*Oof* yourself," I replied, unnerved. Then, "Sorry, I just—"

I waved my free arm at the motor home's large living-area window, which looked out into the clearing. At my gesture, Ellie snapped the lights off and we both froze, standing there in the darkness in the large, luxurious RV of a man who'd been murdered recently.

"There," whispered Ellie, and then I saw it too, going by right outside the RV's window. It was a dark blue ball cap with a sunrise emblem embroidered on it in orange and yellow thread and the word EASTPORT lettered in red.

"Drat," I muttered. It was Bob Arnold's hat, and underneath it was Bob Arnold. Now he was coming around the RV's front fender, squinting unhappily and wielding his own flashlight; in a minute he would be inside.

I looked around at the chaos in the dead man's motor home, the ransacking's aftermath strewn everywhere. And here *we* were, right in the middle of it, so it looked as if *we* must be the ones who'd—

"Jake! This way!" Ellie's voice came from the vehicle's rear bedroom. Bob's feet sounded on the steps outside.

He was our friend, but there wasn't a broom in the world big enough to sweep this mess under the rug. I'd have slithered down a drain like Linda the snake if only I'd fit.

Hastily I followed the sound of Ellie's voice down the motor home's hallway, between the bathroom, the laundry area, and another small room that Hadlyme had been using as an office. Now it, too, looked as if a whirlwind had gone through it: drawers yanked open, papers scattered.

But I didn't care about that anymore, just about getting out of here; these new modern RVs were really quite spacious and comfy, I thought as I hurried along the hall, and if I ever did get out of this I decided I would buy one and drive it to somewhere that nobody could find me for a minute's peace for a change.

But right now, the "getting out of this" portion of the program still seemed most important. Behind me the vehicle's metal door creaked open, then clicked shut. Next I heard Bob moving around, his flashlight shedding stray beams into the hall.

"Here," Ellie whispered in the darkness, making me jump. She was in the small louver-doored closet in the bedroom, shoving aside the few clothes not already tossed out onto the floor.

"I've seen these vehicles on TV," she whispered. "They all have at least one other exit."

Right, it was a fire-safety feature, I supposed. And sure enough, this vehicle did have a sort of hatchway leading out to an indoor-outdoor-carpeted cargo compartment over the rear wheels.

I scrambled across the carpet behind Ellie, closing the hatch from the closet behind me. The cargo area's exit to the outdoors was lever-operated; Ellie found the handle and pulled it, and the next thing I knew we were on the ground, running.

But not, unfortunately, to Wade's pickup truck—never mind that I'd had my heart set on its nice, warm passenger compartment with my nice, warm husband waiting inside.

Because—surprise! When we reached the secluded area of the campgrounds where the pickup truck had been parked under the big old trees, the truck wasn't there anymore.

Any second now, Bob Arnold would be coming back out of the RV, scanning the immediate area for whoever'd been in there before he arrived.

I nudged Ellie, and she nodded silent agreement; we mustn't be found here, looking as if we'd just been rooting around in a murder victim's belongings, must we?

No, we damned well mustn't. "Come on," I whispered, hurrying her around the clearing's edge to where we'd started: Lionel's cottage.

"Wait, we're not going back in there, are we?" She glanced over her shoulder across the clearing, but Bob wasn't following us.

He hadn't seen us. Yet. "Nope," I said. "But behind the cottages there's a sort of path down to the beach. We can come back up farther along the shore from here and keep Bob from seeing us that way."

I'd glimpsed the path earlier, at low tide when there actually had been a beach of sorts down there, stony and rugged but at least offering a place to stand.

Now the tide had come in, and when we peered over the bluff, the beach was gone. All that showed in the moonlight were rocks, crashing waves, and tangles of seaweed, the kind that will catch you and snarl up your arms and legs before dragging you under to drown.

Assuming, I mean, that the rocks haven't already fractured your skull . . . but there was no help for it.

"This way," I said, hoping hard that I sounded more confident than I felt, and started down.

A small, weathered rail fence ran along the bluff's edge. We ducked under it as sticks and gravel kicked loose by our feet rattled out ahead of us and cascaded away downhill. And then suddenly I was cascading downhill, too. . . .

Sliding and half falling, I clung to bushes, exposed tree roots, and then a *wiggling* thing. A *fistful* of them, squirming, writhing . . .

"Agh!" I let go, and just then Ellie must have as well; gravity took over and we began sliding faster down the path toward a flat, slippery-slide sort of rock formation at the foot of the cliff.

A flat, *wet* rock formation . . . Fright seized me as I realized what was coming. "Ellie, we've got to try not to fall into the—"

But it was too late. I hit the sharply downsloping rock, bounced very hard, and *shot* out across it into the crashing waves.

"Oh!" I exhaled, flailing uselessly as without hesitation the frigid water seized me, swirling me out toward the really deep stuff. Desperation made me strong, but for all the good my tries at swimming did, I might as well have been already unconscious.

Then I went under, tumbling and rolling, desperate for air but not getting any—not even knowing which way the air was until at last the waves hurled me upward again and I managed to suck a breath in.

"Ellie!" I yelled, not seeing her, but it came out a strangled yelp and then I was under once more, gargling and gagging.

I bounced off another rock, rolled on jagged gravel, got a slippery not-good-enough grip on a fat weed-slimed rope of some kind, and—

My brain kicked in. *Wait a minute, a rope?*

My hand wrapped around it. From the long, slick, muscular feel of the thing, it was either a rope or an octopus tentacle, which was what my oxygen-starved brain cells suggested. But by then I didn't care if I was holding the hand of a giant squid; I grabbed onto it and pulled, then pulled some more until finally I hauled myself up onto that flat rock again, choking and coughing.

"Ellie?" Each precious, agonizing breath came out bubbly with breathed-in salt water, and my eyes, nose, and throat felt acid-burned.

"Ellie!" Panic impaled me as I gazed around frantically for her but couldn't see her anywhere. Around me the ice-cold waves crashed down ferociously and a chill breeze knifed wickedly into me.

Ellie . . . I opened my mouth to shout for her again, but my teeth were chattering so hard that I couldn't. Hot tears scalded my cheeks, mingling with frigid spray that went on drenching me, and even now my grip on the flat rock was loosening. Then—

Then a shape separated itself from the maelstrom. It was her, clambering unsteadily onto a tiny wave-slopped bit of beach that still remained, looking just as cold and miserable as I felt.

But she was alive. "Jake!" she cried as, energized by relief, I scrambled off the rock and hotfooted it across two more, fortunately without slipping and breaking my neck or anything else.

"Oh, I thought you were—" Beaming, she threw her arms around me. But not for long; we were too wet and clammy.

"Come on," I said, and helping each other make our way along the rocky shore until we got to another path, longer but not so steep, and scrambled exhausted up through little stones until we were back to the edge of the campgrounds again.

When we peeped through the underbrush, Bob Arnold's car was still there, and now a second squad car was pulling up alongside the first. So we slunk off the opposite direction, through blackberry bushes with thorns as sharp as hypodermic needles.

Mosquitoes were there, too—lots of them, out having an end-of-summer blood fest; after my watery adventure I'd have thought my own blood would be too cold to interest them, but by the time we got out to the main road at last, it was a wonder I didn't need a transfusion.

As I'd been praying it would be, Wade's truck was there in a driveway behind some trees, unseen by the cops when they'd gone by.

I staggered toward it, feeling in the back of my pants for the envelope I'd stuck there and by some miracle finding it intact. But then I realized what I *didn't* have, and stopped short:

"I . . . I lost it," I blurted through lips trembling with cold.

Wade stared puzzledly from behind the wheel, trying to make sense of my drowned-rat appearance. I tried again:

"I l-l-lost . . . th-the . . ." But I couldn't do it, and suddenly it was all just too much. "I *l-lost* . . ."

Ellie tapped me on the shoulder. I turned, heartbroken. But: "No, you didn't," she said, holding out the cigar box.

Five

Ten minutes later we pulled into my driveway on Key Street. By then Wade had the heater blasting and even as soaked as I was, it was all I could do to force myself out of the warm cab, especially when I saw all the other vehicles in the driveway ahead of us.

My dad's truck was the last one in, its shiny fire-engine red paint gleaming pristinely under the yard light; how he got it was a story I'll tell another time, but he loved it and after a long, many-faceted battle of wills, Bella had let him keep it.

Next came Sam's work truck, another essential vehicle, wedged between Mika's little Kia sedan and my old Honda—both essential as well. After that came a flatbed trailer crowded with lawn-care machines, including two riding lawn mowers, an old rototiller, and a post-hole digger.

Correction: the pieces of a post-hole digger, rolled up in a tarp. Sam meant to reassemble them into one that actually dug, and there was a plow blade around here somewhere, too, ready for snow-plowing season, which would arrive in about fourteen seconds.

Sighing, I squeezed past the digger parts that stuck out over the flatbed's edge to retrieve a xylophone and a toy car that Ephraim must've dropped there; the last thing we needed in that driveway was any more vehicles.

The last thing we needed in the house was a xylophone, too, but never mind; we'd already dropped Ellie off at her place, so now I went in, shed my clothes unceremoniously, and stood in a hot shower until my body had stopped shivering and my blood no longer had ice crystals in it.

Downstairs, Wade put a steaming mug of coffee in front of me. In my jammies and slippers and with my warmest robe wrapped around me, I sipped gratefully, glad for the brandy he'd added to it.

"So what was the deal with Bob Arnold?" I asked. "Why'd he show up, do you suppose?"

The rest of the family was in bed. Wade had a beer in his hand. "Dunno," he said, setting it down.

"I was lucky Bob didn't spot me," he went on. "Maybe he was just on regular patrol? I mean, that campgrounds might get some vandalism, way off the beaten track like it is."

He angled his head at the cigar box. "So what do you figure's in it?"

It was drenched after its dunking, but we'd peeled off the tape wrapped around it and opened it while we were all still in the truck; we'd found a sealed plastic container inside.

"I don't know," I said, "but I'll bet it was what somebody was looking for in Lionel's cottage. And in the RV, too."

The plastic container was the size of a bar of soap, and we hadn't been able to get it open no matter how we pulled at it. Now Ellie's big screwdriver from her satchel lay on the table beside it, and if that didn't work we could always use an old-fashioned hammer.

Ellie came in quietly through the porch door, fresh from her own shower at home and with her blond hair pushed up into a damp topknot.

"Oh, good," she said, "you found my big screwdriver."

She'd taken it off her boat, then lost it when she dropped the satchel earlier; I guessed once she found I was gone, Bella must've been investigating out there under the window and brought it in.

Now I shot Ellie a look before she could report on how we'd soaked the cigar box. Wade remained reasonably on board with all we had done so far; still, he didn't need to know every detail about the watery portion of our trip to the campgrounds, I'd decided. Back in the truck I'd just said we'd had to take a wet detour.

"Here goes," he said, running the sharp edge of the tool's blade along the seam where the plastic container's top and bottom met. "There," he said, pulling the box halves apart at last.

Inside lay a small, faded color photograph of a young family—a pretty, fresh-faced young woman; a little girl about four years old; and a baby in the woman's arms. No writing was on the photograph's back, and none of us recognized the people—not even Ellie, who'd grown up in Eastport and knew just about everyone in town.

I'd set the envelope I'd filched from Lionel's cottage on the radiator to dry on my way in; now I fetched the envelope and opened it, finding the certificate inside wet but still legible.

"Twenty years ago," said Ellie, eyeing the certificate's date. It was for a baby boy named Wallace Benoit; the mom's name was Anna, and the space where the father's name should've been was left blank.

"Benoit," Ellie said thoughtfully. "Not ringing a bell."

Wade didn't recognize it, either. He went to the alcove and pulled out the phone book; he searched the pages but found no one by that last name in the area.

"Not that it means anything," he said. "Folks have cell phones now. They're not in the book's listings."

So we were stumped, but just then Bella, roused I supposed by the activity in the kitchen, came in and peered over our shoulders.

"Oh, I know them!" she exclaimed at once. "Or I knew the girl, anyway. . . . My, how time flies. It's terrible what became of them," she mused. "The baby's dad took off, I recall, left her without a penny, and not all that long afterward she jumped off the Deer Island ferry, poor thing."

Just then Mika came into the kitchen, sweetly pretty in PJs and a pink flannel robe but paler than I liked seeing, and with a wan, not-very-comfortable look on her face. Tossing her glossy black hair back over her shoulders, she got out the olive oil, warmed it in the microwave for a few seconds, and found the eyedropper in the utility drawer.

"Ephraim's got an earache," she explained, pouring the oil into a custard cup just the way I had back when Sam was little.

"By the way, I went down to the shop and made more doughnuts," she said, coming over to the table to look curiously at the things we'd found.

The birth certificate, twenty years old. And the photograph of a woman with children.

"Chocolate ones," she said. "And a couple dozen more chocolate wafers. Okay?" she added a little anxiously.

"Absolutely," I assured her, when what I really wanted to do was fall down and kiss her feet.

The Moose would be open tomorrow come hell or high water, I'd already decided, since during a festival there was no such thing as too much sweet stuff; if it weren't for my daughter-in-law we'd have been up all night baking even more things for the display case.

Wade got up from the table and went back up to his shop, where after a minute I heard the radio go on; the Sox were in the playoffs again and the game was in California.

Mika turned to go also, carrying her warmed olive oil dish.

"Oh, and I almost forgot. A police detective came by the shop while I was there? A woman detective, wanting to talk with you?"

A zing of worry went through me. As long as I was busy snooping I could almost forget that I was still in imminent danger of being charged.

But I was, whether or not I forgot. "She said to meet her in the diner at nine tomorrow morning, if you can. . . ." Mika's voice trailed off doubtfully. "Why, though, are you in trouble?"

"Nope. Don't worry about it," I replied, so after grabbing a handful of plain saltines from the cabinet, she headed back upstairs.

"Hmph," Bella said when she'd gone. "I'm telling you, that girl looks green around the gills."

I agreed; Mika's usual radiant glow had faded to a waxy sallow color, and after what my dad had mentioned, I feared I knew why.

But the middle of the night wasn't the time to discuss it, and after a bit more compulsive fussing around with a paper towel and some spray cleaner, Bella went back upstairs to bed, too, to her and my dad's apartment on the third floor of the big old house.

"Thanks for not mentioning my unscheduled swimming lesson," I said as, carrying my brandy-laced coffee, I followed Ellie outside. A few moths fluttered softly around the porch light over our heads.

"No problem," she said quietly. "Lucky for me, George and Lee were already asleep when I got there, or I'd have had some explaining to do, too."

Faint sounds of ongoing pirate revelry still floated up from Water Street, music and laughter drifting on the fog that had rolled in, haloing the street lamps. But the memory of that dark, mysterious ship floating in the harbor lent the atmosphere an ominous tinge.

I turned from the thought. "So anyway, maybe we've got ourselves a motive of some kind? I mean, what if twenty years ago Henry Hadlyme was the guy who abandoned the Benoit girl, and—"

"And the baby, yes," Ellie agreed. "So let's say for the sake of argument that maybe he left her, and then she killed herself over it like Bella said?"

She turned to me, her face somber. "But where's the baby today, I wonder? And who's that older child in the photograph? And—"

And what did it all have to do with what was going on now? "No idea," I said. But those were our next questions, all right.

"What we can assume, though, is that it wasn't Lionel out there searching tonight," I said. "After all, why would he ransack his own place looking for something he already has?"

From upstairs I could hear Ephraim's wails subsiding to whimpers as his mother dripped warm oil into his ear. The sound comforted me; I didn't know how we'd ever cram another human being into this house, but I didn't like the idea of taking any of them out of it, either, not even a little bit.

"Jake?" said Ellie as something new occurred to her. Not a good something, from the sound of it. "Jake, what if we weren't alone out there tonight?"

Brrr. But she was right. That flitting figure I'd glimpsed. . . .

"Okay, so let's say somebody was there."

By now my aching brain felt like something that had been drowned, frozen, and bounced off a rock a couple of times, mostly because it had. Still, after another swig of brandy-laced coffee, I squeezed a few more dribbles of thought out of it.

"Let's say somebody gets done searching Lionel's cottage," I said. "And Hadlyme's motor home, too."

She nodded unhappily. "And hasn't found anything. That's why everything in both places was so torn up. So maybe they're about to give up, or to search the *other* cottages. But . . ."

"Right, but then *we* show up, and whoever it is has to make sure we didn't find whatever they missed."

"The photograph and the birth certificate . . . so they stayed and watched us. While you were in the cottage, and when we went over the bluff. Spotted Wade, too, maybe, which is why—"

"Why they didn't follow us into the motor home," I finished, "or right up to it, either, so they could pounce as soon as we came out."

Right, because if they had, Wade would've spotted them, wouldn't he? "And by the time we did come out, Bob Arnold had arrived," I concluded.

Ellie nodded hard, her blond topknot gleaming reddish gold under the porch light. "So whoever it is, if they *were* there, they probably know who we are and that we *did* find something."

It was a lot of theory based on few facts: that Hadlyme was the runaway father in question, for instance, was only a guess. But it felt right: that strong sense I'd had of being *watched* out at the campgrounds still hung dankly on me.

"Is George still home now?" I asked, meaning that he hadn't gone to work a night shift somewhere. Probably he hadn't, since he hadn't called Ellie and he wouldn't have wanted to leave Lee home alone. Still . . .

Ellie nodded unhappily. "He's there. You mean because . . . ?"

"Uh-huh. If we're right about the rest of it, then whoever it was out there knows where we are right now, too, most likely."

She didn't like that idea any better than I did. But there we were: "I'd have followed us, wouldn't you?" I asked.

She sighed in silent agreement, then changed the subject. "Sam's getting quite a collection."

On the lawn, she meant—all the yard machinery. "He sure is. I'm going to try getting him to move some of it, but—"

Her car was parked out on the street because our driveway was so full. We went down the porch steps and out the front sidewalk, and she got into the vehicle. "That's not the only extra room he's going to be needing soon," she said, getting behind the wheel.

She smiled up at me. "Bella was correct, that poor girl looks seasick. And Jake, just think about it, when was the last time you ate plain saltines for a late-night snack?"

I didn't have to think long. Before Sam arrived I'd bought those bland, lightly salted crackers by the carton, washing them down with flat ginger ale on the days when I could eat anything at all.

"Yeah, you're probably right." I sighed, looking back up at the porch. By spring, we'd be setting up bunk beds on it.

From somewhere downtown came the *whoop* of a squad car siren, reminding me unpleasantly of my date with a cop in the morning.

"Anyway, good luck tomorrow," said Ellie. She patted my hand. "Now go in and put ice on that forehead of yours before Bella sees it."

Good advice, I realized, touching my temple gingerly; with each minute that passed, now that the evening's excitement had died down, my skull felt more like I'd tried stopping a freight train with it.

"Thanks," I said, but she was already driving away down the fog-blurred street.

The next morning dawned cool and bright, the fog whisked away by a breeze blowing from the north. In the Waco Diner, the fishermen had finished breakfast hours earlier and were out on their boats, leaving the booths and counter mostly empty.

So she was easy to spot: curly brown hair cut very short, red lips, high cheekbones and deep-set eyes, carefully made up . . .

I walked between the diner's long Formica counter and the red leatherette booths running along the wall to the last one.

"I'm Jake Tiptree. You wanted to talk to me?"

I stuck out my hand. She held it briefly, her gaze taking in my face assessingly. "Hi. I'm Amity Jones."

"Short for calamity?" I didn't know what made me say it—

nerves, maybe. It wasn't every day I got interviewed by someone who, when the conversation is over, might arrest me for murder.

But I regretted the remark when she looked rueful. "Actually, it is. Don't ask me why they named me that, though, I've never been able to get a straight answer about it."

She waved at the seat across the booth's table. From behind the counter the waitress eyed me, nodded, and brought coffee.

"Parents, you know?" Amity Jones went on as I sat. "Can't live with 'em, can't sell 'em for parts."

One of mine had been a federal fugitive and the other one was a murder victim, so I understood. But it didn't create any warm bonds between this police detective and me. She got out her badge wallet, flashed the badge, and showed me her ID.

"Before we start, you should know that I'm not here to arrest you, or even to question you officially, and I'm not recording you, either."

I sipped coffee. None of what she'd just said sounded likely. My face must've expressed what I thought: cops can lie to you.

She let a smile curve her mouth. "Look, I understand why you'd be skeptical. But Bob Arnold says that you didn't kill the victim."

"Oh, really." I'd been expecting a barrage of questions, not a demonstration of Bob's stand-up-guy qualities.

The smile widened. "Really. Want to know what else he said?"

Just then the waitress brought the check. Amity Jones lay some money on top of it and got up. "So, do you?"

Oh, of course I did. But more than that, I wanted to know what game Amity Jones was playing with me.

And I hadn't really wanted that coffee, anyway. She pulled on an expensive-looking black leather jacket over her outfit of black turtleneck, gray tailored slacks, and heeled leather boots. "Come on, let's take a walk."

Outside, vendors' carts pumped out tantalizing aromas of candy floss and sausage rolls, pizza and popcorn, and fried dough. Among the booths selling pirate-themed accessories ranging from eye patches to toe rings with silver skulls welded onto them, we walked along Water Street toward the boat basin.

"Bob says that if you killed Hadlyme, he'd be buried by now in a place where nobody would find him."

I glanced sharply at her. Bob Arnold had gotten chatty with this woman, apparently. And I wasn't at all sure that I liked it.

The black sailboat still floated at anchor just inside the boat basin. "Not sure if I should be flattered or insulted," I said.

We strolled out onto the fish pier, its surface constructed of railroad ties spiked to wooden support beams, the whole thing held up by steel pilings driven into the granite bedrock below.

"Yeah, me neither, actually." She eyed the black vessel with a frown as movement appeared on deck. The bright glint of sunlight on binocular lenses flashed briefly, then vanished.

"He meant that if you'd done it, you'd have done it better," she said, turning toward the boat basin, where a couple of lobster boats were coming in, their crew dressed in yellow rubber overalls and boots.

"Do those boats just sit out like that all the time? No guards or watchmen?" she wanted to know.

She referred to the ones still tied up at their slips, and the rest that would be coming in; I guessed she hadn't yet seen the dock lights on the breakwater, bright enough to read by.

And even without them . . . "You don't need guards for the fishing boats," I said. "Some fool starts messing with one of those, he'll be lobster bait."

Behind us on the street, a couple of cherry bombs went off, and then a pennywhistle began tootling. I faced her impatiently.

"Look, if a walking tour is what you want, that's fine," I said, "but enough dancing around."

We started back, past the long metal gangway leading down to the floating docks alongside the fish pier.

"Why don't you just ask me what you want to ask," I said. "And I'll either answer you or not."

We'd reached Overlook Park, a small amphitheater-shaped area with a view of the water. Curved rows of flat white granite blocks, each set a little higher than the one in front of it, served as the amphitheater's seats.

"Bob Arnold's my third cousin," Amity Jones offered out of the blue as we sat.

I found my voice. "Oh, really?" I uttered stupidly.

On this bright morning, the boat basin was nearly empty. Only the Coast Guard's big gray patrol boat sat at her berth, two young Coasties busily sweeping, swabbing, and polishing, inside and out.

"Mm-hmm," Amity Jones replied absently. She was looking in the other direction, toward the black sailboat—the *Jenny*, I recalled now—which had begun coming around so her stern, or the boat's rear end, in case you'd forgotten, faced the shore.

"How'd they do that?" she asked puzzledly. "Move, I mean, when their sails aren't even—"

"Engines," I replied. Inboard; the propeller's bubbly turbulence showed below the stern's waterline. But even if it hadn't—

"Has to be," I went on, "because on a boat you need power, wind or engine—or even oars, in a pinch—to steer."

Even Ellie's boat was out, I noticed now, but I knew she had promised Lee a boat ride and it was a beautiful day, so probably they were doing that.

"So did you already know Bob Arnold was a distant relative of yours when you came here?" I asked as we got up.

It explained why he'd confided in her, I thought, and it wasn't even particularly surprising that the two of them were related; in Maine, just about everyone is if you look back far enough.

"My mom's a genealogy nut," Amity Jones said, nodding. "But he didn't, I guess. Or anyway, he didn't know until I told him."

We walked uphill past the tall red-brick buildings that housed the pet supply shop, an art gallery, and some high-end gift shops.

"Smart guy, your police chief," she went on. "He deserves more respect than he gets from our department, I'm guessing."

She glanced back again at the *Jenny*, still nosed out toward the bay. Someone was hanging halfway out over the transom at the boat's rear, doing something with some mechanism or other.

"Yeah," I said, "he's smart, all right." But privately a needle of doubt began poking me; was he smart enough to resist her flattery?

Because maybe she was sincere. Certainly he deserved the praise she'd offered. But when you added it to a family connection . . . well, I just hoped he hadn't told her much about me, was all. Who knew which innocent detail might end up being my undoing?

At the corner in front of the post office building, a guy was selling sausages out of a cart. "Red hots! Getcha red hots!"

"Mmm," Amity Jones remarked appreciatively, "snappers."

The long bright-red sausages were a Maine favorite, encased in a substantial skin that popped juicily when you bit into it.

"Mmm is right," I said, as the tantalizing aroma of sizzling fat drew me in. "Here, my treat," I added, pulling out my wallet.

I guessed a couple of sandwiches and a soda wouldn't count as attempted bribery, and as it turned out I was correct. We sat on the post office's curved granite steps, balancing the food on our knees and watching the pet parade go by, the mostly cooperative animals all tricked out in capes, bandannas, and eye patches.

"Oh, this is heaven," she remarked, washing down the last of her hot dog with a swallow of Moxie. "I was over here last week, just by coincidence, but nobody was selling anything as good as this stuff."

"You like Moxie, do you?" I think it tastes like tree roots stewed in crankcase oil and filtered through an old boot.

I hadn't missed her remark about being here the previous week, either, but that wasn't a big deal. Lots of people come to Eastport in summer.

"Moxie? It's like mother's milk," she said, crumpling the hot dog wrapper and getting up. "And I don't care how recent breakfast was, this made for a great snack, thanks."

She was young, maybe in her late twenties, I thought, and still able to eat all day long without gaining an ounce. But she was right, those red hots were delicious.

"Listen," I said finally, "isn't this a little unorthodox? No probing questions, no . . ."

She shrugged. "What, getting a sense of what people are like before I charge at them, start accusing them of things?"

She gathered up her bag, shrugged her jacket straight on her shoulders, and looked me in the eye. "Don't worry, I'll get to that part when I'm ready. And with who I'm ready for."

A troop of Scouts scampered up to the red hot cart and began clamoring for hot dogs and sodas. She watched them with a smile.

But somehow, it wasn't a convincing smile. "Besides," she said, "I've got a few people to talk to. You're not the only one with a reason to have done it."

It was the first time she'd even mentioned Hadlyme's murder. "The young people who were with him, you mean?"

Amity Jones looked wise. "Maybe. But telling you that would be unorthodox, too, wouldn't it?"

I could see in her face that she was getting ready to go, that her goal for meeting with me this morning had been accomplished.

And maybe she'd meant it, maybe I really wasn't her main suspect in Hadlyme's murder; not yet, anyway. But I'd never felt less sure of anything in my life.

Still, there was no sense in letting her know that. "I've got to get going, too," I said, the sight of The Chocolate Moose sign down the block reminding me that it was time to open the shop.

Cookies, cakes, chocolate doughnuts . . . sure, they were all baked, thanks to Mika and Ellie, but they weren't going to sell themselves, were they?

I took my and Amity's hot dog wrappers to a trash bin nearby and dropped them in. A pink pig in a pirate costume trotted by, his curly tail quivering, and a donkey followed wearing a straw hat with his long ears poking through two holes.

Amity Jones looked over at me, smiling and opening her mouth as if to say something, and then the explosion happened.

After the blast, a lot of screaming and shouting broke out. Car alarms honked and building alarms wailed; children bawled, although I didn't see that any of them had actually been hurt.

Thick black smoke rose from the middle of Water Street, between Overlook Park on one side and The Chocolate Moose on the other. I ran toward the shop as people milled around me, some carrying youngsters and others frantically searching.

The Moose's front window was miraculously intact, although the crater in the pavement in front of it, still smoking, was at least a foot wide. As I stared, Bob Arnold swung in and jumped from his car, his eyes scanning the crowd for injuries while he spoke into his radio, summoning help.

"What should I do?" Amity Jones had caught up with me and wanted to make herself useful, but she knew better than to interrupt Bob.

Heck, right now a Sherman tank would probably think twice about interrupting him. "Just walk down the street," I told her, "and watch for people who need help. And if *you* end up needing any help with what you find—"

Flying glass wounds, fractures, even heart attacks . . . so far I didn't see any bodies lying around, but it had been a big explosion.

"If you need anything, just ask for it. Someone will help you," I said confidently, because in Eastport someone will. Then a second blast went off somewhere near the boat basin.

This time the already-shocked glass in The Chocolate Moose's front window dropped out, crashing to the sidewalk. Next came the dull *thud-thud-thud* of a lot of secondary explosions, and the siren on the Coast Guard headquarters' roof began droning.

Ellie, I thought. And her little girl . . . They could be in the boat basin right now. *Or what was left of them. . . .*

"Go," I told Amity Jones, and took off in the other direction.

Shoving through the crowds surging off the breakwater, I tried peering past them down the slanting metal gangway and out along the finger piers. But all I could see was smoke; at the boat ramp I skidded down seaweed-slimed concrete to the water's edge, still not seeing Ellie.

Then I spied an orange life vest bobbing nearby. But it didn't bob quite enough, as if it was weighed down by something. Swallowing hard, I waded in, then reached out and snagged the vest's straps with my fingers and pulled.

Stuck. But on what? With my heart in my throat, I hauled mightily on the thing with both hands, hoping against hope.

A navy blue uniform shirt with the life jacket wrapped around it lurched unwillingly to the water's surface. The shirt had a torso and two arms inside; more pulling revealed a belt and a pair of pants.

All dead weight. My feet slipped crazily on the wet ramp, but at last a man's head emerged from the water, pale and drenched.

"Come on, come on . . ." As I hauled on the limp, wet body, I became aware that a stream of curses was coming out of me, every bad word that I could think of and some that I hadn't realized I knew.

"Don't you dare die on me . . . open those eyes . . . take a *breath*, dammit . . ."

Everyone on the breakwater was too far away to know what I was up to, or too involved in getting their kids to safety to do anything about it. I knew that even once I got him out of the water, no way would I be able to do effective CPR on this kid all by myself.

So instead I hauled him up into a sitting position, yanked his loosened life jacket up above his shoulder blades, and slammed my open right hand into the middle of his upper back so hard that his long-dead ancestors probably felt it.

Again. "Come *on* . . ." But he still didn't breathe, and he looked so very dead at this point that I might've given up if he hadn't also looked so much like Sam at that age, with his long eyelashes and soft, inexpertly shaven jawline.

So I kept smacking him, and I was swinging my arm back to deliver yet another blow when the limp lifeless-seeming body I was supporting coughed, lurched, and puked up about a gallon of seawater. Clambering to my feet I waved frantically at one of the Coast Guard guys now sprinting toward me, and when he arrived I left the young Coastie to his care.

Because I still hadn't spotted Ellie. . . . At the foot of the metal gangway, a crowd of other Coast Guard personnel had converged on what was left of their big gray patrol boat. Twisted metal, burnt plastic, and shattered safety glass, all polished and shipshape just a few moments earlier, was now burnt, melted, or simply gone—

The oily smoke hanging in the boat basin, although chokingly thick, had spots thin enough to see through. But no pretty little blue Bayliner floated in Ellie's spot by the finger pier; on the other hand, it didn't look as if one had sunk there recently, either.

So where was she? I trotted back up the gangway and scanned the water: under the deceptively clear blue sky, nothing that looked like her little Bayliner showed on the bright waves.

All the fishing boats were hurrying back, though, their rumble coming distantly from every direction on the bay; dark puffs of diesel engine exhaust spewed urgently from their stacks.

Suddenly Bob Arnold was beside me. "Jake."

I turned wildly to him. "Ellie went out with Lee earlier, and now I can't—"

He put his hands up, trying to calm me. "No. No, Jake, they're okay. Both of them, I just got a call."

The first crazed rush of people off the breakwater had thinned. Vendors stood by their souvenir tents and food carts, wondering aloud whether to wait for further developments or just close up and go home.

"What?" I demanded confusedly as another bad thought hit me. Suddenly I was terrified that Mika might've taken Ephraim downtown to watch the pet parade. Or Mika *and* Bella might've . . .

A trio of squad cars and an ambulance screamed down Washington Street past the post office building, fueling my anxiety.

"She called," Bob said, looking into my face so I would focus on him. "Ellie had her phone out there, and she heard the explosions."

I was gasping, hyperventilating, and those hot dogs I'd eaten threatened revolt. Trying to calm down, I put my hands on top of my head and forced myself to breathe slowly.

"I told her not to come in here to the boat basin," Bob went on, "to tie up instead at the old dock at the end of Staniels Street and someone would pick her up."

Relief washed over me. "Okay, but I've got to go home first and make sure everyone there is—"

We hurried back up the breakwater together, past Rosie's Hot Dog Stand and out onto the street. Everywhere people were scanning around and calling to one another, gathering their spouses and kids.

"Yeah, they're all safe and sound," Bob said, and at my curious glance he added, "I was at your house when the first boom went off. I had just talked to Amity Jones a little earlier, see, and—"

Glancing around, I spotted Amity talking to the drenched young Coastie I'd yanked out of the water. Someone had thrown a blanket over his shoulders and sat him at one of the picnic tables behind Rosie's.

"She seems to think you're quite the hot ticket," I said. "Like you're not the country bumpkin cop she was expecting. And what do you know, it turns out you're cousins, besides," I added a little acidly.

Catching my tone, he eyed me sideways. "I might've humored her a little on that," he allowed, and then I got it.

Because he really was smart, wasn't he? Oh yeah: "Buttered her up one side and down the other is what I did, actually," he went on. "Glad to have her expert help on such a terrible crime, etcetera."

He looked out over the water toward the black sailboat still anchored off the end of the fish pier. It was strange that her stern still pointed toward us even though the other boats on moorings all aimed the other way, on account of the breeze and outgoing tide.

Which meant the *Jenny* was under power, since as Ellie had noted to me earlier and I'd told Amity Jones, a boat needs power—oars, wind, engine, whatever—to have steering ability. And only steering could keep a vessel sitting at right angles to an ebbing tide. . . .

"Hey, Bob?" I said, noticing something else. "What's that pale smoke coming out of the . . ."

Smoke . . . or was it vapor? Whatever it was, little wisps of the stuff hung around the *Jenny*'s stern.

". . . so Amity Jones will maybe give me a hint about which way the wind is blowing, you know?" Bob was saying.

I'd been foolish to think that flattery or even a family connection would turn his head. "Bob, do you have any idea
what's behind this?"

I waved at the Coast Guard vessel, still smoking from a ragged
hole in its hull; now four blue-uniformed young people were
hauling their injured crewmate off the deck, carrying him in an
improvised blanket hammock. I couldn't see the injured man
himself, but from the looks on his colleagues' faces I probably
didn't want to, anyway.

"No idea," Bob said, squinting at the black sailboat again.

The Coast Guard boat was the only vessel in the basin with
guns on it, I noticed. But I doubted that they would fire now,
all bent and twisted the way they were.

"I don't get it at all," said Bob, still gazing thoughtfully at
the *Jenny*. "Because unless something got planted on Water
Street"—something explosive, he meant—"then whatever it
was that blew up must've come in off the—"

Water. Right, like maybe a . . . "Hey, Bob?" Something moved
on the *Jenny*'s rear deck again. "Bob, what are those holes?" In
the *Jenny*'s stern, I meant. "Like, are they portholes, or . . ."

But they were too small for portholes. Suddenly as I spoke, a
large gray rubber Zodiac boat pulled from behind the wrecked
Coast Guard vessel and headed out of the boat basin at high
speed. Two Coasties stood alertly at the Zodiac's helm, with
two more stationed amidships looking wary and holding . . .
yikes.

"Hey, Bob, those guys on the Zodiac have got—"

"Yeah," said Bob, pulling out his radio. "Guns. Big ones, too."

One of the Coasties shouted through a bullhorn. In response
a puff of smoke erupted from one of the small holes in the
Jenny that I'd just been considering.

A line of deceptively small splashes zipped one after another
across the water, stopping just short of the Zodiac. The Coastie
with the bullhorn put it down fast; then the Zodiac fired some-

thing at the *Jenny*'s hull, a bigger shot than whatever the schooner had.

Splinters flew, and a wide white gouge showed in the vessel's dark paint. In the next instant one of those stern holes made a sort of *pfft!* sound, and an instant later a loud boom erupted from somewhere on Water Street.

"Damn," Bob said, and ran toward the mayhem, leaving me alone.

Six

Clattering down the metal ramp again, I slammed onto the wooden dock at the foot of it and rushed to the end of the nearest finger pier. No more explosions came from Water Street, only the sound of cars starting and pulling out as people evacuated downtown as fast as they could.

Meanwhile, Ellie might've told Bob Arnold that she'd take the Bayliner over to the Staniels Street pier. But I knew Ellie and I didn't believe it; for one thing, she'd have had no way to get back to town from there and wouldn't want to wait for a ride.

And anyway, even with Lee aboard, thinking that Ellie was going to navigate *away* from whatever was going on down here was ridiculous. She'd told Bob what he wanted to hear, was all, and then she'd have put Lee ashore somewhere safe before coming to where the action was.

But now I was getting worried; she'd had plenty of time to get here even with a stop to drop Lee off. Down on my knees on the pier, I inched out and craned my neck sharply to look out around the end of the breakwater.

To the east lay the island of Campobello, about a mile distant; to the north, the Cherry Island lighthouse strobed faithfully even in daytime. Beyond, Head Harbor Passage spread choppy and blue in the distance, but there was no Bayliner out there anywhere that I could see, either.

Maybe if I inched myself farther out on the dock, I'd be able to see more toward the south end of the bay. . . .

Of course there was also a risk that a big fishing boat would come along the end of the breakwater at the wrong moment, just as one of them had earlier, and clip my head off as easily as lopping a flower off the end of a stem.

But at the moment I hardly cared; I'd have tried calling Ellie, but I still hadn't found my phone, and if I didn't see her soon I would have to find a boat that could go out and search for her.

As I thought this, Tim Franco scrambled off one of the fishing boats tied to a pier and hotfooted it up the metal ladder to the breakwater's concrete deck, too intent on some errand or other to bother with the ramp.

Personally, I wouldn't climb one of those ladders if a whole crew of pirates was after me with drawn swords. But the work on the fishing boats didn't let up even for explosions, apparently.

Still clad in the red swim trunks and U Maine sweatshirt he'd been wearing when we towed him in from Head Harbor Passage earlier, he trotted down the breakwater to the street, then turned left toward downtown. I could ask him, I supposed, to take me out on the water to look for Ellie in his little boat.

That is, if I was willing to trust myself to that fuel pump of his. Even I wasn't ready for that much adventure quite yet, though, so instead I squinched myself farther along the dock's edge until my head was all the way out over the water, and then even a little more until my shoulders and half my chest were sticking out over the waves, too.

Any farther and I'd overbalance myself and fall in. But from where I was—balanced precariously, my gut muscles getting a workout because I had to stay stiff as a board to keep my upper body from collapsing downward—I could see down the bay.

Almost. A little more and I'd have a good view all the way to Lubec. So I inched forward a little farther, and—darn, maybe now it was too far, since suddenly I was way, way out there, with only my hip bones in solid contact with the dock planks.

Still, from here I could glimpse . . .

Nothing. No boat showed through the whitecaps' snowy foam or the shimmery mists above. Not Ellie's familiar Bayliner or any others. And then as if to compound my disappointment, I realized:

I'd been able to squinch myself out here, all right, wiggling forward on my belly an inch at a time until my head, shoulders, and torso were extended out over the waves.

Squinching *backward*, however, was another matter. An *impossible* matter, as it turned out, because there wasn't enough of my body left on the dock planks to squinch with.

"Oof," I said, and then, "Uh, hello? Anybody?"

But no one was around. Tim Franco was long gone on whatever errand he'd looked so urgent about, and everyone else I could see was either up on the street or way over on the far side of the breakwater, dealing with the shot-up Coast Guard cruiser.

Meanwhile, those gut muscles I mentioned, the ones that held me stiff as a board so that I could stick out off the end of the dock's planks? Well, they were getting tired. Any moment they were going to fail me; in fact, the pain already knifed through my middle and back, rising rapidly to the level of a scream.

But I couldn't do that, either; right now if I moved so much as a muscle the wrong direction, I'd end up in the drink. And although I could swim, the water was very cold and the dock pilings were seaweed-slimed; I couldn't promise myself that I could get out without help.

So I was stuck and on the point of collapsing, the upper half of my body already angled unwillingly ever closer to the waves.

Finally I closed my eyes and sucked in a breath, preparing for my face to go under. There were no good options available, but maybe I could kick-and-flail my way over to the boat ramp and crawl up to shore.

Maybe. . . . A wave slopped up over my nose, startling me. I gagged on salt water, felt more cold waves, and—

Somebody grabbed my feet. "Jake!" cried a familiar voice.

I let myself be dragged backward, trying and failing to protect my already-scraped middle from the rough edges of the dock's planks. Finally I slid back up onto the dock itself, choking and gasping and spitting out globs of thick, slippery seaweed.

"Jake, what in the *world* do you think you're *doing*? You could have *drowned*! If I hadn't come along you'd have . . ."

It was Ellie's voice, blowing off steam from the fright I'd just given her. But she wasn't the only one who'd gotten a scare. Gasping and with my heart hammering the inside of my chest, I rolled over and sat up.

"Where'd *you* come from?" I demanded right back at her. "For Pete's sake, I thought you must be—"

I waved out at the blue water, for which I'd just acquired a new, even-healthier respect than before.

"I tied up at the Chowder House," she said, meaning the dock where the shoreside eatery's customers could arrive by water, "and sent Lee home from there."

Just as I'd thought. She'd been out there on the water, all right, just not while I was looking. I struggled to my feet.

"Look at you," Ellie said scoldingly, taking my arm. "Wet and cold . . . come on, though, we'll go up to the Moose and get some nice hot coffee into you . . ."

Yeah, sure we would, I thought woozily. My head thudded dully where I'd bonked it the night before on the rocks at the campgrounds.

". . . and you'll be fine," Ellie said as I let her guide me along the floating dock and then up the metal gangway to the breakwater's deck.

At the top, an Eastport squad car with its light bar flashing was parked slantwise across the pavement, blocking access to the outer part of the breakwater. Armed Coast Guard personnel stood sentry at their guard house and gate entrances.

"Wow," I said, gazing dazedly at them. "They're not fooling around, are they?"

A helicopter *whap-whapped* overhead. A National Guard group had been training in nearby Quoddy Village and they were arriving now, too, jumping out of their vans and ready to go in their combat gear.

"No kidding," said Ellie, pointing at the water. From down the bay a squadron of fishing boats still steamed purposefully toward Eastport. They all had marine-band radios, naturally, and by now they'd have heard about what'd happened just as Ellie had; her radio was still working if you smacked it hard enough, I gathered. If not, she wouldn't have gone out.

Probably it would wait until she really needed it and then break for good, I thought pessimistically as we hurried along Water Street toward the shop. I looked around for Amity Jones but didn't see her. I did see our poor blast-damaged Chocolate Moose sign, now missing one of its googly eyes and both buck-teeth.

"Oh," Ellie said softly, staring at the shattered window beneath the ruined sign.

"Yeah," I said. "We're going to have to get some plywood." And after that about a thousand bucks' worth of glass . . .

I peered through the empty frame, sighing at the mess in there. The rest of the shops at our end of the block were damaged, too, and a few of the proprietors were walking around looking stunned.

Luckily, all our baked goods were still in the cooler in the kitchen. And although the festival would obviously have to be put on hold, very soon more people would be down here, wouldn't they?

Covering windows, sweeping up bits of glass, and putting things to rights . . . it would take a lot of work, fueled by—

"You thinking what I'm thinking?" We made our way into the shop.

The bell over the door tinkled forlornly. Glass crunched under our feet. "Oh, you bet I am," said Ellie.

"We'll get out the biggest coffee urn and the extension cord, gather up the doughnuts and the . . ."

Back in the kitchen, everything looked normal except for the yellow police tape still stretched over the cellar entrance. I opened the cooler and found that in our absence, Mika must've been down here baking even more:

Another big batch of chocolate doughnut muffins, four trays of chocolate snickerdoodles, enough Toll House cookies for an army, and a large mocha sheet cake with fudge-nut frosting sat under the cooler lights, all positively radiating deliciousness.

". . . and we'll set up a table right out on the street," Ellie said determinedly, unwilling to let all those expensive ingredients go to waste just because the pirate festival was postponed.

Besides, people were going to be hungry. So we got to work: trays, a cash box, the power cord, and a table strong enough to hold that coffee urn, for starters. We got it all ready to move out onto the sidewalk, not rushing but not wasting time, either.

Neither of us brought up Henry Hadlyme's murder. I didn't even mention Amity Jones. Instead for an hour or so we put all that aside to focus on what we *could* understand: chocolate and all the delicious items you could create with it, and how we could best help after the terrible thing that had happened.

But finally: "They're going to make us leave sooner or later, you know," I said. We were in the kitchen, gathering up the napkins and paper coffee cups with our trademark moose printed on them to put on the sidewalk table.

"The police," I went on, "they'll say it's dangerous, that the boat might shoot at us again, or—"

"Or what?" It was Amity Jones standing behind me in the kitchen doorway. I hadn't heard her come in.

She held out the little bell that had hung over the door. "Found this on the floor."

More likely she'd spotted it and plucked it from its hook before its silvery jingle could betray her. That was my theory, anyway.

"Can we help you with something?" I snapped. I was not in the mood for strangers, and especially not ones whose motives were murky.

She shrugged. "No. I was hoping I could help you."

She waved toward the store's damaged front section. We hadn't even swept up the broken glass yet.

"Anyway, you're right, the county sheriff's deputies are going to clear everyone out of downtown," she said. "But if you two want to stay, I can say I need to question you here on the premises."

I still didn't trust her. She'd had my guard lowered earlier, sure, but upon reflection even her story about being Bob Arnold's cousin sounded fishy to me. And that business about her visiting here a week earlier just by coincidence?

Yeah, that too, now that I thought about it. "I saw you reviving that Coast Guard guy," she said. "Nice job."

Ellie glanced curiously at me. "I just sat him up and smacked him," I told her. "He spit up the water he'd swallowed on his own."

Just about the last thing I wanted was to be made out as some kind of hero; all I really wanted was to be home in bed.

Or under it, where it was dark; my head was killing me. I got a headache pill from the cabinet over the sink; swallowed it with more fresh coffee, which was bliss; then stepped outside with Amity Jones right behind me.

On the sidewalk I let her help me unfold our long table and set it up. "So what are they saying?" I asked her. "The cops, I mean, about what happened."

"Nothing. So far, nobody's got a clue what's going on."

I shook out a red-checked tablecloth and spread it over the long table. Out on the breakwater, men were using a crane to position huge concrete barriers to block off vehicle access.

"SWAT team is coming. They've got an armored truck and some, uh, weapons. Larger"—Amity Jones specified delicately—"weapons."

To blow that damned black-painted boat out of the water with, I hoped, stretching out the orange extension cord. A sheriff's squad car rolled slowly down the street toward us as I worked, and Amity stepped out to talk to its driver briefly.

Afterward the car rolled on by without stopping, its driver not even giving me any side-eye. I faced Amity questioningly.

"I told him Bob Arnold asked you two to stay here and set up an aid and refreshments station for all the personnel who'll be coming," she explained.

"Oh. Okay, then." So maybe she wasn't a complete bull . . . uh, I mean she wasn't a complete liar.

Her neat outfit looked rumpled and dusty, with a splatter-shaped dark stain on those good gray slacks of hers, I saw now.

Blood, I realized. "Get that doing first aid, did you?"

Ellie was bringing chairs out. Amity sank into one of them and shrugged tiredly.

"Guy got glass-sprayed when windows shattered. It seemed bad at first, but he's okay. Pressure, tourniquet . . . heck"—she waved at her bloody pants leg—"I probably look worse than he does at this point."

"Yeah, huh?" I felt my heart unhardening slightly. "Anyone else hurt?" I felt a pang of guilt at not having asked sooner.

She shook her head. "Nothing bad. Could've been a lot worse."

"Well, good for you for helping. You want some coffee, glass of water or something?"

Amity looked grateful, and happier still when the drink Ellie brought turned out to be a Sanpellegrino lemon on crushed ice.

"You guys sure do know how to put on a festival," she said with a sigh when she'd finished it. Across the street, past debris-littered Overlook Park and the boat basin, the dark sailboat still hunkered ominously.

"Right, we sure do." I matched her sarcasm while wondering how we'd get rid of the menacing-looking vessel. "Can't anybody find out who it belongs to, at least?"

Because that might go a long way toward figuring out who was firing explosives from it. "Too bad we don't have artillery of our own," I added.

Probably the Coast Guard had weaponry that could handle the problem, a gunship or something, but it would take hours for that help to get here. Besides, what I really wanted was for us to sink those bastards ourselves, just blow a big hole in the boat: *glub-glub*.

"There aren't any registration numbers on the hull," Amity Jones said, "so there's no way to track an owner down until somebody manages to board the thing, and maybe not even—"

"In fact," I went on over the sound of her voice telling me why things couldn't be done, "it's a darned shame we don't have a—"

But then I stopped in the middle of covering more paper plates full of snickerdoodles with plastic wrap, because we did have one.

A cannon, that is. Not the reproduction one that Wade had used in his demonstration but a no-kidding military weapon, nearly two centuries old but perfectly functional, safety tested by my very own husband for use in the pirate festival's closing ceremonies.

Ellie looked mystified. "Jake, what's that smile about? You look like you swallowed a canary."

When I wasn't wrapping cookies I'd been arranging plates of cake slices and other tempting goodies on the table outside. Now even the coffee urn stood wheezing at the center of the table, brewing more of the dark ambrosia that Ellie makes out of ordinary Maxwell House.

So I was free to go find some—

"Cannonballs," I replied to Ellie's question, glancing again at the dark boat, its gun ports still aimed straight at us.

They, I supposed, were why the Coast Guard hadn't just swarmed the vessel immediately to find out for sure what was going on, not to mention stopping it in its tracks; they didn't want to provoke more shooting.

Wait for the big guns to arrive was the plan, I supposed, and I could understand their caution.

But I wasn't feeling cautious. "Yep, I'm thinking about some good old-fashioned cannonballs," I said, feeling a smile spread on my face. "And you know what?"

They both looked back at me, Ellie in amused resignation and Amity with the sort of thoughtful expression that means someone is wondering what size net to use on you.

I grabbed a snickerdoodle and took a big bite. "I think," I said through the cookie's crispy sweetness . . .

I chewed some more. "I think there's a few of them . . ."

They really were very good snickerdoodles.

"I think there's a few of them piled up behind the hay bales in my garden shed, and . . ."

Cannonballs, I meant, not cookies. And the cannon was there, too, if I wasn't mistaken.

"And I'm going to go get them!" I finished.

Back at the house, Wade sat at the kitchen table and listened carefully. He was angry about the explosions downtown, just as I was. But he didn't think that the cannonballs were a good idea, or the cannon, either.

"Jake, it's one thing to fire it for exhibition purposes, like I meant to. But I wasn't ever planning to use a full powder charge in the thing. Seriously, the last time it was fired in anger must have been in the early eighteen hundreds."

By full charge he meant powder enough to hurl a heavy projectile far enough, and with enough force, to damage the *Jenny*.

"But Wade, if we could sink the *Jenny* . . ."

Before coming inside to talk with him I'd hauled half a dozen of those cannonballs—each heavy enough that I had to carry one at a time—from the garden shed, where they'd been stacked in a pyramid, to the lawn, where we could back up Wade's truck to load them.

So now I really wanted to use them, if only so I didn't have to haul them back into the shed again.

Well, and for other reasons, too. But: "It could explode," he said. "The cannon, that is. The whole thing could fly apart, and I'd be the one who was lighting it off, by the way, standing right behind it."

Hmm, that did put a different complexion on the matter. I was still very ticked at whoever was shooting at us from that sailboat, but not enough to want Wade to lose important body parts over it.

Or any parts, actually. "Besides, if we do sink the *Jenny*," Wade added, "it'll be on us, whatever might happen afterward. And we have no idea what that might be."

I eyed him over the cannonballs lying on the grass like part of a giant's game of croquet, thinking about how much I didn't want to carry them again.

"You know," I said, "I love you, but you're annoying when you're correct."

Laughing, he grabbed up three of the round black projectiles, wedging two under his arm and palming the other as he straightened easily. "Hand me one more, will you?"

I bent, fastened my hands around one, and muscled myself back up into a standing position. The thing was about the size of a coconut, and so heavy it felt as if it might drag me hands-first right down through the grass into the earth.

When he was fully loaded, I followed Wade back to the shed where he stashed the cannonballs once more, and the old cannon that I had dragged out of there, too.

But then he paused. "You know," he said, frowning thoughtfully at the pint-sized piece of antique artillery, "maybe I'll just take that thing up to my workshop and clean it up a little before I stow it away."

The stink of cleaning solvents floated unpleasantly through my mental memory. "Dad just put an exhaust fan in his studio's window," I said, "to get rid of the turpentine smell in the house. So can you do it—"

Wade was already nodding. "Outside, sure," he agreed.

He picked the cannon up. "No sense exchanging one set of fumes for another, is there. I'll take it out back, though, where it's not visible from the street."

Which made sense; he'd already had one antique weapon stolen recently.

"Are the cops downtown saying anything about who might be on that sailboat?" he asked, changing the subject.

"They're not." I told him what Amity Jones had said about no registration numbers on the *Jenny.* "I gather reinforcements are on the way, but so far all anyone's done is set up a perimeter to keep civilians out of the line of fire."

Around me the peace and quiet of Key Street was punctuated only by the sound of my grandson, upstairs yelling his head off about not wanting to take a nap.

I could've taken one, no problem; over the past twenty-four hours I'd had enough exercise for two weeks, and my head still felt like a used pinata.

"I guess they're trying to come up with a plan," I finished. Which was all I knew, and it still seemed to me that putting a hole in the side of that boat was a good idea.

But it wasn't up to me. "Anyway, thanks," I told Wade, then went inside and climbed the hall stairs up to my dad's studio on the third floor, wondering again not just who was on the *Jenny*, but—

"What do they want? And what if anything has it got to do with Hadlyme's murder?" I wondered aloud after filling my father in on new developments.

"Because let's face it, for both those things to be happening in Eastport at once," I told my father, "is an unlikely coincidence."

Or coinky-dink, as Sam would've put it.

"Ayuh." My dad peered out from behind his easel. For his painting session today he wore a paint-spattered white smock over a sweatshirt and jeans, a navy bandanna knotted around his neck, and a purple beret perched jauntily on his head.

He was still working on the portrait of my mother. "Used to do it that way, myself," he remarked, squinting at his easel again and then adding a touch of red.

"What? Used to do what yourself?" I demanded.

But I could guess; decades ago when my mother was alive he'd been a radical activist, with emphasis on *radical*. That meant he'd built bombs, not to put too fine a point on it, and placed them where they'd do the sort of damage that his counterculture client had asked for.

Not to people or animals; he had an unblemished record of "do no harm" when it came to living creatures of any kind. But if you needed destruction done right, safely, and to make a political point, he was your man with a plan.

But that was then; he'd paid for his deeds and now rarely discussed them, which was why what he'd said surprised me.

"It's not enough for things to go boom," he added, eyeing me wisely over the top of the easel.

"The explosions," I said slowly, "they have to be . . . ?"

He nodded, one bushy salt-and-pepper eyebrow arched. "Done in the right order, for one thing. So first you'd set off a smallish one under a trash can, say, just enough to get people . . ."

His gaze was on the canvas, but a reminiscent smile curved his lips. "Interested," he finished.

He touched the brush to his work. "Get the bomb squad, fire trucks, bunch of New York's finest all crowded around where you want them to be, maybe even the Commissioner might show up, if . . ."

Another brush-touch. "If there were cameras," he added.

"And then the real thing would happen somewhere else."

The real explosion, that is. The one that mattered: a Brink's truck, a politician's limo. None of them occupied, all thoroughly destroyed, the cops all somewhere else.

So nobody got hurt. Or caught. He looked up again, aimed the crimson-tipped paintbrush straight at me. "All to create . . ."

He made *Come on* motions with his fingers, wanting me to supply the answer. "A distraction," I said finally, thinking, *Of course. . . .*

"Very good. Now while you're here, would you just turn your head a tiny bit? That way, yes, just a . . . good. Done."

Who, me? "But Dad, why d'you want me to . . . ?"

I walked around the easel. The woman in the painting still had dark wavy hair, deep-set eyes, and full red lips pursed in a smile.

"Mom was beautiful," I said. In the painting she wore a dark emerald-green sweater that showed off her swanlike neck and creamy skin. Now I thought it looked familiar.

"Yes. Yes, she was," he said, looking pensive.

"But Dad," I said, still thinking about all that destruction downtown being a distraction for something else, as he'd suggested. "That's my sweater in the painting, isn't it? The green one?"

He put his brush down, turning to me. "Yes to both questions," he said with a gentle smile. "But that's not your mom. I can see how you might think so, but . . ." He waved me nearer. "Jacobia, don't you see? This painting is of you."

By midafternoon when I got back downtown, the county sheriff's deputies had finished cordoning off the blasted section of Water Street and had set up sawhorse barriers, exempting only our treats-laden sidewalk tables and the coffee urn.

"Do not," Amity Jones warned Ellie and me sternly out in front of The Chocolate Moose, "go past the sawhorse barriers, or somebody will surely arrest you for interfering with a police investigation."

In reply we both nodded obediently like the pair of cooperative little puppets that we were.

Or that we wanted her to think we were. "So where am I in all this, now?" I asked, setting out more paper cups, creamers and sugar packets, and stir sticks.

An army of state cops had hit town in armored vehicles with the Maine Tactical Activity Squad logo stenciled on their sides. So we were doing a land-office business in coffee and snacks—we'd be donating the proceeds to the cleanup effort, of course—but I still wanted to know if I was about to be charged with murder.

"I don't know, yet." Amity Jones eyed me. "I do know about the cutlass and the stuffed parrot, though. Where they both came from, I mean," she said darkly.

The weapon used to kill Hadlyme, the bird perched on his dead shoulder. "You don't think that's all a little obvious?" I asked.

Because really, the guy might as well have had a sign taped to his back: JAKE DID IT. "That I'm being set up?" I added.

"Right," she snapped back at me, "or maybe that's just what I'm supposed to think."

"Sure, the old double-reverse fake-out," I retorted. "Like I'd have come up with that," I added sarcastically.

But I wasn't feeling anywhere near as confident as I sounded. Amity Jones had gotten ornery since earlier in the day, and I wondered why.

Meanwhile, though, more pushback was in order, it seemed to me: "You being a detective and all," I said, "you should've figured out by now that murderers aren't smart enough for complex plans."

Her eyes were still unfriendly. "Yeah. Except sometimes."

She left our long gingham-covered table full of baked goods and coffee makings and got into her car, a dark blue state-issued sedan with no markings and no visible cop gear, and lowered the window.

"Too smart for their own good sometimes," she added ominously, then drove off, leaving me feeling even less confident than before.

"Too smart, my great-aunt Fanny," I grumbled. "Well, I happen to think *she's* just a little too smart for *her* own—"

"Jake." While Amity Jones had been keeping me busy, Ellie had been freshening up the table, refilling the cookie and cake trays, and checking on the coffee urn.

"What?" I demanded, watching the dark sedan make the turn onto Washington Street, then head uphill past the post office building.

Good riddance. But not for long, I thought. In the few hours since the explosions, for some reason she'd turned against me. So—

"*Jake!*"

I spun around impatiently, then stopped short at the sight of my daughter-in-law.

She wasn't supposed to be inside the cordoned-off area. Only Ellie and I had permission to—

"Please?" she begged winsomely, looking adorable in her crisp white blouse and bakery apron and a pair of black slacks.

Flat black shoes with fake jewels on the toes were on her feet, and a pink silk ribbon tied her hair back.

"Oh, Mika," I said. Broken glass littered the street, and the cops hanging around looked grim. "I'm not sure it's a good idea . . ."

Ellie was just then selling cookies to a pair of SWAT officers; now she glanced sideways at me. If Mika stayed, we could leave, her look said clearly, and Ellie clearly wanted to go.

"Just for a little while. I need to get out of the house," Mika coaxed, and I felt her on that one. When I'd left a little earlier, the baby had been crying again while Bella tried soothing him to no avail, Wade was in his workshop running a power saw, and Sam was dropping a snowplow blade—another one, dear heaven—off a flatbed truck into our driveway.

"Please," Mika repeated quietly, then took matters into her own hands by stepping in front of Ellie to wait on the next customers.

"I'll handle it all for a while," she said decisively; not for the first time I noticed the iron will behind all that prettiness, and boy, did she ever know how to use it.

But even then I couldn't just leave her, especially if she might be pregnant. "Uh, hey, guys?"

The officers buying food and coffee turned. "Look," I said, "we don't want your money, all right?"

Their eyebrows went up. We'd already collected a lot for the cleanup fund, and now we needed a favor.

"You're helping us, you shouldn't have to pay. But," I went on, as Ellie and Mika turned curiously, "there is one thing we'd really appreciate."

I waved at an armored vehicle parked halfway down the block just opposite the fish pier parking lot.

"Could you, uh, ask them to move that truck up here and position it right in front of The Chocolate Moose?"

The officers looked at me, at the truck, and at Mika, her sweet expression appealing, and agreed to my request; minutes later the big, heavy armored vehicle squatted massively in front of the Moose, protecting it and anyone in or near it from any more shots fired by the *Jenny*.

Which left me and Ellie free to get our bags and our jackets out of the shop and ourselves into Ellie's car, and then we got out of there.

"So listen, do you think I'm . . . pretty?"

Ellie drove fast and well, heading out of town past the bank and the IGA toward the mainland. On the apple trees crowding both sides of the road by the airport, masses of crimson fruit dappled the green leaves backed by a crystalline sky of deep Wedgewood blue.

Ellie cocked her head at me. "Sure I do, Jake. You're very attractive."

Her tone said I might as well have asked if she thought I was from Mars, and I didn't blame her. Ordinarily my looks are the least of my worries in the sense that I'm clean and my clothes are clean, too, usually, and I brush my teeth often and get a haircut regularly.

But makeup on me looks like paint slopped on thickly no matter how delicately I apply it, so I've given it up. As for style, most days I'm a cross between L.L.Bean and our local thrift store, the New to You shop.

Hey, I'm dressed appropriately for my daily activities, so what can I say? I was fashionable in New York, but in New York I was also miserable.

"But what brings that question on?" she asked, swinging the car around the long curve past Carrying Place Cove.

I shrugged impatiently. "My dad's working on a new painting. And he says it's of me, but I—oh, never mind."

The woman in the painting wasn't merely attractive. She was lovely. And try as I might, I just couldn't see myself in her; not that I even wanted to, particularly. . . .

Except that I sort of did. It was confusing, was what it was.

"Forget it," I said. Even talking about it made me feel anxious. So I changed the subject to the other thing that was bothering me.

One of the other things. "At least we got some protection for Mika."

Ellie nodded, her eyes on the road. "Have she and Sam announced their good news yet?"

Good news. Yeah, maybe. I turned in the passenger seat.

"No, they haven't. But I'm pretty sure they're going to. And Ellie, we do not need any more people in that house. With the six of us adults and a toddler already, it's a wonder some of us aren't camping out in the yard, it's so crowded inside."

"Babies are fun, though." She smiled reminiscently, meanwhile driving like the devil himself was after us.

"Sure they are," I replied, glancing into the rearview mirror in case maybe there was one back there, then shifting to double-check that my seat belt was securely fastened. "But . . . Ellie, where are we going?"

"To check on something that Bella said last night," she replied. "About the photograph we found, with the woman and two little kids in it?"

"Anna Benoit," I recalled aloud. "Who jumped off the Deer Island ferry after some guy abandoned her."

Ellie nodded, accelerating toward the mainland causeway. "So I went online and looked her up to see if there was an obituary, and I found it."

"And?" On the causeway, a few stragglers out of Eastport were headed the same way we were, some of the cars with skull-and-crossbones banners still flying from them.

In Pleasant Point, the usual traffic cop sat in his squad car, parked in his usual spot outside the tribal community building. Ellie slowed; the guy ahead of her didn't, and the squad car pulled out.

We eased on past, with me trying not to feel smug. The state took the land that the road's on right out of the middle of the town, and personally I think drivers who speed through there should have their licenses snipped into bits.

But that's just me. "And," Ellie said, "it turns out poor Anna Benoit had relatives around here after all. They just don't share her last name. And with that information, maybe we can get somewhere with all this. Fix it, even."

"Fix it? But how?" She was trying to encourage me, but I didn't see the usefulness of her discovery. "We've got no suspects, no motive, and not even a theory of how exactly the crime was committed," I went on. "So I don't see . . ."

Past the clusters of small brick houses in Pleasant Point, we drove across a wide, tranquil salt marsh where Canada geese flocked among the cattails, resting on their way south. Next came a grassy ball field, last winter's sand pile, and some metal buildings with trucks garaged in them.

"Well, other than him being stabbed, I mean," I added glumly. "We know that much."

Small mobile homes on roughly cleared quarter acres dotted the grassy expanse that edged the salt marsh.

"But how'd they get that parrot?" I went on. "And the sword? And how'd they get Hadlyme down into our cellar in the first place?"

"It doesn't matter," Ellie cut in as we reached the intersection at Route 1, waited for an eighteen-wheeled logging truck loaded with sixty-foot tree trunks to go by, and then turned north.

"None of it does," she said. "All we need to know is *why*."

"Oh, and now you have a plan for finding that out, do you?"

On Route 1, she glanced in the rearview and hit the gas again, past the Farmers Union grocery, the small white post office, and the New Friendly restaurant. Once we'd left them behind, the hayfields and neatly kept woodlots flew by at an alarming rate.

I hoped all the cops in the county were back in Eastport, not out here running speed traps.

"Yes," she said as, to my right, a small cemetery tucked back among the trees flashed into view: white stone markers, angels and crosses slanting every which way, wreaths and flags and coffee cans holding bunches of fresh flowers.

"Because while you were helping that Coast Guard kid," Ellie went on, then stopped talking entirely as something in the rearview mirror suddenly captured her attention.

"Huh," she said mildly, and then it was upon us: a white sedan roaring up, keeping pace with us on the narrow blacktop.

I didn't have time to do much but gasp at the driver, glaring evilly at us through the eyeholes of a pirate mask with dark arched eyebrows, a scarred cheek, and a wide cruelly curving red mouth.

"Ellie?" I managed. Then the white car accelerated, pulling past us and swerving back into the right lane again just in time to miss being obliterated by another oncoming eighteen-wheeler.

The big truck's horn blared in outrage, the driver in the cab high above us shaking his fist and shouting something in his fury at having just nearly bashed the white car to smithereens.

Then the truck was gone, too, while my eardrums still vibrated painfully with the aftereffects of being hammered on by an air horn. The white car had already vanished out ahead of us, and now I wished that those Eastport cops really were out here waiting for speeders.

"Well!" Ellie said brightly when the event had gone by, so fast I could hardly believe it had happened at all.

Her eyes were wide and her smile looked plastered on. "I guess someone really is keeping an eye on us!" she said.

Outside, the landscape zipped by like slides run very fast through a projector: fieldtreeshousefieldtreeshouse . . .

"Yeah, I guess. Unless it's just some goofball pirate festival person playing a prank. But hey, Ellie? Uh, you can slow down now."

Deliberately she relaxed her hands on the wheel, wiggled her shoulders to loosen them, and flexed her neck, wincing.

"You could be right," she allowed, letting her foot up a little. But she didn't sound convinced.

Me either. *Keeping an eye on us.* Yikes. Somehow that notion hadn't sunk in before, but now it did with a vengeance.

"Ellie, where are we going?" I repeated insistently, meanwhile scanning the side roads and driveways we were passing just in case that white car was lurking in one of them.

She nodded, swallowing hard. "Right, I started to tell you, I found some relatives of Anna Benoit."

Ellie kept glancing in the rearview mirror, but no more cars were roaring up behind us. "But that was her married name," she said.

She slowed, then took a sharp left onto a wide unpaved roadway between a row of mailboxes nailed to the top of an elderly sawhorse on one side and a steel drum set at a 45-degree angle into the earth on the other. The drum was for sand and salt, I guessed. The private road was built and maintained by the landowners along it, a common practice in rural Maine.

No power poles, either, I noticed. Ellie slowed to a crawl as gravel pinged the underside of the car. Trees and brush pressed right up to the edge of the grassy ditch running along both sides of the road.

I didn't see any evidence that anyone lived back here until a big brown dog ran out barking to the end of a narrow track leading off into the woods. A roughly hand-lettered wooden sign that read CARROLTON was stuck into the ground at the start of the track.

Beside the sign, a big rubber trash can with a bungee cord over its lid stood waiting for a trash pickup; by some private hauler, I supposed, since there wouldn't be any municipal services this far out in what the locals called "the williwaws."

Nearby, an outboard engine lay rusting, half in and half out of the ditch. "So who do you suppose that pirate-mask guy was?"

"No idea." Ellie concentrated on not hitting the biggest pot-holes in the dirt track. I peered back at the outboard engine. Grass grew up between its corroded propeller blades.

"Ellie, are you sure this is the right . . . ?"

We bumped down the weedy track between stands of crim-son sumac and yellow goldenrod; here on the mainland, early autumn had already arrived. Next, we passed an ancient garage collapsing in on itself in slow motion, its roof shingles mossy green, and we eased forward into an oak grove, fallen acorns popping and crunching under our tires.

"I'm sure," she said firmly, then stopped the car.

We were in a patch of dappled shade at the end of the dirt track. Nowhere to turn around, I noticed uneasily; when we wanted to get out of here, we'd have to back out.

"Or at any rate, this is the only Carrolton I could find in the area," she said, and then to my obvious next question:

"I asked at the post office," she added simply.

Of course. As Wade had pointed out, almost everyone used a cell phone now, which meant that you couldn't even look up their number in the phone book, never mind an address.

And in any other place but here, I doubted that you could just walk into the post office and get that information, either. But if you were here and you were Ellie, people knew you; liked you, too.

So they would tell you things. "Here goes nothing," she said as she got out of the car.

Reluctantly I figured I might as well get out, too. But I didn't like it. Too quiet, too isolated, too—

"Hey! Who's out there?" a voice demanded from some-where.

"This way," said Ellie, beckoning from a narrow break in the thick underbrush that was all around us. Recognizable under-brush . . .

"Oh, good," I said, "barberries." Even worse than blackberry bushes in the scratch-you-all-to-hell department, the glossy bright-red berries on long, viciously thorny branches were like little drops of blood in the golden light slanting through the trees.

"Hey!" yelled the voice again, louder. "I'm warning you!"

I felt warned, all right, especially since along with the voice came the sound I'd really been dreading: the *clickety-ka-chunk!* of a slide-action shotgun racking a shotgun shell into the firing chamber.

I recognized it from trips to the firing range with Wade; they'd been an important part of our courtship. So even though Ellie had already disappeared into the fading greenery ahead, I stopped short, trying hard not to get flayed by barberry thorns while also hoping not to get blasted by a 12-gauge.

And that's where I was, wondering where Ellie had gotten to and already bleeding from an uncountable number of small stinging thorn wounds when it hit me that those thorns were . . . they couldn't actually be *jumping* out at me, could they?

But something was. Small airborne forms darted angrily about in the bright late-summer afternoon. And they weren't thorns, I saw now in horror, they were—

"Oh!" I gasped as something cold and wet nudged the back of my leg. I leapt forward with a yelp just as I realized that those pale golden shapes in the air, darting and floating around me, were . . .

Bees. Irritated ones, not liking my intrusion. Flailing and swatting, I burst out from the barberry thicket into a clearing.

"Hey! Get away from me, you . . ."

In the clearing, a small A-frame house with its porch set up on cinder blocks was the main building. Around it stood more structures: a whitewashed chicken house and a wire-fence enclosure complete with chickens, an open shed full of split firewood plus more logs dumped in front of it, and an old tool shed, its propped-open door revealing an assortment of carpentry tools and garden implements inside.

A chicken that apparently had its neck wrung recently—I

thought this on account of its head being turned around the wrong way, and also it was dead—lay on a chopping block. A stained ax leaning on the chopping block said that further head-related trauma was imminent.

And on top of all that, there was a woman standing on the A-frame's porch aiming a shotgun at me, which as far as I was concerned was absolutely the last straw.

"If you're going to shoot me," I said, marching forward while brushing away bees, "just hurry up and get it over with, will you?"

"Jake!" Ellie murmured with caution, "be careful, she's—"

"Yeah, I get it." A bee stung me on the wrist. "She's crazy, I see that."

I slapped the bee, squashing it. "Also she's as tough as any man, hunts and fishes and makes her own whiskey. Shoots the pop-top right out of a beer can at ninety paces, blah-de-blah-blah."

I didn't bother looking at the woman while I said it, and to tell you the truth I didn't care what she thought of it, either.

For one thing, the bee that stung me had friends, and they were mad, too. So I was a little busy. But for another, I had pretty much had it up to the eyes with this whole day: drowned guys and explosions and cops who thought I'd killed somebody, not to mention the white car that had just zoomed alongside us.

And come to think of it, my dad's painting, too; on my best day I'd never looked that good, so what was he up to?

Messing with my head, that's what; all I wanted to know was why. But this was no time to wonder about it. Waving away more angry bees, I discovered that downeast Maine's answer to Annie Oakley still had that damned weapon leveled at me.

The brown dog emerged from a thicket and danced around Ellie, bouncing and begging to be petted. Up and down, up and down, as if it had springs on the bottoms of its feet.

The woman with the shotgun spoke. "Those bees ain't going to let up until you get out of their territory."

"And you'll shoot me with that shotgun if I get any farther into yours," I retorted.

In reply she jerked the barrel sideways, signaling for me to approach. Under her narrow-eyed glare, I hustled across the clearing and up onto her porch. Like the rest of the house it was made of raw lumber slammed together with big nails, many of the porch supports and corner posts still with bark clinging tightly to them.

Door in the middle, a window on either side, big stone chimney up and out through the center of the sharply peaked roof . . .

Ellie scrambled up onto the porch beside me. The bees hadn't bothered her. Go figure.

A frayed rag rug covered the rough decking boards around the bentwood rocker by the front door. Next to the rocker, a table held an oil lamp with a smudged glass chimney, a box of wooden matches, a battery-powered radio, and a pair of eyeglasses.

A knitting basket containing a ball of thick yarn and a half-finished sock still on the needles hung from one of the rocker's arms. The woman with the shotgun peered closely at Ellie and me.

"What the *hell* do you two want?" she demanded. She had a plait of thick iron-gray hair and dark eyes deeply set in a lined, weather-beaten face.

A perennial garden, blowsy with autumn, spread to one side of the cottage. I took a deep breath, introduced myself and Ellie as well as I could, then reached out and pushed the weapon's barrel more to the side.

The woman bristled faintly. I shrugged—*Hey, what do you expect me to do?*—and she relaxed a little.

But she didn't engage the safety mechanism on the weapon. "Oh, I know what it must be," she said, her lip curling contemptuously. "You're here to ask me about that little son of a bitch, aren't you?" she asked.

Drat. I'd wanted to ease her into it.

"That *dead* little son of a bitch," she added, her eyes glittering with satisfaction.

"Um, actually—" Ellie began, but I interrupted.

"No, ma'am," I said. "It's not about him. Not directly, anyway."

Another deep breath. *Here goes nothing.*

"We're here about your murdered niece, Anna Benoit," I said.

Seven

Inside, the house was all one big room downstairs, with knotty pine paneling made from real pine and salvaged steel beams stretching across the ceiling, holding it up.

I took in as much as I could from where I stood. The kitchen held an old soapstone sink with a hand pump on it and a squat black woodburning stove with a kettle simmering quietly on the back burner. A notch-eared white cat slept in a cardboard box by the stove.

"Sit." Karen Carrolton hadn't turned a hair at my comment about murder, but she'd let us in. Now she waved us to the large cluttered living area, where two plaid-upholstered armchairs and a brown-and-yellow tweed sofa formed a semicircle in front of another stove.

A coffee table was piled with papers in neatish stacks. Plants in pots on windowsills looked watered and well-kept, and the red and yellow onions, newly harvested and spread out across newspapers on a table, looked nearly dry enough to put away for the winter.

From her garden, I supposed. The net bags for storing them were all laid out neatly there, too. The brown dog's bed was near the stove in the living area; when he finished sniffing us he trotted to it and hopped in, turning fussily before settling with a happy groan.

Karen Carrolton returned with a tray that held mugs and a coffeepot. She set it down, then pulled a creased snapshot from her fray-edged trouser pocket and held it out.

Different picture, but it was of the same woman we'd seen in the photograph from Hadlyme's motor home. "That's Anna. And . . . him," she added sourly.

I took the photograph from her. It was Hadlyme, all right, younger and thinner and with a good deal more of that frizzy yellow hair than he had now, but still with a sneeringly contemptuous smile on his face, and those sharply calculating eyes.

From the way he had his hand flat against her back I couldn't tell if he was about to embrace Anna Benoit or give her a shove. Two things were clear, though: she was very pregnant and, to judge by the look on her face, very unhappy.

"We lived in town then. In Eastport, all in the same house, me and Phyllis—that was Anna's mother—and our other sister. Oh, I wish we'd moved out sooner, then maybe she'd have never met him."

No grief was in her face, just an icy stillness, as if something in her had frozen when the girl died and had never thawed out.

"But how," she asked, meeting my gaze, "did you know she was murdered? Because I said so at the time, I insisted to the police and everyone else that she must have been, but—"

"I didn't know it," I admitted. "I guessed. So you'd let us in."

And so you wouldn't shoot us. But to me it was already the only thing that made sense. Jumped off the ferry, my great-aunt Fanny.

Karen said nothing, digesting what I'd said while pouring the coffee with a steady hand. From its rich, faintly chocolate-tinged aroma I knew that while she might be off the grid in most ways, her coffee-making skills weren't primitive.

"Anna had been married before, had a child already, but

then . . ." I was guessing about this, too, from other hints in the old photo—the older child, mostly. I let my voice trail off into a question.

"Yes." Karen sat in the chair by the dog's bed, then reached down and patted him. "Her first husband—they'd married very young—died in a fishing accident. Not that he was any prize, either. They were living in their own little house by then, of course."

She shook her head. "Drowned off the boat he was working on, a loose line snagged his ankle and . . . well. Afterward, Anna and little Abby were alone."

Sipping coffee, she gathered herself. Then: "That was her first child's name," Karen added. "Not that Anna acted like she knew that poor little girl even existed once *he* came along."

Hadlyme, she meant. "He swept her off her feet, did he?" I asked gently, and Karen eyed me scathingly in reply.

"Off her feet and onto her back," she said meanly, but then she sighed. "Anna was lonely. And he was . . . he could be charming when he wanted to be. When," she added, "there was something in it for *him*."

Karen bit her lip and shoved an escaped hank of her wiry gray hair back from her face, then went on. "She was wild about him, Anna was. Thought the sun shone out of his behind, and that's the truth."

Her voice hardened. "He thought so, too, of course. Came here from Bangor with his parents, but they died in an accident soon after they arrived."

She shook her head, remembering. "Went off the road in their car one icy winter's day, and that was that. *He* survived, of course."

I drank some coffee. It was delicious. Everything about this place, in fact, said Karen Carrolton had built herself a good life here, even if it wouldn't suit everyone.

It made me feel guilty about wondering if she'd killed Hadlyme to avenge her dead niece, and if she had, about hoping I could prove it and get her arrested. But better her than me, I told myself.

"So he'd been on his own for a little while," Karen went on. "Eighteen, he was, maybe."

That surprised me. I'd been thinking of him as older.

"We were as good to him as we could be, at first," said Karen. "Not liking him by any means, but if Anna was happy, then . . ." She paused, remembering. "But we weren't good enough for him, he made that clear right away. She was like a pretty toy to him, but he still had to get out of here as quick as he could."

She sipped coffee thoughtfully. After all her bluster over our arrival, she seemed glad for the chance to talk.

"Without her," Karen added flatly.

And there, of course, was the rub. "But he did stick around for a while?" Ellie asked, and Karen nodded.

"Saving up, I guess. Worked around here in restaurants, married Anna when we all started looking sideways at him, wondering when he'd do the right thing. It wasn't like nowadays when a girl can just move in with a fellow."

I understood; even as recently as twenty years ago, things were a little different here in Eastport than they were out in the big world. You could move in with a guy, sure, but it wouldn't help your social standing any, and even now the awful idea of "making an honest woman of her" hadn't evaporated entirely.

"So she did move in with him, though? Once they were married?"

I finished my coffee; Karen poured more. "No. He kept promising but never delivered. Stayed with us sometimes, and sometimes he slept wherever he was working, in the back room or whatnot."

"Didn't want to spend money on somewhere decent enough to put a baby and toddler in," Ellie guessed, and Karen glanced appreciatively at her.

"Correct. He never spent a dime on Anna or the baby, or the

older child, either. Not one red cent. And then he ran off to the city first chance he got and made a name for himself there, got to be a fancy chef and then he started up a TV career. Just the way he always said he would."

Karen's dark eyes glittered at the memory; a short laugh escaped her. "Much good that name's doing him now, though, hey?"

It wasn't a question, and in that moment I could totally see her running Henry Hadlyme through the heart with a stolen cutlass.

The silence in the room lengthened, so complete I could hear my ears ringing, and my headache was killing me.

"Karen, did you kill him?" Ellie asked finally, and at the sudden look on the older woman's weathered face I glanced around for the shotgun, not wanting to be at the business end of it again.

"No," she snarled, "somebody else had the pleasure of that. He killed her, though, I can tell you that much. Had to've been him."

She set her cup down on the coffee table between a stack of old newspaper clippings and a pile of insurance papers.

"Almost right up until the moment she died, Anna had everything she wanted, or thought she did: a husband; a father for her older child, Abby; and then the baby boy . . ."

"Wallace?" Ellie put in. The name on the birth certificate.

Karen nodded again. But something about what she'd said still didn't sound right.

"I don't get it, you mean he came back? Changed his mind and decided to stay in Eastport?"

Because why would he forget all his ambitions, just settle down here in this remote island town and—

"Oh, no." Karen rolled her dark eyes. "He'd said they'd all go, the four of them. Make their way in the big world together."

The dog whimpered in his sleep; she reached down absently

to pat him. In the silence the clock on the mantel behind the woodstove ticked hollowly; without at all wanting to, I imagined what it sounded like at night with nobody else around.

"And she believed him," she finished. "The poor little fool."

Ellie got up. "Excuse me, but may I use the facilities?"

She gestured toward the window, through which we could see the corner of a small cedar-shingled building with a half moon cut in the door, out at the far edge of the yard where goldenrod grew in tall yellow clumps.

Karen shrugged. "Suit yourself. Watch out for the bees. They ain't in a good mood after all the ruckus you two made out there."

If they don't start a ruckus, there won't be a ruckus, was my opinion about upsets involving any stinging insects, but never mind; Ellie agreed and went outside.

When she was gone I got up too, and wandered over to the window. As I suspected, she wasn't heading toward the building with the half moon cut in the door. I turned back to Karen.

"How do you think he did it, though? Killed Anna, I mean, since I assume he wasn't on the ferry with her."

If he had been, the whole town would've known about it and been sure he'd killed her, and even after all this time his return would have gotten the local rumor mill spinning like an airplane propeller.

But it hadn't. "I don't know," Karen said. "Paid someone to push her, maybe. Or he could've blackmailed someone into it. He always did know the worst things about people."

That didn't surprise me. She glanced up defiantly at me, her expression fierce.

"Don't get me wrong, I'd have killed him myself if I could, and to whoever did finish him, they have my gratitude and I wish them the very best." Pausing, she took in a breath. "I hope he *suffered*," she exhaled fervently.

I didn't have the heart to tell her he probably hadn't, that no signs of struggle had been visible down there in the Moose's cellar. Instead I kept moving around the room, glancing casually at things: a jigsaw puzzle laid out on a card table with an oil lamp beside it, a wicker basket full of stove kindling mingled with newspaper spills all rolled up and ready for fire-starting.

Old gold-framed photographs lined the fireplace mantel: a young woman in a prom dress—Anna, maybe. A tiny dog in a wooden apple crate, just barely managing to hold a large apple in its small teeth.

There were no photographs of children. "So what happened to the little girl and the baby?" I asked Karen. "After their mom died?"

"His father took Wallace and put him in care, and I did the same for Abby." She blurted it defensively as if ready to be reproached for this. I noticed too that she didn't want to say Hadlyme's name.

"He was the baby's dad, after all, so he could," she went on. "But that's all I know. I never saw them again."

Her face twisted with pain. "I couldn't take care of them, and neither could my sister, and Anna's mother was already dead. Anna's death killed her." She stopped, biting her lip. "And anyway, they say a clean break is best," she finished harshly.

Just then Ellie came back in, saw Karen's expression, and wisely remained silent.

"Once I got over the shock of the whole thing, I agreed it was their chance for a better life than I could give them," Karen added.

But if you asked me, she'd never gotten over it. Not that her living like this, with no modern conveniences and nobody around, was so odd; it wasn't, especially here in downeast Maine, where quirkiness was in the air, it seemed like, and everybody had their share.

No, it was the look in her eye that held me: past caring about the law or what anyone thought of her. Like there really wasn't much you could threaten her with anymore.

"It was for the best," she finished simply. "The children got parents who could give them a future, Henry got out of here so I didn't have to look at him every day, and I got peace to grieve in."

If she hadn't been a tough old bird, she might've sobbed, I thought. But she was and she didn't.

Barely. "Jake," Ellie interrupted quietly, "we should go."

I took the cue; I picked up my mug and carried it to the kitchen, where the kettle clucked faintly, simmering on the woodstove.

"I didn't see a car anywhere around out there," Ellie was saying conversationally to Karen, back in the living area. "However do you manage way out here without one?"

"Don't need much," Karen answered shortly. Our little talk had taken the goodness off the day for her, I imagined, and I felt bad about it.

But what's done was done, as she probably would've put it, and anyway I didn't have much other choice, any more than she'd had all those years ago.

"And when I do need to go somewhere, I walk out to the main road and stick my thumb out," she finished.

Which wasn't as outlandish as it sounded, either. People did still pick up hitchhikers around here. For one thing, everybody knew everybody, and for another, you might need a ride yourself someday.

Rinsing my mug at the old soapstone sink in Karen's kitchen, I admired a dozen geranium clippings putting out roots in half-pint jelly glasses full of water.

"*Grr.*" I looked down; the brown dog stood there.

"Oh, yeah? You and whose army?" I retorted.

Despite his efforts, he didn't sound very threatening even when he fastened his choppers firmly into my pants leg and wouldn't let go. I walked back out to the living area with the dog still dangling off me like some furry parasite, growling and kicking.

"Uh, help?" I said, trying not to laugh at the poor thing; he was so obviously embarrassed already. Ellie crouched to pry him loose, his stubby legs already making frantic little running motions even before he hit the floor and scampered away.

"Listen, about your sister, the one you mentioned earlier," I said to Karen. "Do you think you could possibly let us have her phone num—"

Ellie stood, dusting her hands together, not looking nearly as amused about the funny little animal as I'd expected.

"Well," she interrupted me firmly as the dog scrambled away to wherever he liked hiding, "it's been just lovely chatting with you, Karen, and thanks for the coffee. But we've got to go now."

She yanked my arm, smiling at me in a toothy not-happy way that made me think we'd really better skedaddle.

"Come on, Jake," she urged.

I caught on and followed her.

"So long!" She called back over her shoulder as she pushed me out the door, then urged me off the porch and through the clearing toward the barely discernable break in the barberry bushes that led to the path.

"Ouch!" Also, the bees were there. And the thorns.

"Just keep going," said Ellie from behind me. "And when you get out to the road, get into the car right away, no dillydallying."

A bee dive-bombed me, then another. I stopped and tried to figure a way forward past the humming cloud of them hovering just ahead.

Purposefully hovering, it seemed to me. *Menacingly . . .*

"Walk slowly. Don't swat at them," said Ellie, who kept a few beehives of her own near the chicken coops in the garden behind her house. "Let them land on you if they want to."

And then came the part that really unnerved me: "Keep your

mouth shut, breathe through your nose, and whatever you do, don't—"

A sudden rush of something, like a big invisible hand, slammed into the barberry bushes to my left. An instant later came the *pow!* of a shotgun being fired.

"—*run!*" Ellie finished, forcefully shoving me forward.

"Holy criminy, she *shot* at us," I kept saying as we drove back to Eastport. "Was it what I said at the end there, about her sister?"

"Hmm. Maybe," said Ellie. "But let's just catch our breaths for a little while, okay? And celebrate being alive."

"Fine." I leaned my fortunately still-intact head back against the car seat. It still hurt like hell, but right now I was just happy to have any head at all.

Or any breath left to catch. A foot or so to the left and that shotgun would've cured whatever ailed me for good. But by the time we got into town I could at least talk without gasping.

"I guess we'd better check in at the shop."

Ellie pulled over in front of The Chocolate Moose, its sign still dangling forlornly and its front windows still blown out. Most of Water Street was now cordoned off with sawhorses and yellow tape, from the fountain in front of the old bank building at one end all the way to the fish pier, at the other.

But our shop was still accessible, and the armored vehicle still hulked protectively out front. Once inside, we sent Mika home with our profuse thanks and a bag of chocolate frosted doughnut holes, which I knew were Bella's favorite.

"For a pregnant lady, Mika sure does take care of business," Ellie remarked, looking around the shop as my daughter-in-law drove off in her car. "She must be feeling better, to do all that baking."

"Ellie, we still don't *know* she's—"

But Ellie just rolled her eyes at me in reply, and anyway, she was right; while we were gone, Mika had swept up the rest of the mess from the explosions, put the front of the shop in order as best she could, considering that it didn't have any windows left in it, and ordered new glass to be installed in the windows and door as soon as possible.

The work order details were noted on a pad on the counter by the cash register, in her clear, back-slanted handwriting. She'd also done a brisk business in doughnuts, cakes, and cookies, judging by the fact that there was barely anything left in the glass-fronted display case and a good deal more money in the cash drawer than there had been before.

"Yes, she does manage to get things done," I agreed as I hurried out to the kitchen. If business was going to go on being this good, that display case needed refilling yet again, and fortunately our cooking gas was propane from a tank located in the alley out behind the building, and it hadn't been damaged.

I'd just gotten started on making more doughnuts when a helicopter roared overhead again; then from down the block a voice boomed suddenly through a bullhorn: "COME OUT ON DECK WITH YOUR HANDS VISIBLE!"

"Right, that's going to work," I reacted scathingly, picking up the spoon I'd dropped; I hate being startled.

Ellie peered out, taking care not to cut herself on the daggers of glass still sticking out dangerously from the window frame. It had been about six hours since the *Jenny* had shot at anything.

"Probably the cops are just tired of standing around," I said as I got out the mixing bowls, measuring cups, and other tools we needed for a serious session of baking.

"Still, I can't imagine they want to provoke another barrage," Ellie said, troubled. "They've pulled in more vehicles, though—cop cars and a few more of those big armored things like the one parked right out front here. And one guy with a megaphone."

She joined me in the kitchen, where I'd set the doughnut batter to chill and begun the ingredients prep for perhaps the best cookies in the world: double-chocolate ginger wafers; they're a great deal of trouble to make, but on the other hand I'd just had a no-kidding near-death experience, and felt entitled.

"So, she shot at us," I said while chopping candied ginger into slivers. Now that I'd had a chance to think about it, I was more shaken by the event than I'd realized. "With a shotgun."

"Yes. She just missed us," Ellie replied somberly as she got out the butter and eggs. "Or someone did. So now the question is—"

"Ellie, the question is whether we should go on with any of this at all," I interrupted, because I wanted to keep myself out of a jail cell, sure, but not at the cost of my friend's life.

Or my own, even. "I mean, come on, someone *shot at us*—"

"Who shot at you?" Bob Arnold stood in the kitchen doorway. We hadn't heard him come in. I made a mental note to put the little bell back up over the door as soon as possible.

"Who?" Bob repeated the word pleasantly but his round pink face didn't match his tone. He wanted answers, he wanted them now, and—

"I'm not kidding. I want to know who shot at you, I want to know why, when, where, and how"—he took a breath—"and if either of you knows anything else about any of this whole damned-fool mess that you haven't been telling me, I want to know that, too."

He was wearing his blue uniform, boots, and all of his duty-belt paraphernalia, including his sidearm.

Especially his sidearm, actually. "I mean," he finished, "like right-the-hell now."

Even though he didn't look much like a tough cop with that thinning blond hair and those pink rosebud lips of his, when he wanted to, Bob Arnold could be very persuasive.

"Or maybe I should just run the both of you in for obstructing," he added with a frown.

He was our friend, but right now he was absolutely all business, and we could forget about letting anything slide even an inch. And just nearly getting shot drains a person emotionally, as it turns out; I still felt as if I'd had a large hole blown through me, frightwise.

"Okay," I sighed, glancing at Ellie, who nodded agreement. So she got him some coffee from the fresh pot she'd started the moment we'd walked in here, and I got him a piece of fudge cake from the few left in the display case, which by a miracle had not shattered.

And while he devoured what was probably the first solid food he'd had since breakfast, we told him the whole story: about how we'd searched Lionel's cottage and Hadlyme's RV, about finding the birth certificate and photograph, and about our visit to Karen Carrolton's rustic compound way out in the puckerbrush.

"So you think the girl in the picture got abandoned in Eastport by Hadlyme twenty years or so ago," he said. "Then she fell off the ferry. Or jumped or got pushed, whatever, and now you think *that back then* has something to do with *this here now*," he summed up neatly.

"Yes," I said, using a wooden spoon to cream finely minced candied ginger into some butter, along with a cup of sugar.

"We think it must," said Ellie, "because first of all, obviously Jake didn't kill him, which means that someone else did."

I loved her for saying this. "And," she went on, "it had to be someone with a motive, also obviously, and here is one: somebody here with a reason to hate Hadlyme, and if you ask me the guts to do it."

Karen Carrolton, she meant, and I couldn't deny that all of that was true, but—

"Karen doesn't know her ass from page eight," Bob said flatly, holding out his cup for more coffee.

Ordinarily Ellie might've let him get his coffee himself, but right then it felt good to have a cop sitting there in the shop with us. We'd serve him coffee, he'd protect us . . . hey, it worked for me.

"I mean, I like Karen," he added, sipping. "But you just can't believe everything she says."

Sighing, he put the cup down. "But let's say for argument if it did happen, then it all must've been just before you moved here, that right, Jake? And Ellie, I figure that's when you'd have been away at school?"

Ellie nodded. Her boarding school career had lasted only two semesters; after that, as she'd described it, she'd never looked for happiness beyond her own backyard again.

"Well, I'll ask around about it," he allowed reluctantly, "but I'm telling you, if she's firing off shotguns at people, then she's gotten even wackier out there in the woods than I realized, so don't get your hopes up."

He harrumphed, ending discussion on the subject. "Anyway, I want to know more about this shooting business."

She hadn't seemed that wacky to me—not until the gunfire part of the program, anyway. But who knew what info might get me off the hook, suspicion-of-murder-wise, *and* hoist the real killer onto it?

So while Ellie and I finished getting those double-chocolate ginger wafers whipped up and into the oven—melted chocolate, eggs, vanilla, and the dry ingredients—we told him about Karen Carrolton being armed when we got to her place.

"But once we introduced ourselves, she got comfortable with us and so on, we didn't feel threatened," I added.

Bob raised one eyebrow.

"Well, not until the end," I corrected myself. "I'd asked her some questions she didn't like, I guess."

I went on beating flour, baking powder, soda, and salt into the chocolatey mixture in the bowl. "When the shooting started. But . . ." I hesitated. "But before that there was a car. A white car, it came up behind us very fast on our way to Karen's."

So the white car's driver couldn't have known yet where we were going. "Maybe there's no connection," I added, not believing it. But how could there be? Ellie hadn't even told me where we were going, I thought, which was when it finally dawned on me that somebody had been following us.

Bob sighed as he got up. "I haven't seen any car like that out here on the island. You didn't get a plate number?"

I shook my head; Ellie, too. "No, there wasn't time."

"And if I ask Karen about shooting at you, she'll just deny it," Bob pronounced with a grimace. "I swear she'd take the bull in the china shop by the horns, throw him into the glassware just to hear the crash," he went on, pausing in the shop's shattered doorway.

He went on: "Fact is, the only illegal stuff in that story you two just told me is the illegal stuff you did yourselves."

Searching people's cabins, rooting through their mobile homes . . . His pale blue eyes fixed on me.

"And none of it's going to save you from an arrest warrant once Amity Jones collects a case against you, talks to a D.A."

Hope pinged me. He didn't sound very friendly toward Amity Jones. Earlier he'd seemed more neutral about her, but now . . . what the heck, I gave it a shot.

"So," I began tentatively, "do you . . . are you sure you have to tell her about it? The illegal stuff, I mean."

Another snort. He eyed me sternly. Of course he would tell her, why wouldn't he? But then, "Nah," he said.

He shook his head ruefully, as if even he couldn't believe it. "I ought to. It's my job to, and it'd serve you right if I did, you pulling a bunch of stupid stunts like that."

He was getting wound up just thinking about it. "Did either of you even think about how somebody might get there ahead of you? And catch you there, and maybe decide to get rid of you?"

At the campgrounds, he meant. "No," I said. "We didn't think much about that. Not in advance, anyway."

I stopped because something else had just then occurred to me, too. Before I could say so, though, Bob made a face of disgust.

"Of course you didn't think about it in advance. Do you ever?"

"Well—" I began, because sometimes we did. Not very often, I had to admit, but . . .

Bob cut me off again. "And like that wasn't enough, the next thing you do is go tear-assing off into the woods, meet up with Karen Carrolton and her shotgun, and she nearly blows your brains out . . ."

"Bob," I interrupted him firmly. "Now that you mention it, I'm not a hundred percent sure she's really the one who . . ."

But he'd already stopped talking and was frowning. Something about that last part hadn't sounded quite right to him, either.

"Yeah, well, just stay away from her, okay?" He backpedaled a little. "What happened to her niece was twenty years ago, *if* it did, and it could be that Henry Hadlyme had nothing to do with it at all."

He was cooling down a bit. "But like I said, I was away in the service, deployed. And anyway, I don't see how Karen Carrolton could be involved in all this business going on now."

He gestured at the empty window frame, the street outside with dusk beginning to darken it, and the water beyond, the dark sailboat sitting there, though we couldn't see the boat from this vantage point in the store.

"You're right," I conceded, "she'd had to have hitchhiked into town, gotten herself and him into our cellar just at the right moment, and stabbed him to death with a cutlass that belongs to Wade."

"And how would she have gotten *that*? Not to mention the stuffed parrot," Ellie put in. "I mean, how would she even get—?"

"Yeah, yeah," Bob said, pinching the bridge of his nose tiredly.

"Or arrange to have Eastport attacked from the water, for Pete's sake."

He picked up a chocolate doughnut from the plate of them that Ellie had quietly brought out and applied himself to it.

Chewing, he continued, "State cops have ammunition experts here trying to figure out what kind of ammo could explode like that," he said around the last of the confection.

"Wait a minute, what?" I said. "They think the sailboat and the explosions are somehow connected to Henry Hadlyme's . . . ?"

Bob sighed heavily. "I don't know what they think. They're not running everything they do past the local police chief, believe it or not," he added sarcastically.

He licked chocolate off the tip of his finger. "But a very smart man once said that coincidence means you're not paying attention to the other half of what's happening, and I've never forgotten it."

I looked at Ellie, and she looked at me. He had a point, that maybe we hadn't given the idea enough thought.

"Have they found out whose boat it is yet?" I asked, because the answer to that would go a long way toward sorting this all out.

Bob shook his head. "Maybe there's some paperwork on the boat that says, but getting on is still a no-go."

Getting up, he let Ellie put a white paper bakery bag full of more doughnuts into his hands. "State folks are right about not wanting to trigger more gunfire, though," he went on, "or anything else."

He cast a sour glance at the dusk gathering outside. "Not too much damage yet," he went on, "but we've got some pretty old structures here, not built to modern standards in the first place, and now the brickwork's fragile, besides."

Pushing a few strands of hair back from his high forehead unhappily, he added, "Another barrage of whatever that ammo is could take down a row of buildings."

Or start a fire, I realized with a shiver, and if that happened the entire downtown could go up before anyone could do much about it.

"Whole damned vessel could be wired like a booby trap for all we know," he finished before swallowing the last of his coffee.

"Anyway, you asked me, so I'll answer. I'm telling our visiting state homicide cop exactly zilch about what you've just told me."

Relief washed over me that he wasn't going to rat us out to Amity Jones for meddling in her investigation.

"'Cause, yeah, she floated me a tale about us being cousins," he said as he moved toward the door. "And maybe it's so. Lotta people in Maine are related to one another."

Maine family names were linked all the way back to the early 1800s; it was what made Amity Jones's kinship tale so plausible.

"But even if we are related, I still think she's just trying to get me to tell her things," he said from where he stood at the empty window, gazing out to where it was getting dark.

Not *dark* dark, but shadowy enough so that even when I stepped out past him into the street it was hard to catch sight of the *Jenny*. Her murky shape in the harbor blended with the fast-deepening hue of the waves so thoroughly that she'd become invisible.

Or . . . had she? I squinted puzzledly as Bob went on. "Uh, Bob?"

But he didn't hear me. "Whatever she says, what she thinks is that the local cop's too dumb to live and she's got me wound around her little . . . Hey." He interrupted himself as he caught sight of what I was watching.

Down the street, things were moving, armored vehicles jockeying themselves around as if getting into position for something. Radios crackled, men called out to one another, and quite a few previously unseen law-enforcement personnel began scurrying around until all of them were inside the vehicles.

"What the hell?" Bob pronounced as the vehicles began

pulling out, a parade of them rolling by the Moose, turning onto Washington Street, and rumbling uphill on their way out of downtown.

When they had all gone and we could see across the street to the water again, a set of enormous floodlights on the breakwater now illuminated the dark waves.

"Wow," I said as Ellie came out to stand beside me, wiping her hands on a clean dish towel.

"Wow," she echoed. Then: "Listen, about what happened back there at Karen's place."

"Yeah." I'd been so shaken up by Karen's shotgun—if it had been hers—that I never asked Ellie why she'd been in such a hurry to leave.

Bob had already set off down the block toward where a few of the state cops were still milling around, talking on cell phones or into their radios and getting themselves ready to leave, too, apparently.

"You looked around Karen's yard and the outbuildings and so on, I assume," I said, and Ellie nodded.

"And something about what you found—"

Once Ellie made her discovery, whatever it was, we'd gotten out of there like our hats were on fire and our backsides were catching, as Bella would've put it.

She nodded again. She had her bag over her shoulder, I noticed—the same one she'd been carrying out at Karen Carrolton's.

"So what'd you find there?" I asked. "I mean, come on, do I have to guess, or—?"

She pulled something from the tote bag: a pirate mask. The dark arched eyebrows, hash mark scars, and thin red lips drawn back in a leering grin were the same as I'd seen on the mask worn by the driver of the white sedan that had menaced us earlier.

"Oh," I said softly. "So unless this is yet another coincidence, whoever was in the white car must've followed us to—"

"Or was on his way there, anyway," said Ellie. "Which means maybe Karen Carrolton really is in on all this bad business somehow, even if she wasn't the one who killed Hadlyme."

Just then a straggler from the now-postponed pirate festival staggered by with a hook sticking out of one ragged sleeve and a rum bottle clutched in his other hand; a fake gold tooth gleamed from his grin, and a plumed hat sat crookedly on his head.

"Ahoy!" he shouted at the dark water. Across the bay, the lights on Campobello had begun glimmering in the dusk. "Ahoy, there!"

But only a distant foghorn answered, moaning a warning at a fog bank now blurring the horizon to the south.

A bell buoy clanked, and down in the boat basin a diesel engine idled grumblingly. The evening's last few gulls sailed in, crying and circling to settle for the night in their roosts under the wharves.

But no anchor chain rattled and no small noisy waves slopped the sides of the mysterious dark sailboat *Jenny.*

Not here, anyway; in the spot where she'd floated all day in the harbor, only an unbroken expanse of dark water remained.

The *Jenny* was gone.

"Easy," said Wade at our dinner table after Ellie had dropped me off. "After dark they could get out of the harbor with no trouble."

He drank some beer. "Drop the lines, start the engine, is all."

"But wouldn't somebody hear them?" Sam objected, forking a slice of meat loaf onto his plate.

It was leftover meat loaf, but the way Bella made it—sliced, with leftover gravy poured over it, then baked again until the meat loaf sizzled and the gravy bubbled—that stuff was heaven.

I ate a bite of my mashed potatoes, then another. After the

day I'd had and the little real food I'd eaten, it was a wonder I wasn't just shoveling it into my mouth with both hands.

"Ellie said there was a diesel engine idling down in the boat basin," my father remarked. "Could've masked the *Jenny*'s."

Wade nodded, forking up some more steamed green beans from fresh out of the garden, so delicious you could eat them like candy.

"Could ask Tim Franco. He's always down at the boat basin or on a boat. Back in town, I noticed. Maybe he knows something about it."

Bella nodded. "I know his grandmother. I saw her in the IGA today, and she said that he's back. He had work for a week, but then . . ."

Her voice trailed off, perhaps echoing Tim's grandmother's disappointment. Then Mika piped up from where she sat patiently encouraging her toddler son to eat some of his yummy meat loaf.

"Why can't he keep a job?" she asked as Ephraim turned away, wrinkling his nose.

She hadn't known Tim for years the way we all had. Everyone liked him, but . . .

Wade spoke up. "Tim gets . . . bored," he said gently. "Hard enough to find work in our"—he put a twist on the words—"economically depressed area."

Oh, it was that, all right. People worked hard and helped one another out, but there wasn't much spending cash floating around.

But Tim was a special case: a good starter-outer but with no grit for the daily grind once the novelty wore off, and as I'd heard from his own mouth, with not much insight into the problem, either.

As a result, he never had money and always had grievances on the topic. I put some blueberry chutney on my meat loaf.

"Surely the Coast Guard will find them and apprehend them,

though," I said, returning to the subject of the *Jenny*. "Now that they're not sitting there threatening the downtown."

Bella was busily stowing away her dinner while sneaking tiny morsels of her own meat loaf to Ephraim. These he ate happily while supervising us from his high chair.

"With all the Coast Guard's fancy electronics, I don't see how anyone could hide from them for long," she agreed between bites. But:

"If the boat's out on the water, that's true," said Wade. From his work as a harbor pilot, he knew all about this stuff.

"You can't slide much past 'em in their own territory," he went on. "But once a vessel gets outside of U.S. waters—"

The U.S.–Canadian border ran down the bay's middle, an invisible line that only fishing boats bothered about, usually: we didn't poach their lobsters and scallops, and they didn't poach ours, etcetera.

But when it came to nonfishing law enforcement . . . "Do you mean they can't be chased across the line at all?" I said.

Wade brushed back his hair with a calloused hand. "The Coast Guard, or any other U.S. law enforcement authority, can't just barge into Canadian waters and apprehend the *Jenny* or anyone else."

Sam took a break from eating steadily and silently, replenishing the calories he'd expended all day on mowing lawns, tending gardens, lopping dead tree branches, and giving shrubs their autumn pruning.

"If I were them, I wouldn't go that far, anyway. Too risky. I'd just pull into some little cove and lay low," he said. "Wait till not everybody was looking for me. And then—"

He snapped his fingers lightly in front of Ephraim, who blinked and grinned after a startled instant.

"Presto! I'd vanish," said Sam, smiling back at his son. "Slide off like a ghost some dark night when no moon's out, get clean away."

Ephraim giggled, but I didn't. "They'd have to know about where the little coves are," I said slowly.

Around the kitchen table, people were having just one last forkful of potato or a final dab of meat loaf before downing the last of their beer or ginger ale and crumpling their napkins.

"Which means," I went on, "that it would need to be someone from around here. Or that someone's helping them, knows about . . ."

Mika got up and slid Ephraim from his high chair. She looked peaked again and hadn't eaten much, the half slice of meat loaf and spoonful of potato she'd taken all mostly still there on her plate.

As if to forestall comment about it, she smiled brightly at me while hoisting Ephraim onto her hip. "At least they *are* gone," she commented quietly. "So the festival can go on as scheduled, maybe?"

"Yes," Bella agreed, taking the baby and jouncing him gently so he crowed with delight. "And life can get back to normal."

After depositing him in his playpen, she began clearing plates. The men had already made quick work of utensils and serving dishes, and at the sink Wade was up to his elbows in soapsuds, washing glassware.

"Um," I said. "Not exactly normal. Not quite."

I'd already asked her if she knew who around here—besides the shotgun-happy Karen Carrolton, that is—might recall Henry Hadlyme's tragically abandoned sweetheart, Anna Benoit.

"I wish I could remember more," she said now, "about what you asked me. There's a name on the tip of my tongue, but . . ." Her big grape-green eyes fixed troubledly on me.

"Don't worry about it. This will all turn out fine," I assured her.

I wished I were as sure of that as I'd made myself sound, though, and she was still eyeing me suspiciously. So I changed the subject.

"Bella, you've seen the painting my dad's working on, right?"

Dad was busy helping Wade with the glasses, and the clatter they made while going about their chore made this my chance.

"The one he's got on the easel now," I specified, "of the girl in the green sweater?"

Her expression softened. In the artistry department she believed that my dad was a cross between Rembrandt and Picasso with possibly a touch of Michelangelo thrown in for good measure.

"I've seen it. And isn't it elegant, though?" she asked, beaming proudly. "I think it's the nicest likeness of you I've ever seen. Who knew your father was so talented?"

"Mm-hmm," I said noncommitally, and she scurried away looking satisfied, back out to the kitchen to supervise the menfolk in their attack on the glassware.

I, however, was not satisfied, since as I've mentioned, the best I can say about my own looks is that I clean up okay, given enough time and effort.

So instead I went to the front parlor, meaning to ask Sam and Mika about the painting but stopping in the doorway when I found them in quiet conversation about something else.

". . . rent a place," he was saying, and she was shaking her head.

". . . afford it?" She sounded doubtful.

"I think we have to," he said, "there's not going to be enough room for . . ."

Which was all I needed to hear. *Oh, of course she is pregnant,* I thought as I backed from the doorway and headed upstairs. They just didn't want the rest of us concerning ourselves about it yet.

But sooner or later we would have to, because Sam was correct: there wasn't enough space in their room or in the one we'd planned to turn into Ephraim's tiny chamber, little more than a broom closet at the top of the stairs, for another child.

At this point I'd have vetoed getting a parakeet, we were so jammed. And there were no other rooms in the house, which was what I was fretting about yet again when it hit me from out of left field:

"Before my time," Bob Arnold had said about the tragedy of Anna Benoit's abandonment and subsequent drowning.

Bella hadn't remembered it, either; she'd been living in Lubec with her horrible first husband in those days. But now I recalled the sister Karen had mentioned, saying that the sister had been around here back then and getting angry when I had pursued the subject.

Back, I mean, when Anna Benoit jumped, or fell, or was pushed off the Deer Island ferry—

The phone rang. "Mom!" Sam called to me. "It's Ellie!"

Eight

I picked up the extension, and from the sound of Ellie's voice I knew at once that she had just come to the same realization I had.

"Jake," Ellie said, "I can't imagine why I didn't think of it earlier, but—"

I could. Someone had been shooting a shotgun at us, for heaven's sake, scrambling our brains with the sudden awareness of our own mortality. Even now, after several hours had passed, I still felt as if I could barely remember my own name.

"—there's someone else who might be able to tell us—"

The happy clamor of the tail end of dish-doing floating up the stairs, and I happened to know that there was an important baseball game that Wade was eager to watch on TV tonight.

So I was, as they say, at liberty. "So maybe," Ellie said, "we should take a ride tonight and—"

My dad went upstairs to his painting studio and shut the door. The shower in Sam and Mika's bathroom went on, as did the TV in the front parlor, and Ephraim began fussing from his playpen until Bella went in to soothe him.

I leaned against the wall exhaustedly. "Ellie," I said, "it's a good idea, but . . ."

Outside, one of Sam's lawn machines roared to life as he began working on the only yard in town that he hadn't cut yet: ours. Lucky the riding mower he'd chosen had a headlight, I thought.

". . . to fetch himself a rabbit skin to wrap the baby bunting in," sang Bella in a voice that sounded exactly like a creaking hinge; hearing it, Ephraim's crying shut off like a switch.

Everyone in the house seemed well settled in for the evening, in fact, just as I wished to be. "Ellie, all I want is a bath and a nice glass of—"

Outside, the mower's engine fell silent. "Jacobia," Bella said quietly from behind me. "I just recalled who it is that might—"

"Wade?" Sam called from the back door. "Hey, Wade? Didn't you leave that little cannon of yours on the porch out here?"

He had left it there to let the cleaning solvents he'd used finish drying before he brought it inside; I knew this because I'd nearly tripped over it, bringing in the green beans from the garden.

He'd prepared it for another weapons demonstration, too, I had gathered. I'm no expert, but after years of being married to Wade I'd at least been able to tell that the cannonball, explosive charge, and fuse were already in it.

"Willetta Beck," pronounced Bella.

"Willetta Beck," Ellie said simultaneously. "I just now re-called the name. She's Karen Carrolton's sister."

". . . 'cause that cannon's not out here now," Sam finished, and I heard Wade rising hastily from his chair in the parlor.

So the cannon was really gone, and I didn't like that a bit; for one thing, the last time someone stole one of Wade's weapons, it hadn't ended well. . . .

Ephraim let out a wail they could probably hear over on Campobello. Not for the first time, I wondered if a nice, quiet jail cell might turn out to be a relief.

On the other hand, jails—and prisons, heaven forbid—are the noisiest places on earth. I contemplated this fact for a moment while the baby's cries subsided to wretched sobbing.

"Pawwot," he wept. "Pawwot."

Parrot. I'd ordered a new one online, but it hadn't arrived yet.

"Yeah, you know what?" I said into the phone. "I'll meet you at the Moose in five minutes."

When I got there, the glass had been replaced in the front window and the door was fixed, right down to the little silver bell hanging over it once more.

Even our poor battered moose-head sign had received first aid and now looked only slightly more googly-eyed than before it got blasted.

"I got George to come down and fix all that," Ellie explained.

In Eastport, George was the one you called in case of sparks in your chimney flue, leaks in your cellar, or a skunk under the front porch. Now Ellie was putting the finished double-chocolate ginger cookies into the cooler; the white chocolate slivers stuck into their glossy dark-chocolate frosting were the delicious finishing touch.

"Willetta Beck," she repeated, stripping off her oven mitts.

I gazed around at all she'd accomplished. A chocolate brioche and two dozen more Toll House cookies were cooling on the counter.

"Do you, like, operate at warp speed when I'm not around? Is that your superpower?"

She laughed. "No, I got Lee to do some this afternoon at home."

Ellie's daughter was a terrifying little paragon of just about any virtue you could name: good student, decent violinist, team member for three sports, volunteer at the animal rescue, etcetera. She even sang in the church choir.

I kept waiting for her to bust out and show her punk side, to dye her hair fuchsia and get nose piercings or something, but she never did. She just kept motoring along like a kid with her eyes on the prize and her head screwed on straight.

The prize, at this moment, was a stash of saved allowance money big enough to augment the college scholarships she meant to secure.

"Turns out that if you pay her, my kid's a pretty decent little chocolate-themed baker," Ellie added, smiling.

Which was good to know, because that baby-bunting business might be sweet, but it was going to put quite a crimp in Mika's helping-in-the-shop schedule, especially if she and Sam no longer lived in the Key Street house with us.

Although if they stayed, someone would have to start sleeping in a hammock on the porch.

"Who's Willetta Beck?" I asked.

Ellie plucked two fresh cookies from the cooling rack, poured two coffees dosed with cream, and settled us at a café table.

"Willetta is Karen Carrolton's sister," she said. "I recalled the name when I pulled this out of the mailbox a little while ago."

The latest issue of the *Quoddy Tides*, Eastport's biweekly local newspaper, lay on the table between us. PIRATES! screamed the headline, but there was nothing about the murder or the explosions; it had gone to press before they happened.

"Huh." I bit into my cookie. As the flavors of ginger and chocolate mingled on my tongue, the happiness centers in my brain jumped up and started dancing around.

Which is, of course, exactly what those cookies are for. "So where's Willetta, and what is she doing now?"

Ellie shrugged. "Don't know what she's doing. She used to have horses, I think. Went to shows and gave riding lessons and so on."

"And you think she'll be able to help us . . . *willing* and able," I amended, squinting at the newsprint some more, "because why, again?" Then I looked up from the paper. Outside, the fog had rolled in at last, blurring everything to a romantic, streetlight-haloed softness.

"I have no idea whether she will or not," said Ellie. "I just thought, especially since Karen seemed so upset by the idea, that we could go visit Willetta and ask."

The *Jenny* was still out of the harbor. All the state cops had departed, too, or at any rate their big armored vehicles weren't clogging up downtown anymore. Which meant—

Which meant we were alone here with whatever—*whoever*—was out there now, lurking in the gloom. Because—

"What?" demanded Ellie, seeing the look on my face.

"Did you read the article?" I held the paper up. A short one-column piece below the fold was titled LOCAL WOMAN ESCAPES CRASH.

The local woman being Willetta Beck. Ellie shook her head. "No, I got as far as her name and then the oven timer went off, so . . ."

I slid the paper across the table. "Yeah, well, I think somebody else got the same idea that you did. That she might know something."

Ellie took the paper and read aloud: ". . . escaped serious injury after another vehicle forced the car she was driving off the River Road in . . ."

She looked up. "Jake, it says the car that forced her off the road was a white sedan." Like the one that had menaced us.

Ellie stuffed the newspaper back into her satchel and cleared our cups and napkins. In the kitchen, she went around making sure things were turned off and put away while I peered out the window again.

We didn't need anybody stopping us to ask where we were going. "Nobody out there," I reported. "Except for a few more pirate wannabes staggering out on the fish pier," I added.

I could see the plumes on their hats waving under the yellowish dock lights that illuminated the wooden pier like the setting for a stage play.

"Good." She came out with her sweater and bag over her arm and hustled me to her car. Twenty minutes later we'd crossed the causeway to the mainland and were on the part of Route 1 known as the River Road, headed north toward the town of Calais.

"Willetta *was* in the phone book," Ellie commented. "So now I know where she lives."

"I see." The St. Croix River gleamed at intervals between the trees along the road, and beyond it lay New Brunswick, Canada, dark and forested.

I changed the subject. "Someone took Wade's antique cannon off the porch," I said.

Ellie glanced at me without comment.

"We've never had anything stolen off the porch before." Or from the house, or out of the yard . . . "Wade called Bob Arnold to let him know. Of course, there are a lot of strangers in town for the pirate festival," I said. Meaning that the thievery didn't have to be linked to Hadlyme's murder, or to our snooping into it. "But—"

"But coincidence," said Ellie, "and the other half of whatever's happening?"

"Precisely." I leaned back in the car seat as more slivers of the St. Croix flashed by between dark stands of trees.

"To spot that cannon, someone would have to have paid pretty close attention."

To our house, Ellie meant. "But maybe somebody just wanted an authentic pirate festival souvenir," I replied hopefully.

But I wasn't convinced. Along the road, the dark stretches began giving way to a few yard lights, small houses with cars parked on them, and here and there a row of mailboxes on posts. After that came a hilly S-curve with dark granite rising straight up on one side and dropping off sharply toward the river on the other.

"This must be it," said Ellie at last, as a narrow driveway

opened between two big maples. Pea gravel crunched under our tires as Ellie turned in, and we made our way slowly along the narrow track.

A faint light flickered ahead, brightening as we turned into a circle drive with another massive maple towering at its center, its branches overspreading the driveway.

At the circle's far side, a moss-lined brick walk curved toward a small white cottage with dark shutters and a brick chimney. Smoke twirled from the chimney in pale wisps, ghostly against the dark sky.

Pink geraniums bloomed from tall clay urns at either side of the door and from the window boxes at the windows shedding warm yellow light onto the bricks. When Ellie rapped the horseshoe-shaped brass door knocker on the red-painted door, excited barking erupted inside, followed by the sound of footsteps scuffing along a bare floor.

"Hello?" The woman who answered peered out at us, surprised by two strangers at her door but not seeming displeased. "Can I help you?" she asked sweetly, her faded blue eyes moving from my face to Ellie's.

Her hair, white and fine as spun glass, stuck out in careless tufts from her head. The dogs peered from behind her, one white-faced old golden retriever on either side.

Ellie introduced us. "We met your sister, Karen, earlier today, and we'd like to ask you a few questions. May we come in?"

I expected we'd be refused. But, "Oh, of course, why don't you come into the parlor? I'm having a drink, perhaps you'd like one?"

Oh, dear heaven, would I. After the day I'd had, I felt like a mile of bad road. We followed Willetta Beck down a narrow red-tiled hall made narrower by the overflowing bookcases on both sides.

"Pretty horses you've got out there," I remarked, just to have something to say. We'd parked by a rail-fenced pen where two blanket-draped ponies stood peaceably munching something out of the feed bags they wore.

"Silly things, they're a pair of rescues. Won't eat unless you shove their noses in it," Willetta said with affectionate scorn as she led us into the parlor with its braided rugs, doily-clad tables, and floral-chintz-upholstered chair.

It was full of books, too: on shelves flanking the sheer-draped windows, in stacks on the floor, and spread out on the settee she'd been sitting in.

A string quartet played softly from a pair of speakers on the mantel. "Sit down, won't you?" Willetta invited while the dogs nosed us pleasantly, their feathery tails wagging.

Willetta was having bourbon on ice, and I accepted her offer of one just like it; Ellie, seeing as she was driving, had iced tea with a sprig of mint in it.

"So"—Ellie turned to business—"you're probably wondering why we dropped in on you like this."

But Willetta Beck didn't seem surprised. "Yes, well, actually I'd heard that you two were . . . what's the polite word?

With her hands wrinkled and sun-spotted, her face thin-skinned and grooved into runnels, she was obviously quite elderly. But when she moved, she was quick and limber as a woman in the prime of life.

"Snooping." I supplied the word, and she laughed merrily.

"That's one way of putting it. But are you here to ask me about the . . . accident? I guess you've read about it in the *Quoddy Tides*?" There was a small flesh-colored bandage on her forehead. "If it was one," she added. "I must say, though, it seemed very deliberate to me. One moment I was alone on the road and the next . . ."

She bit her lip, recalling the event, then went on decisively. "No, it *was* deliberate. The police and the EMTs didn't believe me, of course. I could tell they thought it was one of those things where the old lady gets flustered and runs into something."

The "something" in this case being a ditch, at least according to the *Tides*. "But I don't get flustered, and I know what happened."

I got up, carrying my drink. The books stacked on all the surfaces were about horses: horse health, horse nutrition . . . She saw me examining them.

"Yes, it's a bit of an obsession with me. Always has been."

She waved at the crowded mantel over the ceramic-tiled fireplace, where a small blaze leapt pleasantly. Engraved silver cups, trays, plaques, and horse-shaped statuettes crowded the mantel, along with a dozen or so each of framed ribbons, diplomas, and photographs.

"In my day I was quite the horsewoman," Willetta said. "Nowadays everyone's afraid I'll fall off and break a hip."

She gave me a look that was no less piercing for the skimpiness of her lashes or the fading blue of her intelligent wide eyes.

"They don't know it, but it's how I'd prefer to go, really. A nice ride and then a crash, maybe a brief pneumonia on my way out."

She laughed trillingly again, not seeming in the least to be a candidate for "going out," as she put it. In the kitchen something wonderful was simmering, some kind of a stew.

"But I don't dare say it aloud," she added, "or my health care provider"—she gave the words a dry twist—"will put me on the old-lady suicide watch."

One of the dogs lay down on a hooked rug in front of the fire. She watched it thoughtfully for a moment. Then:

"But if you went to see Karen, it's not my car crash you're here to ask about. You want to know about Anna, don't you?"

Ellie and I glanced at each other in surprise, bringing another laugh from Willetta.

"Please," she said. "It's been on the news that Henry Hadlyme died. Was murdered, that is. And Karen called me this afternoon."

For the first time her voice hardened. "Also, I think being run through by a sword qualifies as murder, don't you? I mean

I doubt it was accidental." She rolled her eyes. "And of course it was about Anna. Who could ever believe anything else?"

"And you think your own car accident, that in your opinion was *not* accidental . . . that it also had to do with—"

She cut me off. "I was on the ferry that day all those years ago, you see. I was going to visit my friend on Deer Island. We were planning a picnic."

Well, there was a surprise, that she'd witnessed Anna Benoit's final voyage. Her voice softened with the memory.

"Some people brought their cars—the ones who were going on to the next ferry at the other end of the island, to New Brunswick. But Anna and I were on foot. We stood by the rail watching the porpoises."

Ellie spoke up. "Did Anna say anything about—"

Willetta Beck shook her head firmly. "About Henry? No. Maybe I should have asked. But she looked as if she wanted to be let alone."

Out in the kitchen a timer dinged; for the stew, I imagined, which now smelled as if she were running a French restaurant in here. Ignoring it, she finished her drink and continued.

"I went to the ferry's other side when we got to the Old Sow whirlpool. I wanted to see the piglets, you know? The bunches of baby whirlpools that the big one throws off?"

I recalled them from our trip of the previous day, the dark, glassy swirls that looked so harmless but weren't. "And did you? See them, I mean?"

"Oh, yes. Dozens. The current was strong that day, and I recall thinking that it was like seeing into a volcano, so powerful." She looked up. "But cold, of course, instead of hot. Even the spray flying up into my face was like ice chips, I recall."

"Was anyone else out on the deck besides you two?" I asked. "And where she stood, was it where anyone else could see her?"

"No, there was a van on the ferry, and it was between her and the ferry's pilot house," Willetta replied. "So I'm sure the pilot was being honest when he told the police he didn't see what happened."

"And you didn't, either," said Ellie. "Because if you had, you'd have told the police about that."

"Correct." She got up to poke the fire, which had collapsed.

"I was watching the whirlpool, as I said, when I heard a scream. Other people heard it, too, and ran to where Anna had been standing." She sighed heavily. "But it was too late to save her, she'd already been carried away, and with the tide running hard and the currents surging the way they always do out there . . ."

I understood; if you want to dispose of a body, the Old Sow is the place to put it. It could end up in Nova Scotia, or on a beach in some rarely visited cove on some island, or it might never come up.

"Her body," Willetta Beck said, "has never been found."

The dog on the rug shifted and sighed. It was cozy and warm in here, and I felt a sudden reluctance to go back out into the dark. Somehow talking about a girl's long-ago fall—if it was one—from the Deer Island ferry made the night seem menacing, especially when Willetta Beck went on:

"Someone must have pushed her, though. I'm certain of it. Always have been, though at the time the police called it an accident."

Ellie frowned, getting up. We'd both noticed that Willetta Beck hadn't put another stick of wood on the dying fire or offered another drink, hints enough that our visit should be drawing to a close.

"But there are railings on the ferry," Ellie said, "always have been, so how could—"

"Exactly." Accompanying us to the door, our hostess nodded enthusiastically. I noticed again how limber and in good shape she seemed, then glimpsed a possible reason at the end of the hall.

Another room, one that we hadn't entered, was full of exercise equipment: a stationary bike, some free weights, a screen with VCR tapes stacked by it . . .

No wonder she seemed so surprisingly fit for her age: she worked at it. Ellie glanced in, also, taking in the elaborate setup.

But not commenting. "You'd have to try pretty hard to fall off that ferry by accident," she said. "And if Anna *didn't* jump, then . . ."

Willetta opened the door for us. Behind the rail fence the two ponies whickered quietly under the yard lights.

"But why don't you think she jumped?" Ellie asked suddenly.

Her car was only a few yards away under the trees by a small barn that I hadn't noticed earlier, but we lingered on the red brick path gathering our sweaters around us to gain a few last moments.

"From what I've heard, Anna had reasons, and surely that's a simpler explanation than . . ."

In the warm yellow light streaming out of her snug, civilized little dwelling, Willetta Beck's face looked older and harder, her pale blue eyes flat disks gazing into the night.

"Murder?" She finished Ellie's question and turned to us. "I'll tell you why," she said. "The way I told the police, only they didn't listen."

Ellie stepped out onto the driveway, her feet crunching on the gravel, and stopped as something about the small red barn attracted her attention.

"Just an old lady wanting to get in on all the excitement so she could have something to gossip about with her old-lady friends, they probably thought," Willetta Beck went on.

She'd been elderly even then, I realized, mentally revising her age upward; hard to believe, but now I supposed she must be at least eighty.

Ellie had made her way into the shadows by the rail-fenced horse paddock, on the other side of her car. Willetta still gazed the other way, toward the road and the car lights flickering at the end of it.

"Well," I said. "Thanks for the drinks."

Her old eyes turned slowly to me and she held out a hand, which was strong and steady, her grip firm with nothing tentative about it.

"Thank you both for coming," she replied. Ellie was getting into her car. "Come back again and I'll introduce you to the ponies."

But then she added quietly, so only I could hear, "I know why you came. And believe me, if I could have killed that horrid fellow myself, I would have."

I stepped away reflexively, the malice in her voice so repellent suddenly that it was hard to believe this woman had been entertaining us in her parlor moments earlier, as sweet as you please.

"But as you can see . . ." She lifted her arm, and for the first time I saw her right hand. It was shrunken, withered, and malformed, with a long scar running up into the sleeve of her sweater.

"Fell off a horse as a girl," she explained matter-of-factly. "Not that it ever kept me from doing anything. I learned to adapt." Then, watching Ellie pull the car up to where we stood: "And Henry's stab wound was inflicted from the front, I assume?"

I allowed as how it was, and she nodded almost wistfully, as if she really did wish she'd done the inflicting.

"If he'd been stabbed in the back, I might not be out of the picture in the suspect department. I did hate him enough, and in fact I was in downtown Eastport that day," she said.

More news. "And you hated him because . . ."

"Why, because he murdered his poor little wife, of course. Or had her murdered, paid or maybe even blackmailed someone to do it."

It struck me again, just as it had when Karen Carrolton said it, that these were a lot of conclusions to jump to. "To get rid of her," I said, "so he wouldn't be stuck here with her and the baby instead of following his dreams to New York?"

I didn't think so. He'd already left, and already established that he wouldn't be sending money, but Willetta Beck nodded, accepting this further step in the narrative.

"And stuck with the older child, too, of course. When I think of what poor Anna must've been going through. . . ."

Ellie was now in the car waiting patiently, but I could tell by the way her fingers twiddled restlessly on the steering wheel that she was practically bursting with some new fact she was dying to tell me about.

Willetta Beck continued, "But as I was saying, I do think you'd need both hands to stab somebody from the front, wouldn't you? Because they'd try to fend you off, of course, and you'd have to . . ."

A chill went through me; she'd imagined it very clearly . . . unless of course she really had witnessed the event or participated in it. I ended the conversation as smoothly as I could, allowing over my shoulder that a visit to the ponies sounded delightful and we'd be sure to do it soon.

Then, in a final flurry of pleasantly meaningless words and phrases, I reached the car at last, and Ellie and I crunched back down the gravel driveway under the trees, out into the night.

"You're not going to believe this," Ellie said, switching on the car's heater as we sped back toward Eastport.

"I already have something I don't believe," I replied. "Henry didn't kill Anna. Why would he?"

The night rushed by, the dark swathes of evergreens crowding up to the road punctuated by lights from the little houses spaced widely apart.

"He didn't have to kill her to get free of her," I went on. "He was already gone. Anna couldn't have made Henry Hadlyme come back to Eastport, or send money, either, so why . . . ?"

Ellie shrugged, her eyes on the dark road ahead. "Willetta's got what amounts to an alibi, though: that she's not physically capable of—"

She stopped suddenly as a large catlike animal ran across the road in front of us; took the embankment on the far side in a single long, lithe stride; and vanished into the woods.

"Bobcat," she commented, pleased to have seen one.

Me too; the tufted ears and stubby tail were a rare sight even around here. But then I yawned. Being suspected of killing someone was tiring, I was beginning to find out.

"On the other hand . . ." Ellie returned to Willetta Beck's supposed disability. "If she can manage horses, why wouldn't she be able to—"

"Only if she took him by surprise," I said. I let my head, still thudding away painfully, loll back against the car seat.

"Because, just think about it," Ellie agreed, "he's got two arms to hold her off with, and she's got just one, and her good hand's holding the . . ."

Right, the cutlass, which she'd have stolen from Wade's weapons display down on the breakwater. And how would she have gotten the stuffed parrot?

"Besides, Hadlyme was no Mister Universe," I put in, "but still he must've outweighed her by sixty pounds. And he was what, forty or so years younger than she is?"

The car's smooth motion and Ellie's good driving lulled my head pain a little. "And if her attempt failed, he'd be alive and able to say who'd attacked him," I finished.

So maybe this whole trip had been a waste of time. I sighed heavily.

"You know what, though?" said Ellie after a while of no talking; we were both very tired. "There's a white sedan in her barn."

I sat up sharply, my eyes snapping open. "No kidding? But why didn't you . . . could you tell if it was the one we saw near Karen Carrolton's earlier?"

In the dashboard's glow Ellie's lips curved faintly. "You didn't give me a chance. But it was there, all right. Can't swear it's the same one, but it would be quite the coincidence if it's not."

I twisted around to peer out the car's rear window; no one was following. Not now. Not yet. . . .

"But how could that make sense? Willetta Beck fakes an attack on herself, says a white sedan ran her off the road . . . why?"

Ellie took the turn onto Route 190, headed toward town. Soon we were on the causeway with the dark water spread out on both sides.

"And this happens right after a similar vehicle nearly does the same thing to us," I added.

Ellie watched the roadway carefully. "The timing's interesting, that's for sure."

Just off our right bumper, our headlights illuminated a trudging racoon; when she'd steered carefully past, she went on:

"And then there's the *Jenny*."

Right, because what could the mysterious gun-equipped sailboat have to do with Hadlyme's murder?

And yet it must be tied in somehow, since otherwise it was more than the mother of all coincidences; it was flat-out unbelievable.

We swung around the long, dark curves past the Eastport garage, the old power plant, the airport with its runway lights glowing and its hangar buildings gaping, and finally the Bay City Mobil station, closed for the night.

"Want me to take you home?" Ellie asked as we pulled onto Water Street and stopped in front of the Moose.

Everything downtown was silent and dark, even the last of the fake pirate stragglers all gone to bed. It was what I should've done, too, but with my skull pounding out a thudding rhythm of misery, I knew I wouldn't sleep.

Besides, Amity Jones was still around here somewhere, likely planning my imminent apprehension for the crime of skewering Henry Hadlyme. And if these were my last hours of freedom, I wanted to be awake for them.

"No," I said. "If all those cops have really gone chasing after that sailboat somewhere, the street will get clear and the festival will reopen. So we'd better be ready."

Which is why over the next few hours we baked a fudge layer cake and began an éclair recipe that would get completed in the morning. Ellie mixed more butter and sugar, beat in eggs and vanilla, and began adding dry ingredients while I made cake frosting and created room in the cooler for the big bowl of éclair dough to begin chilling.

But my heart wasn't in it. By tomorrow morning, I imagined deputies would be on their way here from Augusta, carrying a warrant for my arrest.

And I'd be in custody soon thereafter, I expected, because Amity Jones seemed tough, smart, ambitious, and new at her job, and wanting a win very badly on account of all those qualities.

Badly enough to try using a family relationship to Bob Arnold, for instance, to get information out of him, and maybe even enough to overlook—not deliberately, perhaps, but still—whatever didn't make sense about her suspicions of me.

"Ellie." I stretched clear plastic wrap over the bowl of éclair dough. "Listen, if for any reason I'm not around for a while . . ."

She bit her lip, patting a brioche loaf into shape. We'd made a dozen crescent rolls, too, out of a quick-rising sweet dough recipe she'd invented, and since they were nearly cool I made frosting for them, the simple old-fashioned kind that everyone likes: butter, confectioner's sugar, and melted baking chocolate.

"Don't be silly," said Ellie. "That's not going to—"

"*If* I'm not," I persisted as I dripped hot milk into the frosting, loosening it just enough to spread, "then I want you to run the shop, tell Bella she's in charge of everything at home . . ."

Bills, taxes, banking, insurances, and all the various permits, licenses, and registrations that Sam and Wade need for their work—all of that was my job in our large, many-faceted household.

But Bella was smart, and I happened to know she could focus like a laser when the occasion demanded it, so if she had to, she could do it all just as well.

". . . and find me a lawyer. A *mean*," I emphasized, "lawyer. A lawyer with *teeth*."

Ellie shook her head vehemently, but she didn't argue anymore. She might not like it, but she knew the lay of the land as well as I did, and it was about to get bumpy.

"And just tell everyone else at my house to go on doing their part," I said. "Whatever they're good at, just pitch in and do it, and what they're not, let someone else help."

Because teamwork was what made our household a success, and it would keep things together in my absence, too, or so I hoped.

We worked in silence for a while. "But maybe you won't need to," I relented when we were finished with our tasks, everything put away, the freshly made baked goods laid in the cooler all ready to be set out tomorrow.

I switched out the light over the worktable. "Maybe we'll come up with an answer for what's going on around here, and that'll save me a lot of trouble," I said.

But I didn't really believe it. In the faint yellow glow of the small lightbulb over the sink, the bakery's kitchen was as still as a held breath, all its familiar shapes turned to what Sam used to call night animals.

I'd always told him they were friendly animals, but now I wasn't sure. Outside, I stood on the sidewalk while Ellie locked up.

"You've told me many times, though, that it's good to have a plan for if things don't work out. Just a backup plan, is all."

Ellie looked up, her expression defiant. Her car was still

right there, but I'd already told her I meant to walk home; for all I knew, it was the last evening walk I'd be getting for a while.

But she had other ideas. "You'll go to jail for that horrible man's murder," she said flatly, "when hell freezes over."

And that was Ellie. She'd be fierce on my behalf for as long as she could, no question about that. But there wasn't a thing she really could do about any of it; besides, when I glanced around at an oddly familiar sound coming from down the street, I saw that it was already too late.

Ellie's hand was already on the car's door handle. She squinted toward the odd sound, a liquidy burble that went on repeating itself.

"What the . . ." Halfway down the block on the sidewalk in front of the Quoddy Crafts store lay a small black object. *Trill! Trill!* it insisted as I approached it with my heart sinking.

Lying there all alone as if someone had accidentally dropped it was a cell phone. I grabbed it up.

My phone; I knew it from the SpongeBob sticker that Ephraim had insisted I put on it. "Hello?"

The caller ID screen said the caller was unidentified. Then the screen went dark; someone had hung up.

Water Street was still deserted except for us. I put the phone back into my bag where it belonged and got into Ellie's car, and the ringing began once more.

Unidentified, the screen said again. "Who is this?" I demanded into the device. "What do you—"

"Just listen," said an unfamiliar voice. "If you want to know what's going on and find out who murdered the late, unlamented Henry Hadlyme, get onto the *Jenny.* Do that, and all will be revealed."

Ellie backed out and began driving up Water Street. "The *Jenny*?" I repeated. "But we don't even know where—"

The voice hardened. "Just do what I say. Get on that boat and do it soon, unless you like your revelations . . . explosive."

The phone went dead. "Damn," I breathed as Ellie kept driving out Water Street toward the south end of the island, until the pavement ended in a turnaround overlooking the bay.

"So. My phone wasn't lost," I said as the dark water to the north spread out before us. In the distance, a few lights on faraway New Brunswick's shoreline gleamed.

"Someone got it either out of my bag or off your boat after I dropped the bag there," I said.

Ellie's nose wrinkled puzzledly. "But why?"

Good question. What I wanted was a little sign with the answer on it to drop out of the sky. But no sign appeared; instead, out on the water a flotilla was gathering, local boats getting into good viewing spots for the pirate festival's traditional fireworks show.

The show had been scheduled for midnight. "Oh, I'd forgotten all about that," said Ellie when I pointed out the probable reason for all the marine activity.

"Me too. I guess the state cops must have given the okay for it to go on once the *Jenny* left," I said.

Or possibly, seeing as this was Eastport, where in general the authorities from away could walk east till their hats floated for all we cared, no one had asked.

Then suddenly the answer *did* appear; I should wish for things to come to me out of the blue more often, I decided.

"To get the number," I said. Once I'd thought of it, it was obvious. "They couldn't look it up. They got the phone's number off the phone, then put it where I'd be sure to find it, and then they called me on it."

While watching from somewhere nearby to be sure I *did* find it . . . and I would have, no matter what, I felt certain. Instead of on the street, it would've been on my back porch, or on my kitchen table.

Whoever had just called me on it would've made sure of it. "But why not *tell* us what we're supposedly going to learn," I wondered aloud, "not put us through all the trouble and risk of—"

"Because it's a trap," Ellie interrupted. "Baited with a promise of learning who killed Henry Hadlyme, if I'm reading all this right."

"Because we're getting too disruptive? Poking around into too many . . ."

She turned to me in the gloom of the passenger compartment, her face gravely still.

"Maybe. But now we need to know what *else* is going on . . . what's *going* to go on. Because you're sure they said it was an *explosive* revelation we'd be preventing?"

Which was when it hit me: the bombs fired earlier off the *Jenny.* Or they'd been as good as bombs, anyway—that is, *explosive.*

She put the car in gear. "Anyway, now we can be sure Hadlyme's murder and the gunfire from that boat really are connected."

The car's tires squealed as she pulled out. "And it'll happen again," she said, "unless we do something to stop it. That boat will be back and it'll fire those guns again, I'll bet, and *this* time . . ."

Urgency gripped me; what she said made sense. "Right, but do what?"

Not to mention, *How?* Ellie drove away from the view of the dark bay, out County Road past the tennis courts and the fire station.

"And if the cops haven't found the *Jenny*," I went on, "how in the world are *we* supposed to—"

At Washington Street she turned right, down toward the harbor again. Here the houses were sprawling old family homes broken up into apartments, their mailboxes hung in rows on the porches.

In some of the windows, TV screens flickered; others were dark, their tenants tucked up in bed. I wished that I were, too—the inside of my poor aching head already felt as if fireworks were going off in it—but instead, moments later we pulled into a parking spot on the breakwater, high above the boats in the boat basin.

There weren't many tied up down there. Instead most boats were out on the water readying for the fireworks, loaded with friends and family all bundled up in warm jackets with life preservers tied over them, waiting for the show to begin.

"Good," Ellie commented at the sight of the deserted piers. She turned off the key, then got out of the car and hurried toward the sharply downsloping metal ramp.

"No one's around to try to stop us," she said, starting down the ramp.

I hustled along behind her, trying to think of an argument that would dissuade her from what she was obviously bent on doing.

That is, finding and boarding the *Jenny*. The more I thought about it, the worse an idea it seemed. "Ellie, what about—"

"Lee's at a sleepover with her cousins on the mainland," she recited. "George is in Bangor taking a class for his electrician's certificate, so no one's sitting home worrying about me."

At low tide, the metal ramp was nearly as steep as a ladder. I put a hand firmly on each rail. Just watching her scampering down ahead of me made me dizzy, until at last with a deep sigh of relief I stepped onto the floating dock.

The operative word was *floating*. This naturally caused a lot of swaying, bobbing, and bouncing, and none of those are things I'm good at handling.

"Yeeks," I said, and Ellie took my arm, guiding me forward to the finger pier where her own boat was tied. After hopping aboard, she took my hand firmly and yanked me on, too.

"If I'm right about all this, we've got a couple of hours," she said.

"Why?" The water rippled and heaved. I found a good sitting spot and plunked myself down on it so as not to topple overboard.

"I mean, why do we have a couple of hours?"

A zillion other questions filled my head. Whether I would drown tonight was the first one, of course, but phrases like *why didn't I become something sensible like a lion tamer or a sword swallower* were in there, too.

Meanwhile, Ellie went through her departure routine: turning the batteries on, trimming the engine so that the propeller was all the way down in the water, firing up the GPS screen so we could see where we were going and whether the water underneath us was deep enough, and last but not least, turning up our radio and then smacking it until the speaker spat static before turning it back a little so it was silent.

Then she turned to me. "So tell me, Jake, if you were going to fire weapons at Eastport and you didn't want people to realize what was happening right away, when would you do it?"

Back in the streets somewhere, blocks from the harbor, a cherry bomb popped, and then a second one. And a third. "Ohh," I breathed, catching on. "I'd do it when there are a whole lot of *other . . .*"

My mouth went dry suddenly with the awful likeliness of what she was saying.

"Other explosions," I whispered while she busied herself in the boat's little cabin. She came out clutching a pair of bright orange life jackets and thrust one at me while pulling the other one on herself.

Next she started the engine, the big Mercury outboard coming to life in a watery rumble on the first key-turn, and finally she hopped back out onto the dock again and cast off the lines.

One from the bow, the other from the stern. Nervously, I got up. "Ellie, you know I hate being alone on the boat when we're—"

"Drop it in reverse," she snapped, glancing up at the breakwater where we'd parked the car.

"Besides, never mind that we don't even know where the

sailboat is," I said, "but if it's a trap like you think, why are we even—"

"Jake? Reverse, please. Right now, please. I mean like really right this minute, okay?"

I still didn't like it, but I got the message and did it. She already had a hand on the boat's rail, guiding it away from the dock; then she jumped in.

The boat was by then moving backward very purposefully. "Um, Ellie?"

Moving *fast*. Also, it was dark back there on the water behind us. *"Ellie."*

She was watching the parking area. A car pulled into another of the parking spots up there, its lights strobing the water briefly.

"Start your turn now," she said, meanwhile paying a good deal less attention to my predicament than I felt it deserved.

To the fact, I mean, that we were moving. Backward. With me at the helm, and have I mentioned that I hadn't done this very often in the dark?

Never, actually, was the number of times I'd done it. "Now," Ellie said, and I really had to do something or we'd be on the rocks.

So I turned the wheel, and you can imagine for yourself the many profanities I uttered while I tried remembering which *way* to turn it. But at last I guessed correctly and the boat's stern swung to port.

"Straighten her out." She said it absently while fiddling with something in one of the lockers near the engine.

I obeyed that command, too, and the boat quit turning, only now it was backing toward a forest of dock pilings, as big around as tree trunks and thirty feet tall, and this would have unnerved me even more than I already was except that suddenly two figures got out of the car up on the breakwater, capturing my attention.

The *white* car . . . it was a white sedan. Which was when I said the heck with it, shoved the gear shift lever into forward, and hit the throttle hard enough to make Ellie look up in surprised appreciation.

"You go, girl," she said approvingly as we . . . well, we didn't exactly *shoot* out of the boat basin, but we moved very efficiently past various obstacles: a barge with an industrial crane perched on it; a big concrete block with a massive steel loop set into it, used for tying up really large visiting vessels; some old wharf pilings collapsed teepee-style on top of one another . . .

A lot of things, in other words, but we didn't hit any of them, and in just a few moments—even though it certainly *seemed* like years—we slid smoothly between the massive concrete breakwater and the wooden fish pier out into the dark open water.

Nine

Out on the bay, the sky and the water merged: dark above, dark all around. Behind us, Eastport shrank to toy-town size, while across the water on the island of Campobello, TV screens flickered in distant living-room windows.

I stood at the helm with the cold salty air and the spatters of icy spray striking me in the face, black sky spreading overhead, and a big engine surging with power under my hands. For a moment I felt like a million bucks, as if I could drive the Bayliner all the way to China if I had to.

Ellie came up behind me suddenly. "Listen, get out on the bow for a while, will you?"

"Out on . . . what?" But I let her take the wheel.

"There are lobster buoys out here, remember? They are all over the place just like before, only now in the dark we can't see them."

She handed me the flashlight she'd dug out of the storage bin. "Take this, get out on the bow, and watch for buoys ahead. If you see one, say what o'clock it is. Like, straight ahead's noon and so on."

"Oh," I said, hefting the flashlight hesitantly; I understood the o'clock part. It was the "out on the bow" part that—

Oh, what the heck; I'd already nearly scuttled us on the corner of that damned barge, and after all, what was a little more mortal danger among friends, right?

"I'll save you if you fall in," Ellie said, meaning *don't*, and I understood; in the cold waters off Eastport, my life jacket probably wouldn't do me much good, and plucking me out of the water wouldn't be the problem, anyway. In the dark, *finding* me would be the problem.

Still I scrambled out there, stepping along carefully until I was perched as far forward on the front part of the boat as I could get. Think of the flying scene in *Titanic* and you'll get the idea.

Not until I was down on my belly with my head sticking out over the surging water, though, did I realize how crucial my job here really was. There were *dozens* of buoys out there in the water, each attached by a line to a lobster trap sitting on the bay's bottom, many fathoms below.

And snagging a lobster buoy on our propeller was a disaster that I didn't want to confront right now. . . .

"Two o'clock," I called back urgently.

Ellie changed course and avoided the red-and-green-painted buoy bouncing in the waves, and after that we repeated the process a dozen more times, until my eyes were nearly bugging out of my head.

Finally only a few lonesome buoys still bobbed like brightly painted bits of mischief, and I made my way back to the cockpit.

"Everything okay?" I asked. Ellie stood at the wheel, calmly piloting us through the night.

"So far," she replied, not very comfortingly. But it was better than nothing, so I went below, where I switched on a few of the cabin lights and plugged our handy little two-cup coffeemaker into the accessory panel.

Busying myself didn't make me feel any less anxious, though.

"So listen. What if it really is a trap?" I handed a steaming mug to Ellie while she steered us I-still-didn't-know-where.

"And where *are* we going, anyway? What makes you think you know where the *Jenny* might be?"

"Well, if you were a sailboat," she replied, "where would *you* hide? With a lot of *other* sailboats, that's where. And with other small boats in general."

"Huh?" I drank some hot coffee and felt my brain cells start bouncing around like basketballs until a few of them went through the hoop; painfully, but they did it.

Then, "Ohhh." In the salt-smelling darkness and the roar of our engine, we passed the channel marker off Buckman's Head, a high bluff at the island's south end. From here we could continue south to the shoreline town of Lubec, or—

"Skeleton Cove," I pronounced, and she nodded approvingly; it was a popular anchoring spot for boats that couldn't—or preferred not to—tie up in the boat basin.

"All those boats sitting on moorings there," I said, "you think the *Jenny* might've—"

"That's where I'd go," Ellie agreed, keeping her eyes on the GPS screen as the cross-currents past the channel marker started shoving the Bayliner around.

"Hardly anyone but locals know about it, so I'd slide in among the other boats and keep the sails down. No one's going to be there to notice, and in the dark you look just like everyone else, anyway."

Around us now the tides and the currents were converging to produce a sort of washing machine effect. I hoped we'd get out of it before the spin cycle began. But I couldn't say anything about it; I was too busy hanging onto the rail to work any muscles other than the ones in my fingers.

Besides, she already knew. A biggish wave hit us, and another. "This," she uttered grimly, "is how pirate ships ended up on rocks."

Not what I'd wanted to hear. But then a few minutes later—it only felt like an hour to me—"Okay, that's the end of that," she said with a sigh as we cleared Buckman's Head and the waves calmed.

The next thing we saw was the cargo port complex—buildings and piers and storage warehouses—and on the water the massive shape of the *Star Verlanger*, the ocean-going cargo ship that Wade had piloted in the day before.

Ten stories high and lit up like a city, the big vessel bustled with rumbling, beeping industrial activity: tall cranes; pallet loaders; and, on the ramp leading down to it, trucks hauling flatbed trailers carrying containers the size of railroad boxcars.

In the hubbub we slipped by unnoticed, easing past the port and into the quiet cove beyond. Waves lapped our sides, *slop-slopping* as we slid along. An anchor chain clanked softly somewhere in the gloom, and a mooring ball bumped grittily against the prow of a vessel that had been made fast to it.

Then suddenly small boats were everywhere, floating so thickly around us that I could've jumped from deck to deck. But:

"Ellie, I don't see—" In the distant, fog-diffused glow from the *Star Verlanger*, these boats all looked alike.

She didn't reply, just moved the throttle up a hair, sneaking us in between an old Chris-Craft cabin cruiser and a battered skiff.

"Where?" I demanded, squinting, but then I spotted the *Jenny*, smaller than I remembered but still just as ominous-looking with her portholes dark and her black sails wrapped tightly around her mast.

I wouldn't have noticed her if I hadn't been looking carefully. I was about to whisper something about how Ellie had been right about that when suddenly she let out a string of expletives so creatively chosen and well arranged that my mouth just sagged open the rest of the way in surprise.

"Take the wheel," she snapped, then dropped us into reverse briefly before switching the key to off. Next, she dropped anchor and trimmed the engine up so that the propeller was out of the water.

Finally she scrambled past me to the stern once more and then out into the little well between the deck and the engine mount.

"Come on, don't do this to me," she breathed, peering out over the water at something I couldn't yet see.

Which did not increase my confidence. Meanwhile, we were approaching that big mooring ball I'd heard scraping, and now at last I spotted the beat-up little skiff I'd seen, sliding toward us fast.

The skiff hit us. "Damn," I said, "so much for stealth."

"Jake! Get back here! Grab that grappling hook!" Ellie gestured urgently at a long pole I'd thought must be part of a fishing rod.

It wasn't. "But . . ." I still didn't get what was going on.

"We snagged that skiff's mooring line. Hook the skiff so it can't get away," she said, and when I'd done so she leaned over our boat's side, flailing at the skiff's rail with the curved end of the long-handled grappling hook.

After drawing the small boat even nearer, she tumbled off our stern down into the little vessel. "Do not," she uttered darkly up at me, "let go of that hook."

So I didn't, but even at anchor our boat badly wanted to go one way and that skiff wanted to go the other. Now crouched in the smaller boat, Ellie fought to haul the snagged line away from the propeller.

Finally, the line inched grudgingly up from where it was caught under the prop, and then I really *was* the only thing keeping the skiff from floating away with Ellie still on it.

"Ugh," I said, as my arms seemed to stretch like the rubber-band extremities on animated cartoon characters.

Gasping, Ellie clambered halfway up out of the skiff. "Okay," she exhaled, which was when the grappling hook's wet shaft slipped through my hands and the skiff slid away very suddenly.

"Uh, Jake?" she managed. Her top half was on our boat, but her legs were still in the departing skiff, which now that it was freed of our propeller seemed seriously to be making a run for it.

"Ellie, come on," I urged desperately, reaching out for her as the skiff kept pulling away.

"*Oof!*" she replied, hauling herself ineffectively, so I let go of the hook, grabbed her with both hands, and pulled hard. She rolled the rest of the way into the boat.

Which should've been the end of it. But now the boat hook was floating away. It was a very nice boat hook, and I hated the idea of losing it, so I leaned down and snatched at it, and in my hurry to retrieve it I must've misjudged the distance in the dark.

And that's how I fell in.

Falling into the dark, frigid water of Skeleton Cove was like a punch in the throat, a sledgehammer to the chest, and blast of liquid nitrogen applied to the rest of my body. At once I was so cold, I could barely move.

But in a few minutes I wouldn't be able to move at all, I knew from the safety lectures Ellie had given me. So with my squinched-shut eyes stinging with salt water, I grabbed blindly at what I hoped was the Bayliner's swim ladder hanging off the back of the boat.

I'd missed it twice by the time Ellie noticed that I'd gone overboard; trying to yell had only produced a sickly gargling sound and distracted me from the more immediate project of not drowning.

When she did notice, she moved swiftly to toss me a life ring. I stuck an arm through it, and she hauled me closer until I could manage to clamber up the swim ladder and over the transom and then at last get back into the boat.

That ended the situation's drowning potential. The freezing part of the program, however, turned out to be more long-lasting.

"Oh. My. G-goodness." I was shivering so hard I was sure whoever was on the *Jenny* could hear my teeth chattering.

If anyone was. But there was still no sign of any activity on the dark vessel, now just a few hundred feet from us. No lights, no sound . . . She floated like a shadow with the lights from the distant cargo dock glimmering faintly on the waves around her.

"Don't talk." Ellie tore the life jacket off me and hustled me below, into the Bayliner's little cabin. Luckily we kept dry clothes there, and in a few minutes I was dry, too, drinking more hot coffee and toweling my hair.

But I couldn't stop shivering. My hands kept on shaking, and I didn't dare speak, because I knew whatever I said wouldn't make a lick of sense, as Bella would've put it.

And the icy lump of fear in my chest wouldn't dissolve, either. Finally, though, I went back up on deck and found Ellie just sitting there staring at the *Jenny* with her cell phone in her hand.

"What, are you going to call them?" I waved at the dark vessel. "Tell them we're here and to turn the porch light on for us?"

She looked up, pleased to see me moving around and talking. I didn't tell her that my head felt like it might explode, because why bother? My headache was the least of our worries, and anyway she couldn't do anything about it.

"I'm trying to figure out how we're going to board that boat. Secretly," she added.

I sat beside her. "Look, it's been a good attempt, but maybe we should just go. . . ."

Home. Not only was I nearly at the end of my rope physically, but every time I thought I understood one half of whatever was going on, the other half went haywire on me.

Ellie wasn't about to give up, though. "Do you know where your husband is?" she asked. "And mine, too, and probably even Sam?"

"In bed, sound asleep?" I replied hopefully

Or in Wade's case, sitting up watching the late-night sports shows and waiting for me to get home. I hadn't spoken with him in hours, I realized with a sudden pang of guilt.

But Ellie was already shaking her head. "Remember all those little boats we saw a little while ago, jockeying around to get a good place for watching the fireworks show?" She didn't let me answer. "They were out there because the show's on for tonight, word about it must've gotten around, and that means . . ."

"Oh no," I uttered as what she was saying finally got through to me.

Because it meant Wade was out there. I hadn't been thinking clearly enough to realize it earlier, but every year he was part of the crew that fired off the fireworks canisters from a barge just off Eastport.

And if he went, Sam would go too, probably, and Ellie's husband, George, as well, if he hadn't already left for Bangor when he heard.

"Once he heard the show was on, George would go out and get the girls from the slumber party, too, wouldn't he?" I said, feeling a thrill of horror run through me.

"He wouldn't want them to miss it," she agreed, holding up the phone. "I tried to call them, but nobody's answering."

Of course they weren't. If the men were anywhere near the barge-load of fireworks right now, their phones were off; theoretically there was no danger, but Wade was in charge of safety and didn't want the tiniest spark from a phone or anything else near the explosives.

"No one at your house is answering, either," Ellie said, "and now the phone service is getting spotty. So . . ."

Oh, Lord; Bella loved fireworks. They might've all bundled up against the night's chill and headed downtown, where they'd be right in the line of fire if any should occur.

Which I was fairly sure it would; sure, the *Jenny* was here right now, but it wouldn't take her long to get back over there and into menacing position.

"Try the radio?" I suggested. "The Coast Guard, or call 911?"

She sighed heavily. "Tried 'em both, but the radio's finally crapped out, I'm afraid. It won't go on at all, and 911 dispatch says one of those drones they've been flying around downtown just hit the comm tower on High School Hill."

The comm tower was the way everyone's cell phone signals got routed around here; our island was too remote to use the tower on the mainland. I must've made a face.

"Right," she responded bleakly. "Phone service is iffy until they get someone to go up the tower and fix it."

So maybe *that's* why no one answered the phone at home . . . or it's what I told myself, anyway. But the way things were going around here I didn't feel optimistic about that.

"Meanwhile, we've got about an hour left to do something about all this," Ellie went on. "After that . . ."

Right. I glanced at the time on my own phone. The fireworks would start at midnight if they kept to the original schedule as I expected they would, and by now it was 10:45.

"Ellie, does the *Jenny* have a swim ladder like the Bayliner's, d'you suppose?"

I didn't know for sure what was going to happen in an hour and fifteen minutes if we didn't manage to intervene somehow, but the more I thought about it, the more I was betting on kablooie.

"Yes, I think I saw a ladder. But getting on isn't the problem, you know," said Ellie. "Our getting over there without them noticing is the problem."

I understood. The quiet thrum of our engine coming in here very slowly had been one thing; I could imagine them not hearing that. But the var-*ROOM* of the outboard's startup was hard to miss.

And if this was indeed a trap, the last thing we wanted was to meet their welcoming committee.

"So what if we just *floated* up to them?" I said. "Quietly."

Ellie frowned, her face pale and unreadable in the moonlight. "You mean . . . but . . . oh, I see. Just—"

I jumped up. "Yup. Tide's rising, now. See it all going by us? And it'll carry us along, too, if we let it."

On the water, clumps of seaweed with driftwood tangled in them sailed serenely by on the incoming current, moving swiftly toward the innermost inlets of Skeleton Cove.

And toward the *Jenny*. "Because you're right," I said, "we need to get on that boat. If we don't, whoever called us on my phone is going to do something bad. I don't think they were lying about that."

Ellie got up, pacing the deck in the near darkness. "I'm not sure how close I can get us with no engine. It'll be dicey."

But moments later she was scrambling out onto the foredeck to haul up our anchor. Ripples streamed silently against our hull as we began drifting on a slow, stealthy collision course with the *Jenny*.

"Ellie?" I whispered.

Ahead, the sailboat loomed gloomily like a ship out of a dark fairy tale.

"I'm here," she whispered from out on the Bayliner's foredeck, where she hunkered. "I've got to be ready to drop the anchor again at the right moment, so we get close enough and stay there."

That gave me pause. Her hauling up the anchor and our getting going at all had been such an important moment—

Adrift! Dark water! Collision course!

—that I hadn't thought too much about the stopping part.

But of course there would be one, and as the *Jenny*'s black hull drew rapidly nearer I spied Ellie leaning out with the anchor in her hands. The tide ran fast here, and we'd closed the last few dozen yards swiftly.

"Ellie, look out, we're going to—"

The anchor splashed. Too late, though. Bracing myself, I gripped the rail and hung on.

"Um, Ellie?" Because any instant we'd be slamming into—

But we didn't. Instead our vessel stopped forward-motioning with a jarring lurch and began to swing around until we were nestled flat alongside the *Jenny*'s stern. Her shiny gold name's elaborately curled script gleamed high above our deck, and above that two round white life rings hung from her stern rail.

There was still no sound from her. No handy escalator or elevator from our deck to hers, either, unfortunately. In fact, I did not see any swim ladder, which would've made the whole thing much easier.

I squinted puzzledly, trying to figure out how we were going to get aboard. Then a new thought hit me: Maybe we couldn't. Maybe we'd have to give up in defeat, and instead of this harebrained adventure we'd just have to come up with something else.

Personally I believed I could think about it much more usefully while standing in a hot shower, but—

"Jake." Uh-oh. "Jake?"

That didn't sound good. It didn't sound bad, exactly, but . . .

"Jake, come on out here."

I climbed up and out onto the foredeck, where Ellie still perched somewhere, stepping carefully since it was dark here in the shadow of the *Jenny.*

"Where are you?" I whispered, peering.

"Here," she said, and then I saw her and wished I hadn't, because what *she* was doing was what *I* was going to be doing very soon unless a lightning bolt struck me—at the moment I'd have definitely preferred one—and what she was doing, exactly, was this:

With her sneakered feet balanced precariously on the rail of our own vessel, she was holding on with both hands to the lower rung of a rope ladder hanging down off the stern of the *Jenny*.

Which raised my suspicions at once, even aside from the bolt of sheer fright that the sight of that ladder shot through me, so intense it was like an out-of-body experience.

"How'd that get here?" I said, partly to postpone the whole idea of me being *on* the ladder; oh, I just loathed the notion.

"Because if they just now threw it over," I said, "it means they really did know we were coming, and *that* means . . ."

"Yup. Like I've been saying." Ellie nodded grimly. "Probably a trap. Now, steady my legs," she added, adjusting her grip on the ladder dangling from the *Jenny*'s stern.

I hurried to comply. Falling in at all would be bad enough, I knew from my own unhappy experience, but if she did it here, she'd be stuck *between* the two vessels.

I wrapped my arms around her jeans-clad calves.

"Not so tight." Her whole body swayed with the movement of the two boats, and I felt her feet slip.

"Ellie!" I cried in alarm. Then both her legs wriggled suddenly out of my grasp and she was gone, scrambling away from me up the rope ladder in the dark.

"Come on!" she called softly to me from above. "You can do it!" But then, "Oh, I think there's someone . . . Jake, hurry!"

"Yeah, right," I muttered, still hesitating. But if I stopped to think about it much longer, I would never manage it, and I couldn't let her down, I just couldn't.

So I took a few deep breaths and crawled up onto that rail, and then I just kept on going, damn it, not stopping until I stood with my hands over my head, swaying wildly while grabbing for the ladder.

It dangled elusively as the water and the boats moved, first one way and then the other. Snatching at it, I staggered scarily, then regained the vestiges of balance that I could and snatched at it again.

This time the rough hemp strands of the rope brushed my fingers, then slipped through them. Teetering, I grabbed for it one more time, and this time I caught it.

"You're doing great!" Ellie called softly, her face showing pale from high above me on the *Jenny*.

Wade did this all the time, transferring from the pilot boat to a waiting cargo ship so he could pilot the big vessel into port. *People do this*, I recited to myself, *and I am a people, therefore I can*—

I put my left foot out, settled it onto a rung. The *Jenny* moved away from me. Or possibly I leaned away from it.

But for whatever reason, now my right foot was on the ladder's rung and my left was still solidly on the Bayliner's rail, with me in the air between them.

Also, one hand was still waving around. Then my left foot lost contact with the Bayliner.

All I needed was an eye patch and a sword clenched in my teeth and I'd have fit right in with the pirate festival, boarding this dratted boat. Struggling, I swung my free hand back around to the rope ladder but it kept *moving*. . . .

Moving a *lot*. Then from the corner of my eye I spied why: that cargo ship we'd passed on our way in here was easing away from the dock, deck lights blazing so that it resembled an inverted chandelier shining in the night.

And the ship's massive movement was creating waves; big ones, now rolling into Skeleton Cove.

Grimly, I grabbed for the ladder again with my right hand, then felt my left one slip. *Oops* . . .

The fall took a long instant. Then icy water surrounded me. The terror I felt was nearly as bad, and when I finally came up, gasping and choking, I found I was about to be crushed between the *Jenny* and the Bayliner's hull.

That stuff about your life flashing before your eyes is true, by the way. Meanwhile, I learned suddenly that when I have to, I can swim pretty fast.

But I couldn't do it for long. Suddenly I was out from between the two vessels, no longer about to be ground to a pulp between them. Also, though, I was still floundering, gasping, and splashing.

And to make things even worse, I'd taken off my life jacket when I'd changed out of my wet clothes and hadn't put it back on. So when the round white life ring sailed down out of the darkness at me and smacked onto the waves, I latched on to it so hard that I thought my arms might never unbend.

Which in the next moment turned out to be a good thing, since the life ring immediately rose up *off* the water again, as up there Ellie pulled hard, and went on rising with me hanging on to it for dear life.

Meanwhile, I was once again (a) wet, (b) scared witless—some say the witless part is just my natural condition, but never mind—and (c) chilled to the bone yet again. In moments I found myself level with the boat's rail and then toppling over it, onto the *Jenny*'s deck.

"*Oof*," I said quietly, blinking in the gloom.

No one peered back. "Hello?" I whispered, still ice-cold but beginning to feel hopeful. Maybe we really *had* sneaked onto the . . .

From the darkness behind me two hands swooped, snatching the life ring away. A rope looped around me so fast that I couldn't stop it, lashing my arms to my sides.

"Up," said a voice. A woman's voice . . .

Darn. Glumly I struggled to my knees, then rocked back onto my feet and managed to stand up; not gracefully, mind you, and not even on the first try, but I did it.

Dim deck lights were burning now, so I could see that the boat was much larger than I'd thought, with a long, wide deck area and the black-sail-wrapped mast sticking up in the middle of it.

A wet bar had been set up near the hatchway to the cabins that must be belowdecks; deck chairs, folding tables, and shade umbrellas were attached by bungee cord to cleats set into the rail, along with more flotation devices and some flat-topped wooden barrels that I thought might be used as food-serving stations.

In other words, this place was . . . but I didn't have time to finish that thought.

"Walk," said the figure holding me, and I didn't have much choice about that, either, so I obeyed once more: straight ahead across the *Jenny*'s shadowy deck, through the small open hatchway gaping ominously, and down a set of steps—there were three of them and they were carpeted, I recall that part very clearly—into the dark.

On the bottom step, I thought about turning and running, getting back up onto the deck somehow and yelling . . . but the cargo port and the cargo ship departing from it were too far away for anyone to hear me.

And anyway, before I could do any of those things, someone came up from behind me and bonked me on the head with something.

I saw stars, then nothing at all.

When I came to, I was in a small paneled cabin with a porthole, a pair of side-by-side bunks, and a wooden straight chair. I was on a cot, trussed up like a cartoon heroine who is about to be tied to the railroad tracks. And I had the headache that ate Chicago.

"Hey." It was Ellie, propped in the chair, tied around the waist just like I was but otherwise okay.

"Hey, yourself." I wiggled experimentally, but of course there was no slack in the rope binding my arms to my sides.

"We're underway," she said.

Moving, she meant. The *Jenny* was going somewhere.

"So I guess it was a trap after all," she said.

Yeah, and it worked. Oh, terrific. . . . Sucking in a deep breath, I sat up; good heavens, that hurt.

My head, my arms, my chest . . . groaning, I swung my legs over the cot's edge and tried to stand so I could see through the porthole.

But instead my knees turned to jelly, and I sat down hard again, this time on the floor.

And I was so *cold.* "Jake!"

I rolled over and struggled back up onto my knees. "Wha?" My mouth wasn't working too well, either.

"Come closer," she urged. "And turn your back to me."

"Urk," I replied, but she kept nagging at me until I did it.

"Now, hold still," she said.

Her forehead bumped the middle of my back. "What are you . . . ?"

But then I got it; she had the knot in her teeth and was trying to loosen it. Finally, she created enough slack in the ropes.

"Oh," I moaned, rubbing my arms, but then I got right to work, too, and moments later she was free of her own bindings.

And she was ripping mad. Ellie stomped to the slatted wooden door of the little cabin—two narrow bunks, a tiny washstand, two reading lights, one for each bunk—and yanked on it.

Locked. Of course. "Oh, give me a break," she said disgustedly.

She grabbed the wooden chair and smashed it against the door until the slats broke, then reached through and unlocked the door from the outside.

"Ellie," I breathed, "shouldn't we at least try being quiet? I mean"—I babbled on as she hauled me out through the demolished door—"from everything I've ever heard about sneaking around, one of the first rules is that you need to be very, very—"

"Jake," she grated, "I know. I really do. But what we need most right now is to be *up there on that deck.*"

"Huh?" We reached the hatchway we'd been hustled down through. On the other side of its door, slatted like the cabin's, a battery lamp burned low, its sullen orange glow seeping between the slats.

I put my face to the slats. Beyond it, the lantern shone upward through the murk onto the faces of three people hunched forward.

The deck lamps had been turned off again. The night was silent. "We need to be out there, to find out what they're up to," Ellie said.

She had a point. Besides, down here they could trap us again; they knew the boat's whole layout and we didn't.

"Tying us up and stowing us away *now* doesn't mean they won't kill us *later*. It just means they haven't done it yet, maybe because they're busy getting ready to do something else," she added.

Right again; something *not good*. "There's not going to be anywhere to jump to, either," I agreed, "no place where we can make the swim to shore until we get wherever they're going."

At this point I had a fairly good idea of where that might be, too, because looming behind the dim-lit figures on deck, a familiar shape hunkered. A *black* shape, blocky below and round above . . .

It was the cannon from my garden shed, the one that Wade had cleaned on the back lawn and that Sam had put on the porch so as not to hit it with his lawn mower. Where it could be seen from the street, and had been stolen, and under the circumstances there was no point to stealing it, I thought, unless someone meant to . . .

Voices approached. "Quick!" Ellie whispered as we slipped out through the hatchway door onto the shadowy deck and hustled behind one of the big wooden barrels positioned against the *Jenny*'s rail. Lashed there, because you sure wouldn't want *that* thing rolling around loose when you hit rough seas, especially if it just happened to have a tray of canapes and some champagne flutes on it. . . .

The thought prodded my brain again. Why was this boat set up for food service? Because clearly it was, but right now I had more urgent questions to ponder.

Like whether we would survive this. Crouched in the gloom, we held our breaths as the three shapes that had been huddled around the lantern gathered at the rail. Then a fourth person popped out of the hatchway from which we'd just emerged.

"They got out." It was Amity Jones. Angrily she stalked toward the figures at the rail, gripping a flashlight.

"Well, look for them." I recognized Willetta Beck's voice. "They can't be far, can they?" She sounded shaky but determined.

The others stepped forward, wincing when the flashlight's beam crossed their faces: one was Lionel, Henry Hadlyme's unacknowledged son, in skinny pants and a down jacket. Beside Lionel stood Karen Carrolton, with her thick gray braid and coal-dark eyes, wearing a dark sweatshirt, pants, and boots.

What the heck?" Ellie murmured beside me.

"Yeah," I agreed, startled at the sight of all of them together on the *Jenny*. "I guess murder's a team sport now."

The important word being *team*: none of them could've done it alone, I realized, any more than I could've run my whole household by myself. Together, though . . .

Lionel spoke. "Listen, ladies," he began hesitantly. "I've gone along with all of this so far. So don't get me wrong, but—"

Amity Jones turned smoothly. "Oh, what shouldn't we get wrong, Lionel? The fact that this was all your idea in the first place?"

His mouth dropped open. "My idea? What're you talking about, you were the one who—"

"Children." Willetta Beck's voice cracked like a horsewhip. "Find them, please. You can quarrel later."

Lionel stomped over and leaned against the barrel we were crouching behind, his posture rebellious. After lighting a cigarette, he blew its pale smoke into the chilly night. "Find them yourself."

He flicked the match over his shoulder. "Killing Henry was one thing. He deserved it. But the rest of this—"

The match landed in my hair, which fortunately was still wet, and have I mentioned that I was freezing to death?

"We said we'd help you if you helped us, Lionel." It was Karen Carrolton this time. "That was the deal, remember? Or are you saying now that you want to back out?"

She stepped forward menacingly. Lionel shrank a little but held his ground.

"I'm saying Henry's dead. That's what we all wanted. This stuff about getting revenge on Eastport, too—"

"Is none of your business," said Amity Jones.

I'd almost forgotten she was a cop, but her service weapon glinting in her shoulder rig reminded me, a stray flashlight beam bouncing off its blue-steel grip.

Oh, great. I nudged Ellie; she sighed minutely, nodding to let me know she'd seen it, too. So even if we *did* jump . . .

"Henry was just the half of it," said Willetta Beck. "What he did to your mother was criminal. Not just leaving her in the lurch the way he did, but turning the town against her."

She turned to Amity Jones, who was going around the deck poking that damned flashlight beam at every shadowy place. Soon she'd reach the one we were hunkered in.

"He told everyone she was crazy, hysterical, that she needed to be in care. An *institutional*," Willetta emphasized, "care facility."

"Which by that time she practically was, what with the way he'd lied to her and then abandoned her," Karen put in. "He even told her that if he went away and made good the way he planned, he'd be back."

That flashlight beam bobbed worrisomely nearer. Lionel flicked his cigarette over the rail.

"I know all this," he said impatiently. "So *he* got to look like the hero, leaving in hopes of being able to provide for his family—"

"When all he really wanted was to chase fame and fortune," Amity Jones finished for him, turning away just as the flashlight was about to invade our hiding place. "Not for her, for *himself.*"

"Fine, like I said, I get all that," Lionel retorted. "I've known it all along. But what did the rest of Eastport do to any of you that was so bad?"

Karen Carrolton's reply was even colder than the water around us. "Nothing. They just believed him. Everyone did. It's why she couldn't get a job here, or a place to live on her own. They all believed she was crazy."

"It's why," Willetta Beck added softly, "no one investigated her murder. They just assumed she'd committed suicide, and that was that."

The seas beneath us got rough again suddenly; by now we were coming back through the cross-currents around Buckman's Head toward the boat basin and the lights of downtown Eastport.

"Fine," Lionel said. "I get that. And I understand why Amity is involved, too." His voice softened. "Funny how I've gone so long thinking I had no family. Then I found Horrible Henry—that's what I've been calling him—and now I find out I've got a sister."

Somebody switched some deck lamps back on again, I didn't see who. I looked from Lionel's face to Amity's, seeing as if for the first time: *Of course.*

Two peas in a pod, as Bella would've said, and never mind the different fathers they'd had; I should have seen it sooner, only she wore so much makeup that I couldn't have.

Wore it deliberately, maybe, so nobody would guess. "But

now that I do know, I've got to live with all this somehow," Lionel said. "With whatever really happened to Henry," he added carefully.

Too carefully, I thought, as after a moment Amity spoke up. "I've known who Henry was all along," she told Lionel. "I've known because Aunt Will and Aunty Karen had told me about him."

Lionel leaned back hard against the barrel, which to my amazement didn't shift—not quite. My heart settled back down into my chest.

"After our mother Anna Benoit died, *her* mother died, too," Amity said. "So I had no one. But Karen and Willetta took charge of me and eventually sent me to a convent school in Bangor."

"So you're my . . . my aunts?" Lionel questioned the two older women. "My mother's sisters?"

They nodded together. "When Amity phoned us to say Henry was on his way to Eastport, of course we were interested," Willetta said.

"And after she got you two on board with her plan, that's when she called me." Lionel went silent, working it out in his head; then his voice rose angrily. "You'd known about me, too? Where I was and what I was doing?"

"Yes. But there wasn't anything that I could do about—"

"He took me to Manhattan," Lionel cut in harshly. "Stuck me in a private orphanage where he was working as a cook's helper so he could pay his way through culinary school." He sucked in an angry breath. "By the time I was eight, I'd run away. Somehow I latched on to a documentary photographer who was doing a series on the characters who hang out in Penn Station."

Ellie nudged me, a squint of puzzlement on her face. A thought had just struck her. Me too, suddenly, as the *Jenny* went on making its way through the bounding waves around Buckman's Head.

"Guy wasn't a creep, by some miracle. He started letting me do errands for food and a place to sleep. Pretty soon I knew the darkroom chores, too, and I could pack his kit: film, lenses, lighting gear." Lionel sighed. "And the rest is history. A few years later when I applied for a job on the *Eat This!* podcast team, Henry interviewed me. And he didn't even recognize me."

But Lionel had known Henry. An unpleasant chuckle escaped him. "I'd kept track of him, you see," he added in a voice that made me glad it hadn't been me he was keeping track of.

Behind us, the hatchway we'd come out of gaped darkly; if we got down there again unnoticed, maybe we could find a better hiding place.

"I'm sorry," Amity said, hearing the hurt in Lionel's tone. "I'm sure that he wouldn't have known me either."

Again with the careful talk. She didn't want to admit that she'd seen Henry up close at all before he died.

"Anyway, let's find them," she said, changing the subject. She meant me and Ellie. "If they're overboard, good riddance. If they're not . . ."

She drew a finger across her throat, and considering what else she'd apparently been up to lately—I still didn't understand all of it but what I did know was bad enough—that was enough for me.

"Hurry," I murmured to Ellie as we backed up toward the hatchway opening on our hands and knees.

"Right," she muttered. She knew by now, too, that somehow Amity Jones was at the dark heart of all this.

Whatever *this* was. Inching backward, my shoes bumped against the hatchway's threshold. Beside me, Ellie stopped also.

"What?" I whispered.

"Look." Ellie pointed with her gaze at Wade's cannon, mounted on the boat's stern. All it needed was a lit match.

And as my friend had just realized, we couldn't leave it like that. "Ellie, d'you still have the big screwdriver in that satchel of yours?"

The satchel had been hanging from around her neck when she had climbed the rope ladder. Although the tool wouldn't still be in it, of course; I'd had to ask but there wasn't enough good luck in the world for that big screwdriver to still be—

Without looking she plunged her hand down into the bag—it had been tossed under one of the bunks in the cabin when our captors tossed us there earlier, and fortunately they'd been too careless or distracted to notice it when they left us, so Ellie had found it again—and came up with the screwdriver. Big, chunky handle, thick, steel shaft, sharp-edged blade . . .

She passed it to me.

"The right tool really does make all the difference," I said, feeling a bit more hopeful, suddenly. They hadn't yet dumped us overboard, after all, so we were ahead in that department at least.

Ellie crept backward yet again toward the open hatchway while I made my way toward the stern and the cannon mounted on it. Mounted with screws, I hoped—with heads that this screwdriver would fit. If it didn't . . .

But I didn't want to think about that. Whatever had hit downtown Eastport the day before was going to look like nothing compared to the damage that old cannon could do to a lot of fireworks watchers.

So I had to stop it. I just had to. Also:

"Ellie." She paused. "Ellie, find out who's driving the boat. Get control if you can."

She nodded silently and vanished into the gloom while I slid along the deck toward the cannon, now only a few feet away in the near-darkness. The quarreling foursome still huddled amidships with their backs turned to me.

"You knew I was out there somewhere," Lionel was saying to Amity Jones. "You could've saved me."

From a life as a kid on the street in Manhattan . . . yeah, I guessed he could've used some saving, I thought as I scrunched myself against the *Jenny*'s transom where the cannon was mounted. Not too sturdily, I hoped, since all I had was that one screwdriver.

We were just off Eastport now, sliding past the end of the fish pier. In the lights from the end of it, the screw heads glinted.

". . . could've gotten in touch with *me*," Amity was retorting hotly to Lionel's rebuke.

"Me? I didn't even know you existed, I didn't know *anything*," he maintained, but she wasn't buying it.

"Don't give me that, when I called you knew exactly who I—"

"Is that true, Lionel? Did you really know all about us up here?" Karen Carrolton asked.

Her voice was very even and calm. Dead calm. Without wanting to, I remembered the chicken with its neck wrung in the yard of her little subsistence farm out in the puckerbrush.

"Keeping track of us, too, were you? Maybe even planning a little revenge of your own?" she asked mildly.

Four bolts inexpertly placed through the slots on the base of the cannon held the gun to the boat's transom. Luckily, each bolt had a groove in its top so that in a pinch, a screwdriver blade could slot into it, and in the fish pier lights I could manage to see the slots.

Still shivering hard from the dunking I'd had earlier, I lifted the screwdriver. The *Jenny* had stopped, or at least the shoreline had quit sliding by, but I still felt the rumble of diesel engines idling from somewhere under the deck.

But never mind them, I told myself firmly; we didn't have much time. Ellie had tied a wine-bottle cork on a string through a hole she'd drilled in the tool's handle, so in case she dropped it off the boat, she could retrieve it.

Still shivering, I pushed aside the cork on its string and put the blade's end into the slot on the first bolt head, and—

Splash! The screwdriver hit the water before I realized that I'd dropped it.

Shocked, I looked down at the water where the cork bobbed, far out of reach. Then I looked at my hand, still not quite believing that it was empty.

But it was, and what the heck was I going to do now?

Ten

"*Psst.*" The sound came from below me, down on the water where the screwdriver had vanished.

Which was ridiculous, there couldn't be anybody—

"*Psst.*" But what the heck, this night had already gone nuts; what were a few disembodied voices among friends?

I leaned over the transom, trying not to go where the screwdriver had gone. The rope ladder that had given me so much trouble earlier still dangled there, and at the bottom of it—

"Hey!" Timmy Franco's round freckled face beamed up at me. He was jockeying his rowboat in the backwash from the *Jenny*'s engine with some skillful jujitsu of those hand-built oars of his.

"You guys okay?" He grabbed onto the rope ladder.

"No! We're not." Behind me, the four murder-plotters—or that's what I guessed they were, anyway; however much they wanted to deny it to one another, they sure sounded as if they'd done it all as a team—moved toward the hatchway.

This, I thought, boded ill for Ellie, still belowdecks somewhere. Another sound came from the water. I peered over the stern in alarm.

"Timmy, what're you *doing* down there . . . oh, no. Oh, wait."

But in the moment when I'd looked away, he'd tied his row-boat to a cleat in the *Jenny*'s hull and was halfway up the rope ladder, sure-footed and happy as a little clam.

"Hi, Jake!" He beamed at me over the transom, then hopped over it to crouch with me behind a stack of folded deck chairs.

"What're we doing?" He hunkered down comfortably, hands clasped on his bent knees.

"Timmy, listen, I don't have time to explain, but I need you to get back in your boat, get to shore real quick, and find Bob Arnold. Or—Timmy, you don't have a phone on you, do you? A cell phone?"

He'd had one the other day, out on his boat. But it was too much to hope for that he had one now; even if the phones turned out to be working again, Tim was the opposite of the modern constantly-device-equipped person.

His idea of "online" was a fish on a hook with a frying pan not far behind. But then he surprised me, producing a cell phone from his pocket. I thumbed the on button.

The screen lit up, and Timmy grinned. "Good, huh? Cheap little Walmart special, but it works."

"Very good," I agreed, flinging an arm around him and hugging his shoulders. "Tim, this is wonderful."

"Thanks," he uttered shyly as I punched in Bob Arnold's number.

Nothing happened. Behind me, Tim fiddled at something with the screwdriver I'd dropped, because of course he'd grabbed it up out of the water.

I dialed again: nothing. "Come on, come on. . . ."

This time the call connected and the phone at the other end rang.

"You've reached the City of Eastport police department. Please hold, or if this is an emergency please dial . . ."

Which meant that Bob was so busy, he was sending all his calls to the dispatcher. Then the phone itself went dead.

"Argh!" I whispered, not quite hurling the thing into the drink. Now I would have to go down that rope ladder, which was approximately the last thing I felt like doing, and maneuver my way into Tim's boat, which was the other last thing I felt like doing.

But things were too fraught to let Timmy do it, so getting to shore and finding Bob Arnold was my only option. Or at least I thought it was one until I spotted Tim's rowboat floating away from where it had been tied to the *Jenny*.

Before I could think about what this meant, all the deck lights snapped on. Blinking in the glare, I sank behind the deck chairs and yanked Timmy down with me.

"Keep quiet," I whispered.

"Look," Timmy murmured in reply, nudging me, and I poked my head up just as Amity Jones, Karen Carrolton, and Willetta Beck trooped up through the hatchway and out onto the deck again.

"I know I heard something . . . ," Amity Jones muttered, peering around suspiciously. With the lights on, she didn't need a flashlight anymore, and she was coming our way.

"Come on." When Amity turned her back, I grabbed Tim by his sweatshirt collar and hustled us both up and over the boat's transom and onto that damned rope ladder, again: me first, and then he got the idea and followed.

"Where's Ellie?" he wondered aloud softly.

I wondered it, too. Also, Lionel was missing from the group, and when I recalled the verbal dustup he'd had a little while ago with his half sister, Amity Jones, I felt uneasy about him.

And I still didn't know who was at the helm of this floating gun-wagon. I mean, somebody must be driving, but the probable candidates were all right there in front of me, not at the helm.

Halfway down the ladder I paused to catch my breath. That's how I noticed, behind the ladder, the four round brass-ringed holes in the *Jenny*'s stern, each about three inches across.

"Gun ports," said Tim interestedly, not seeming to understand our neck-deep peril.

They were where all the earlier gunfire had come from, I realized as he went on. "Somebody did a nice job of installing . . ."

Yeah, installing enough firepower to level a city, which still worried me, even though the gunports—and the cannon—were now all aimed out at the water, not at Eastport.

A chain rattled distantly; then came a familiar-sounding splash. It was the anchor, I was pretty sure. So we'd be staying awhile, even though from where I clung I could hear the boat's big engines still rumbling quietly.

In case a fast getaway was required, maybe? Come to think of it, I'd have liked one of those myself. But unless I engineered one of them, it wasn't going to happen; I was fresh out of ideas.

And now as if to put a sour cherry on an already inedible cake, I saw why we'd stopped with the boat's stern and guns facing the bay:

That's where the target was. "Tim?" I managed faintly. "Tim, is that boat I see out there the one for the . . . ?"

"Fireworks," Tim finished for me. "It sure is, only it's not a boat, it's a barge."

The fireworks for the pirate festival that Wade and Sam would be working on tonight, and George, too, probably.

"Must be about time for 'em," Tim said. "Got a lot of explosives on there, wouldn't be safe try'na light 'em from a fishing boat."

Right. But the barge wasn't going to be safe either, if . . .

A mechanism *inside* the gunports whirred, startling me so I just about leapt off that rope ladder; as it was, I was swinging one-handed for a minute there.

"Yeeps," I said, gripping the hemp rungs again.

Out on the water, the dim forms of men moved around on the barge. Mostly they were Eastport fellows, some who used explosives at their jobs on the logging crews and others like Wade and Sam who'd helped out every Fourth of July for years and knew just what to do.

Meanwhile, the tide, the breeze, and the currents had conspired to float Tim's little watercraft out past the breakwater's end, but now it had drifted back nearer to us again, just not quite near enough.

"Tim, if I snag it, could you get back into your own boat?"

It bobbed tantalizingly only a few feet from the rope ladder's bottom rung. I could grab it, I thought, but only if I—

There. One hand on the rope ladder, one foot swung out to give myself a little more reach . . .

And then the wet scrap of rope was in my hand, which would've been fabulous if only my foot hadn't chosen that moment to slip.

"Hang on, I gotcha." Tim scampered down that rope ladder like he'd been born to it, seized the back of my sweatshirt in one hand, and *heaved* me up past his own body onto the rungs above him.

I clung there, shaking. He'd snatched the rope as I went by, and he still had it. Down in the water his small boat waited patiently, an air of reproach seeming to cling to it as if it wondered why he'd let go of it in the first place.

"How . . . how'd you *do* that?" I quavered when I could speak again.

Which of course was not the big question right now, but it was the only one I could think of.

"What?" He looked puzzled, briefly. But then: "Oh, you mean . . . hey, I've been tossing lobster traps overboard an' haulin' 'em back up since I was a tadpole." He brushed off my amazement at his strength.

Then he let go of the ladder himself and dropped down into

his boat. "But I better get goin' now and try to find Bob Arnold for you, don't you think?"

Oh, boy, did I ever. "Yes!" I hissed, and in the next moment he was rowing silently away from *Jenny*, out of sight—leaving me alone there, clinging to a rope ladder in the dark, while out on the water that barge carrying all the fireworks might as well have had a glow-in-the-dark bull's-eye painted on it.

You could, I supposed, miss it from here; the cannon wasn't exactly a precision instrument in the target-hitting department.

The other guns, though—the ones inside the *Jenny*'s gunports. I still didn't know what they used for ammunition, but whatever it was, they shot a lot of it and they shot it fast, to judge at least by the damage they'd already done to downtown Eastport.

And now not only was the fireworks barge in range but all of Water Street would soon be filling with spectators for the fireworks display, which was why I had to do something even though I had no idea what, and Ellie was still on the *Jenny* somewhere, too . . .

Trapped, maybe. Needing me to come and get her. So I reluctantly unclamped one hand from the rope ladder, hauled myself upward, then unclamped the other hand and repeated the process.

At last I reached the top rung and peered over the transom— no one was on deck, again—then climbed over it past the cannon.

If I'd known how to operate it, I'd have made it inoperable, but I didn't. So instead I crept down onto the deck and across to the hatchway leading below. With my back flattened to the hatchway door, I looked right and left, unsure which way to go.

To the foredeck where the anchor chain must be? If I hauled up the anchor, the *Jenny* would drift and those guns wouldn't be lined up anymore with their intended target.

But if that happened, somebody onboard would do something about it. Drop anchor again, probably, and we'd be back where we'd started.

On the other hand, if I went below looking for Ellie, I could get caught there and that would be . . . let's just call it equally unhelpful.

While I wavered, out on the water the barge revved its engine, the men aboard her knowing from past years' experience where to position the barge for maximum fireworks visibility. I scanned around for something I might use for a weapon, but there wasn't anything: no boat hook, no broom handle, not even a hatch cover to clobber somebody with.

But then, wait a minute, I thought. A *sailing* vessel—

The sails, wrapped tight around the *Jenny*'s masts, were canvas with metal grommets set into their edges at intervals. No way could I ever get one of them down alone, even if I could think of something useful to do with it.

Which I couldn't. Where there were sails, though, there were probably . . .

Extra lines. Or ropes, as landlubbers like me still called them. But as I thought this, the women returned to the deck, popping up out of the hatchway as I shrank from it and dropped into a crouch.

This time they didn't turn the deck lights on, probably because the shore was filling with fireworks spectators and the women didn't want to be seen.

"You're sure you know how to fire that cannon?" Willetta Beck was asking Amity Jones worriedly. "So we don't get blown up ourselves?"

"Don't you trouble yourself about it," snapped Amity over her shoulder as she strode to the old weapon on the stern. "You'd be amazed what you can learn just by Googling it."

Fat chance, I thought. Looking it up online was one thing, but actually managing to fire an antique weapon was something else, especially if you didn't want to blow your face off.

Still, in this world dumb luck makes up for a lot of igno-
rance, I've noticed; thinking this while feeling around, I found a
handle to one of the boat's built-in storage bins along the rail.

The women were still looking the other way. The handle
turned, and the bin cover lifted, and inside was . . . rope! Neat
coils of the softest, flexiest, easiest-to-manipulate nylon rope
I'd ever handled.

Before this bunch got ahold of her, I thought, somebody must
have really liked the *Jenny* a lot. Which raised another question,
one I'd puzzled over before. *But never mind*, I thought again.
Amity Jones was getting ready to fire that cannon, so there was
no time for strategy or a rescue mission, not by Bob Arnold or
anyone else.

This cockamamie plan was going to work, or else—
No. Don't think about that, either. Just . . .
Just don't.

I slipped through the dark hatchway and hurried down a
short corridor past a couple of tiny cubicles like the one we'd
been kept in earlier, each with a pair of narrow bunks and a single
porthole. Next came the galley, and now I saw why the cabins
were so small: to make room for an expanded food preparation
area.

Stove, oven, fridge, even a chest freezer were cleverly positioned to use up as little space as possible; pots, pans, and serving implements hung on hooks, and plates were lined up on
edge in slots on a shelf near the ceiling.

The whole place looked smart, efficient, and very profes-
sional; photogenic, too, with its stainless steel surfaces and teak
trim, and those foot-friendly rubber mats on the floor.

This made me even more suspicious about whose boat the
Jenny might be. Or might have been. At the passageway's end,
three carpeted steps led up to another door, this one with a
window in it.

And through the window: fuel gauge, battery indicator, switches for lights and pumps . . . It was the *Jenny*'s helm, where all the controls and instruments were located, as well as the steering.

I couldn't see who was at the wheel. I tried the door handle: locked. I had a moment to wonder why it was locked, and then somebody touched me on the shoulder and I nearly passed out from fright.

It was Ellie. Behind her, Lionel stood sullenly rubbing his wrists.

"Amity Jones can't tie a knot worth a darn," Ellie said with a grin, holding up a length of clothesline.

"Yeah, well, it was tight enough for me," Lionel grumbled. "And she must've wrapped it a million times around my wrists before she yanked it."

"Yes, well, you know what they say: If you can't tie a knot, tie a lot," Ellie replied mildly.

Right about then, I felt like tying one end around my waist and the other to the anchor and jumping overboard; if I was lucky, maybe some kindly shark would come along and put me out of my misery.

"How are you, anyway?" she added, peering at me.

"Terrible," I said, which was putting it mildly. By now my head felt as if someone was in there where my brains were, hammering their way out. "But come on, we've got to be quick."

We went back up on deck, where from out on the barge, men's voices carried across the water as they laughed and joshed with one another now that the fireworks preparation was finished. Amity Jones and her two aunts were near the boat's stern, conferring.

We still didn't know who was running the *Jenny*. But maybe we wouldn't have to. . . .

"Stretch this rope out," I told Lionel quietly, handing him a coil of the stuff I'd found just before I'd gone below.

Because I had a wild idea. "Run it back and forth across the deck," I told him. "That's right, just lay it down there. Make each length parallel to the one before, and a foot or so away."

He did as I asked, and then I got Ellie criss-crossing a set of rope lengths in the other direction. Moments later a loose web of soft, pliable strands lay neatly arranged on the deck's surface, like the diagram for a game of tic-tac-toe.

The women were still all huddled together by the cannon bolted to the stern. "What are they waiting for?" Lionel whispered. "And . . . you do know they're planning to fire that cannon, right?"

He waved at the hashtag pattern made of ropes, spread out on the dim-lit deck between the mast and the cabin hatchway. If you didn't know they were there, the ropes were almost invisible in the gloom.

But I could see them, and to me they looked just like what they were supposed to be: a trap, like the one they'd laid for us. Because as Ellie had said, we were getting too disruptive, I supposed, too likely to trip them up somehow. But now . . .

"I'll bet they're just waiting for the real fireworks to start," Ellie said. "So the explosions will cover the cannon fire."

That's what I thought, too. If it took a while for people to figure out what was happening, it would be just that much longer before anyone tried helping the guys on the barge, who were the actual targets now.

"But why?" Ellie added. "I mean, why would they have anything against the Eastport fireworks committee?"

Lionel's answering laugh came out a soft snort. "They don't. I heard all their plans before they decided I wasn't on their side."

He looked out at the dark water. "It's not those guys they want to hurt. It's everyone else. Like the aunts said, the ones who broke my mother's heart twenty years ago and didn't investigate her death. And their . . . their descendants, too, I guess."

"*Hmph,*" said Ellie. "We'll see about that." She turned to me. "What are we waiting for, anyway?"

I wasn't sure how I'd become the leader for this little adventure. But . . . "Patience," I said.

Onshore, more people crowded along the path above the boat basin and out onto the breakwater. Many had little kids in their arms or perched on their shoulders, eager for the fireworks display to begin.

I didn't see Bella, Mika, or Ephraim, or my dad's skinny figure, either. But that didn't mean they weren't there. Finally:

"Okay, you and Lionel go over there," I told Ellie, waving them both to the far side of the deck.

It was almost time. "Okay," I whispered, "each of you pick up an end of rope. That's right, one at each corner."

Out on the barge, a lighter flickered briefly, then went out. One of those long-nosed barbecue lighters, I supposed; no sense having to stick your hand right in there with the explosives to light them.

Meanwhile, near the cannon, the women's voices grew urgent. From what Wade had said, firing an antique cannon was tricky, and I hoped they'd give up before trying it despite Amity Jones's confidence.

But no such luck. "I'll do it," Amity Jones said.

What they wouldn't have known was how to load the thing; too bad Wade had prepared the weapon after cleaning it. So the cannonball, explosive charge, and a fuse to light it all up were already in there, ready to go.

Amity lit a match. Out on the barge, somebody lit that barbecue igniter again, too, the tiny fire flickering in the dark.

Onshore, the crowd's excited murmuring increased until it was audible even way out here on the *Jenny.*

"Get ready," I heard Amity Jones say.

Get ready, I mouthed to Lionel and Ellie, who each held a rope end. I held one also, and I'd tied the fourth to a cleat on the rail so that the ropes lying on deck were the equivalent of a net, and now I meant to catch someone in it.

Several someones. . . . Amity stepped forward to light the fuse on the cannon, and—

Brring! A bright musical trilling erupted from my back pocket. What the . . . ? *Brringgg!-brringg!*

It was the phone Tim Franco had given me. I grabbed reflexively for it, but the three women gathered by the cannon had already heard it; they rushed toward us.

Which had been my plan all along, actually, although the phone hadn't been. So *here goes nothing . . .*

"Pull!" I yelled, and Ellie and Lionel did. So did I, whereupon the rope trap we'd set up on deck tangled niftily around the ankles of the three murderous plotters hurling themselves at us.

Too bad that even after Lionel had abandoned them, there was still another one.

"Hello, Jake." Timmy Franco's freckled face appeared in the cabin hatchway opening. Then the rest of him emerged, crossed the deck to me swiftly, and seized my wrists in his strong hands.

The next thing I knew, I was on my back with my hands tied.

"Sit up." Ellie and Lionel were tied, too, lying there on the hard deck right beside me.

"*Mmph*," I said, wincing, then lurched up as I remembered: *Wade. Sam and George and the rest, on the fireworks barge . . .*

The crowd still massed on the shore; out on the water, the barge loaded with the equivalent of who knew how much dynamite—

Enough to kill them all, surely . . .

—still floated peacefully. "Tim, *why?*"

He smiled sadly. "Why do you think? Or did you think that when I get old and poor, even poorer than now, you'll take me in to live with you and your family?"

He finished the knot he was tying around my ankles. "So you've been on the boat all along?" I asked. "And after you gave me the phone and rowed away . . ."

He nodded. "Came right back again. You were busy, so I just kept out of sight behind you."

The same way we'd stayed behind the three plotting women: in the dark, we just hadn't seen him.

"And by the way," he added, "in case you're wondering, that rope ladder you're probably counting on, to escape?"

A mischievous grin spread on his face. "Kaput," he pronounced, waving toward the *Jenny*'s stern where it now lay in a tangled heap.

"But Tim, how will you ever—"

Get away? I meant to finish, but he took a different meaning.

"Live with myself?" A bitter chuckle escaped him. "Jake, for a guy like me, the question's a lot simpler than that. It's, like, how will I live at all." He shook his head sadly. "Everybody in Eastport thinks the same as you. 'Good old Tim, never has a dime but he'll get along somehow. He always does.'"

He checked the knots at my wrists. "But you know, winter's coming again, and I don't think I can spend any more nights sleeping rough," he finished. "I just don't think so."

Back by the cannon, the women had regrouped to complete their evil deed. But now it seemed the fuse wouldn't light.

That, or it *had* lit and then fizzled out. And I knew from hearing Wade discuss it that it was risky business, lighting a too-short fuse. To do it, you had to get *really close* to the cannon, and when it went off—

Boom! An explosion split the night. I thought my heart might jump right out of my chest.

But it wasn't the cannon, which still hunkered stubbornly unfired back on the *Jenny*'s stern. Instead a bright-white chrysanthemum with a crimson center bloomed on the dark sky, its fiery tendrils twining.

"They've started," Ellie murmured while Lionel looked daggers at Tim. We were tied up with enough of that loose rope to braid a—

A ladder. Which of course I couldn't do, or anyway not on such short notice. But . . .

Wait a minute. You can climb a rope ladder. But you can also climb a—

You could climb the rope itself, I realized desperately, and more to the point right now, you could slide *down* one. That is, if you really had to. And Tim would've tied his own boat to the *Jenny* again when he came back aboard, right?

So it was down there, probably.

"Ellie! Lionel!" I kept my voice low; somehow I had to get them onto their feet and following me, and they had to do it *fast.*

"Come on, hurry!" Because we weren't being rescued; Tim hadn't ever gone to alert Bob Arnold. Those guys on the barge weren't being saved, either, or any of the people onshore.

Not unless we saved them. Not to mention ourselves.

"Move!" I said urgently. Tim had gone back to the helm, and now was our chance.

I leaned over the rail. Just as I'd thought, Tim's little boat bobbed down there, tied securely this time; that floating-away stuff had just been a ruse to keep me from suspecting him of anything.

The water was still just as dark and cold, though, and it was just as far down as it had been, before. Oh, it all just looked impossible. But we did have one thing in our favor:

After tying us up with the loose ropes that had been all over the deck, Tim hadn't cut off the surplus.

That left a long stout line with . . . yes! A loop already at the end of it. We couldn't do what I was hoping for without one, and I couldn't have managed tying it with my own wrists still bound together.

Ellie and Lionel watched, not understanding, while I scooped the loop-end up in both hands and dropped it over another of the cleats on the *Jenny*'s rail.

"Okay, it's tight," I said. We'd already gotten our ankles out of their bindings by yanking and wiggling; painfully, and with the loss of a fair amount of skin, but we'd managed it. "Now we just need to untie our hands somehow."

"Oh, is that all?" Ellie said skeptically, but Lionel turned his back to me.

"Pocketknife. In my back pocket." My annoyance with him faded slightly, even more when the knife turned out to be sharp.

So I dealt with the ropes: clumsily, but he'd been too hurried to put our hands behind our backs before tying them, so I managed that, too.

"All right now, Lionel, you go first," I said, "and when you get down there, steady the boat. Hurry!"

He looked at me like I was nuts. "Are you kidding? I can't—"

One of the women huddled by the cannon lit another match. In a minute they were going to kill my husband and my son.

And then they'd kill us. "Lionel, if you don't go over that rail right this instant, I'll beat you unconscious and throw you over."

My cheery tone must've convinced him. He scrambled over the rail, surprising me with his agility, and in a moment despite his fears he was in Tim's boat.

"Now you." Ellie looked doubtful about leaving me, but: "Go on," I urged her, "I want someone down there with Lionel right away."

Because he must know that despite his apparent change of heart, he'd be in custody soon while everything got sorted out by the police—and depending upon *how* it got sorted, for a long time afterward.

"He's clever," I told Ellie, "and if he gets away from us, he's gone. And this last part I need to do might take me a minute."

Which was a lie; the truth was, I wasn't convinced I could do it at all. In fact, I was pretty sure I couldn't—and I didn't want her stuck here with me if I got caught.

She looked suspicious. But there was no time to argue, so she did it: over the side, down the rope, quick as a little monkey.

A glance told me she'd made it. Now it was just me against them. I wouldn't have the stomach to do what I'd planned by using the knife, though.

Some things—like not being able to stab people with a pocket-knife, for instance—you just know about yourself.

So I guessed I'd just have to do the rest of it the hard way, with my hands.

Eleven

I crept toward the stern, keeping to the shadows and ducking behind the deck chairs, when Amity Jones glanced around, getting almost within slugging distance.

Out on the water, the barge fired off three bright white flash-bangs and an enormous pinwheel, lighting the whole sky; I froze, waiting for darkness again, then eased forward a little more as Amity Jones fired up another match.

She was still trying to light that cannon. If she succeeded, the fireworks barge—with my husband and son on it, plus a lot of other Eastport fellows—would go up like a gunpowder factory.

And after that . . . "Tim knows what to do?"

It was Willetta Beck. I thought again how uncertain she sounded, as if this was all against her better judgment.

Amity, by contrast, sounded pleased with herself. "Oh, he knows, all right. He got this boat all the way up here from Portland, and once this part is done, he'll haul the anchor again and bring us back around so our stern faces town."

I listened in horror. So that's what Tim had been doing during his week away from here. And those smaller guns, I realized, the ones installed belowdecks with their ports set into the stern . . .

That's why the *Jenny* would be coming around: to fire them at the crowd onshore, one that by now included Mika, and my grandson, probably. And Bella and my dad. Everyone . . .

Fright flooded me, and with it came new determination. I had to stop this now . . . if I could. And if not—well, if not, then my life wouldn't be worth a hill of beans anymore, anyway.

So before I could talk myself out of it, I clenched my hands together, raised them over my head, and stepped up quickly behind the three women making their ghastly revenge plan.

Maybe I couldn't overpower all three of them at once, but I could disorganize them, and right now that's all I really wanted.

To make this work, I'd have to clobber one from behind, then hurl myself at the other two, bowling them over. Okay, now: *One, two . . .*

Not quite believing that I was doing it at all, I brought my two fists down hard on the back of Amity Jones's head. It felt as hard as an anvil, but—

"Oof," she uttered quietly, and dropped as if shot. Behind her, Karen Carrolton and Willetta Beck gaped in surprise.

But their startlement wouldn't last. I stepped back, gathering myself to charge, putting my head down and hunching my shoulders . . . and then I heard it: a soft, purposeful-sounding sizzle.

"Oh, holy criminy," I heard myself saying, and backed away fast.

Amity Jones must've finally got the fuse lit just before I hit her. And now that it was lit, there was no way to put it out, or not any that I knew.

Which meant that in moments Sam and Wade would be dead; Ellie's husband, too—blown to bits when the fireworks barge exploded. And all because I'd failed. I'd been so glad to see Tim Franco when he showed up, it simply hadn't occurred to me to wonder *why* I was seeing him.

But now it was obvious: it was what he'd been hired for, to run the *Jenny* while she was in Eastport and probably to pilot her out of here in the confusion after the mayhem happened. Even who she'd belonged to was starting to become more obvious: that well-equipped galley I'd seen had been built for just one person—but there was no time to ponder that, either.

The fuse sizzled hotly, a small, spitting red dot in the night's gloom. Then it stopped, and the two women still standing nearby peered down curiously at it, probably to see if it had gone out.

But it hadn't.

In the next instant a bright orange flash erupted around the cannon as the gunpowder ignited and a thunderclap smacked the world senseless. It smacked me, slamming me back hard against those heaped deck chairs and out of the way of what happened after that: the whole cannon *flew* backward, whizzing past me sputtering flame, just missing the *Jenny*'s mast to crash straight through the hatchway doorframe.

The hatchway collapsed on itself. Smoke spewed in black billows through the debris, and somewhere an alarm began honking. Frantically I looked over the rail for Ellie and Lionel, too stunned to think of anything else.

I didn't see them. Here on the *Jenny*, all three women who'd been plotting mass murder moments before now lay crumpled on the deck near where the cannon seemed to have ripped loose from its bolts, propelled by the gunpowder blast.

But they were all moving, and when I staggered unsteadily over to them, I found that the cannon hadn't hit them; they were just stunned.

Behind me the smoke from the demolished hatchway thickened ominously, tinged with yellow flame, and unless I was mistaken the deck had begun *slanting* . . .

Then I realized: The *Jenny* was sinking. I crouched by the women. "Are you all right? Can you get up? Because we've got to . . ."

I couldn't hear myself, and as for that crouch, it was more like a collapse.

Kids, don't try any of this at home.

"Listen, all of you, we've got to get off this boat." Hurriedly I turned Willetta Beck over onto her side so she was facing me.

Her mouth moved soundlessly. Then her eyes rolled back, becoming white. In the dark they were all I could see, and what they looked like is yet another thing I urge you not to try experiencing for yourself: yikes.

Even worse, though, was the sight of the shoreline when I looked up, because it was moving again.

We were moving. Also, the deck began vibrating with a distant mechanical chatter: *Those smaller guns*, I realized suddenly. The ones built into the *Jenny's* stern. The gunports Tim Franco and I had climbed past and that he'd commented on. . . .

Tim's at the helm, and he's turning the boat so he can fire those little guns at—

At everyone onshore. And when I say little, I only mean compared to the cannon.

Ellie appeared in the smoky gloom on deck. I jumped away, then recognized her.

"What're you doing? I thought you were—"

"Never mind, come with me," she urged. "Once it tips far enough, this boat's gonna roll, and we don't want to be here for that."

Yeah, no kidding. And she'd scrambled back up that rope to save me, hadn't she? Gratitude welled up in me, even though I didn't have a lot of time to spend luxuriating in warm-and-fuzzy feelings.

"What about them?" I waved at the women still sprawled on the deck, then noticed that Amity Jones wasn't with them.

"We can't just leave them here, can we?" I mean, sure, they were killers. But we weren't. And the boat was leaning a *lot*.

I seized the shoulders of the prone form lying nearest me;

Ellie looked impatient but bent to help. Then Amity Jones rose unsteadily from behind the deck chairs, now sliding across the ever-more-rapidly-tilting deck toward the opposite rail.

Amity looked stunned, but I still thought she could probably save herself without our assistance. Karen Carrolton was going to need help, though. Blood ran from her nose, and a big bump rose on her forehead.

The boat lurched again suddenly. I hauled Karen by her sleeves; Ellie already had Willetta Beck propped against the rail, which was a lot nearer the dark water than before as the boat listed acutely.

"Hurry!" called Ellie. "We'll dump them overboard, and someone onshore will come out and—"

"I'm coming!" I called back, but then I wasn't, as Amity Jones tackled me suddenly, spinning me to face her.

"Oh, no, you don't," she snapped, hurling me down and jumping on me. Eyes wild, she straddled me, reaching for my throat.

"You think you're so smart," she snarled. "Think you're so . . ."

Well, no, actually I didn't. See *mistakes I'd made*, above. But what I did think was that I'd had enough of this little bully.

So who knows, maybe in that moment there was some killer in me, too, as in one swift infuriated motion I drew my knees up, kicked my feet out, and slammed Amity Jones so hard in the chest that it was a wonder she didn't just fly up off that damned boat into the water.

Instead of getting pushed off, which is what actually happened.

I'm not going to go through all the details of hoisting those half-conscious women over the rail of a sinking boat, but it was no picnic. Each big splash was like a gut punch.

People onshore waded in to fish the floating forms out of the drink while Ellie, who'd pushed Amity Jones off the *Jenny* and jumped in after her, now grabbed Amity's hair and yanked her, fussing and fighting, into Tim's little rowboat.

When Amity saw the other small boats gathering and realized that her escape window was closing, she made even more of a ruckus, bucking and kicking until Ellie grabbed her feet and with a quick flip upended her right back into the water again.

This time I didn't feel sorry at all; I may even have dusted my hands together in satisfaction, watching Amity splutter.

But not for long, because the foundering vessel I was still on was now almost in position to fire those below-deck guns at the crowd. Like fish in a barrel.

"Go!" Ellie urged when I hesitated at the rail. *Jump*, I thought, but somehow I still just couldn't.

It wasn't far to the water with the *Jenny* so nearly capsized, and the smoke pouring from the hatch flickered sullen orange, encouraging me further. But there was something I had to do, something my frazzled brain still hadn't thought of . . . and then I had it.

"Phone!" I yelled. Ellie looked up at me as if I was even crazier than before, and by then I really was, of course. But Tim's phone had rung a little while earlier. That meant the phones were working again.

And *that* meant if only I could—

Find it. The two older women had already been ferried to safety; now the crowd onshore was fixed on the spectacle of Amity Jones, swimming *away* from a newly arrived dinghy whose occupant was trying to pluck her from the chilly water.

"Jake, damn it, get down here," Ellie said flatly.

Which gave me some pause, as did the new harder lurch sideways that the *Jenny* took, her deck so nearly vertical that I half expected an orchestra somewhere to start playing "Nearer My God to Thee."

But instead I finally found Tim's phone, which had slid under that pile of deck chairs. This time Bob Arnold answered at once.

"Bob? You've got to—"

A torrent of angry verbiage erupted from the phone as the deck *shivered* under my feet. And still those guns vibrated beneath it, too, their whine now audible between the shouts of the crowd.

Tim must be getting ready to fire them. Had to be, since soon they'd be under water. And so would we . . . but with the *Jenny* on top of us.

"Bob!" I tried interrupting his tirade.

I couldn't imagine how Tim thought he would escape. But things were happening too fast for me to worry about him.

"Jake!" Ellie cried urgently from below me on the water. "Come on! She's going over!"

"Bob, shut up and listen," I said into the phone. "Get the people away from the shore. He's got guns on this boat, Bob, and any minute he's going to—"

The phone went dead. Either Bob had gotten the message and hung up, or the little device had given up the ghost at last. With a curse I flung it away, scrambling uphill on the deck to cling to the rail.

"Ellie!" I yelled, but she didn't respond to me, instead staring past me in horror at something I hadn't yet seen.

But now I did. The fireworks barge, with at least a third of its original supply of fireworks on it, I estimated, had motored in toward shore without my noticing; well, I'd been a little busy, hadn't I?

Now the barge floated fifty yards from the *Jenny*, between us and the people onshore. So if those guns fired, they'd *all* get blown to bits, unless—

Suddenly Ellie appeared right there in front of me, drenched and furious, perched on the rail.

"Damn it, that's the last time I'm climbing that freaking rope," she said, only she didn't say "freaking."

"Promise me," she entreated. "Tell me that this time after I go, you'll jump, too."

So I promised. And then I pushed her. She went over the rail like an angel, arms outstretched, unafraid even after I gave her the shove.

"Promise me!" she cried again as she fell, and I called back, "I will!" And then . . .

And then of course I didn't.

I don't want to make it sound like I was . . . well, I was angry and scared, was all, and I think that something inside my head had already gone haywire. But the demolished remains of the hatchway leading below were in flames, and I wasn't about to jump through them. So I rummaged around on deck until I found a toolbox, and inside it—yes! Tools.

Then I scrambled precariously around to the *Jenny*'s foredeck, where I found still another hatchway door to the helm. It was locked like the first one, but a hard bash with the pipe wrench I'd grabbed out of the box took care of the darling little brass door latch that somebody had installed, and then I was through.

The boat slanted sharply, water lapping the deck. Tim sat in the captain's chair with his feet braced on the console so he wouldn't slide off.

He hadn't heard me; a sinking ship makes a lot of agonized creaking and groaning sounds, it turns out, like a body made of wood that is being torn limb from limb.

"Tim." Sweat-drenched and grimacing, he gripped the throttle in one white-knuckled hand and the wheel with the other. A rifle that I hadn't seen before leaned against the chair he sat in, but I couldn't quite reach it.

And anyway, there was no time; the boat *shuddered*. I grabbed his shoulder. Snarling, he shook me off without turning. He was still trying to steer while shoving the throttle forward desperately, but this ship wasn't going anywhere except down.

"Tim, it's over. We've got to get off right now or we'll—"

Drown, I was about to say, but before I could finish he slammed both fists down on two flat gray knobs mounted on the console.

The rattle of automatic weapons came from behind us, those ports in the stern, I realized. Bursts of gunfire were erupting from them. That's what the knobs were—firing buttons. Someone had reengineered this vessel very thoroughly, and not just in the galley kitchen.

"Tim!" I cried, hauling at him, but he left off leaning on those guns only long enough to shove me away.

I stumbled backward until my head hit something hard. The world flipped over, and suddenly I couldn't see straight. While my eyes were still struggling to refocus themselves, the guns fired again in a long murderous-sounding chatter.

Through the spray-smeared windshield the shoreline was almost vertical, we were over so far. Then water began rising up through the carpet on the floor, and I knew this was it; I had to get out *right now*.

But first I was going to end Tim Franco's deadly shooting spree—

Because I had to. Wade, Sam . . . and if those fireworks exploded so near to land, half the people onshore would be killed, too.

Gathering what few wits I had left, I wrapped my hand around that pipe wrench again. Then I raised it, which was when I finally realized how truly difficult it is, hitting a person on the head.

Emotionally, I mean. Like stabbing, I suppose, it just goes against the grain for most people. That was why I hesitated, and while I did so the most amazing thing happened:

The windshield burst inward, not shattering but crackling in a sudden starburst, then ripping away from its metal frame as something big hit it.

It was an anchor, as it turned out, and behind the anchor

loomed Lionel, rising in front of me like something vomited out of the water.

Pale, drenched, and shivering really hard, his curls hanging in wet, wormy tangles around his face, he looked like death, if death got really angry and crazy.

Dragging himself through the torn-open windshield frame, he grabbed Tim's throat with one hand and punched him so hard with the other that I thought Tim's eyes might fly out the back of his head like a cartoon character's.

But this was no cartoon. Cold water slopped around my ankles, and I kept sliding downhill, meanwhile trying desperately to climb toward the hatchway opening, not yet quite submerged.

But it was going to be. Lionel grabbed me and shoved me out through the windshield. On my way, I grabbed hold of the chain he'd unclipped the anchor from and hauled myself along it.

Waves churned foamily around me. The deck lurched as if trying to fling me off. I scrabbled for the rail, intending to leap over it.

Then Lionel heaved himself up through the windshield opening and began crawling toward me. Tim was still back there in the cabin as it filled with cold salt water. Lights bobbed toward us, boats coming to help. A spark of hope warmed my frozen heart. But then I saw him:

Tim clambered out and hoisted himself atop the cabin roof. There he stood, splay-legged, balanced unsteadily and lifting—

That rifle. Lifting and aiming it, straight at the fireworks barge . . .

"No!" I screamed, but too late. He squinted through the gunsight, and although I couldn't see his trigger finger tightening, I *felt* it. A bitter grin stretched his lips.

"No!" I cried again, and then the *Jenny*'s stern dropped abruptly, tipping the foredeck up hard and knocking Tim backward. Scrambling to save himself, he overcompensated, sliding forward and landing in front of me.

But he couldn't hold on. "Tim," I said, reaching out a hand.

He snatched at it, missed, slid downhill farther from me in the attempt. "Tim, crawl, damn it—"

His eyes implored me as he tried to obey, pumping his feet uselessly against the foredeck's wet, sharply inclined surface. Lionel hurled the end of the anchor chain wildly, hoping Tim could grab it.

But it was no good. Cracking and splintering sounds filled the air amidst the angry hissing of water reaching the fire that still raged somewhere belowdecks.

And then her stern went under. "Jump!" Lionel yelled. "Now, right now, we've got to—"

I got one leg over the rail and looked back, hoping to find that Tim Franco had somehow made it back up the slanting deck behind me.

But he hadn't. Now he clung desperately with one hand to the thin shaft of the doomed boat's slender radio antenna. Then it broke off, and he whirled away as if down a waterslide, vanishing into the waves.

He was watching me as he went, his eyes wide, pleading with me to help him. But there was nothing that I could do about it.

And then I did jump.

The last day of the Eastport Pirate Festival dawned clear and bright.

"Morning," said Wade, wrapping his arms around me as I stood at the bedroom window. "How're you feeling?"

"Excellent." I forced a smile, trying for the fiftieth time not to relive the awful moment when that cold water closed over my head.

The truth was, I felt as if I'd been hit by a ton of bricks. My head thudded, my throat was still raw from all the screaming I'd done the night before, and every muscle in my body hurt.

But I wasn't dead, which I could easily have been. "Fabulous," I added, pulling my clothes on.

It was only six in the morning, and I'd had about three hours of sleep, but downstairs in the kitchen the daily circus had begun and I didn't want to miss any of it; funny how when all of your minutes get nearly taken away from you, each one becomes so precious.

"Toast!" Ephraim's funny, fiercely determined little-boy voice floated up the stairs. "Toast, toast, toast, toast . . ."

Wade looked unfooled by my declarations of health. But he could also see that I didn't much want to talk about it.

Not yet. "So," he said instead. "There really is going to be another one, I guess."

Baby, he meant—Mika and Sam's. They'd broken the news after we all got home the night before. Which was early this morning, actually, but never mind.

Wade sounded just as conflicted about it as I felt. He loved little Ephraim as much as I did: truly, deeply. But if we put any more people in this house it might burst, and I still didn't know what to do about it.

Glimpsing my worried look, Wade changed the subject again. "There are two more mowers in the yard," he observed, peering past me out the window.

Yes, there certainly was another pair of riding machines out there, each with a mowing deck that looked as wide as a freeway. They'd been in the yard when we got home from the hospital.

I'd been taken there in an ambulance despite my protests. Once brought into the emergency room, I'd been looked over very thoroughly, with special attention to my poor noggin—not to mention the X-rays, reflex tests, various neurological examinations, an EKG, and intravenous fluids.

And as it turned out I'd probably had a concussion since I fell and hit my head on the rocks out at the campgrounds. Now I had strict instructions not to exert myself and to avoid a whole list of foods, drinks, and activities that might stress my bruised brain.

Not that I intended to follow many of those instructions, being as today I felt . . . well, not fine. But I was alive. And that, it seemed to me, was a lot to feel good about right there.

"So I guess they don't think I'm a murder suspect anymore," I said, bending to get my shoes.

Only about half my blood rushed up into my head, which made it feel as if it were about to burst like a balloon, and the rest dropped to my feet, which left my knees quivering weakly.

"Yeah, nearly being another victim does tend to dilute suspicion against you," said Wade, retrieving the other shoe from under the bed.

He motioned for me to sit, then slid the shoe gently onto my foot and tied it, and of course I didn't burst into tears at this kindness.

One did leak down my cheek, but I brushed it away quickly before Wade saw it. Bob Arnold had been kind, too, when he'd stopped by the house after we got home, regarding my cuts and bruises with horror.

"Bob filled you in on what Amity said, did he?" Wade asked. Even though it had been late, once he knew I was okay he'd gone back down to secure the rest of the fireworks, stowing them all in a padlocked closet at the Coast Guard station and keeping the key.

"Uh-huh." By the time Amity got yanked out of the frigid water in the boat basin she'd been so cold she'd been delirious, and gabbing about pretty much everything she'd been up to.

I gathered myself and stood, still waiting for what Wade wasn't saying—that is, what an idiot I'd been for ever getting onto the *Jenny* in the first place.

Or maybe it was me saying it, silently but emphatically. "Okay, now," I breathed, trying not to yelp when I moved.

Or when I breathed, or blinked, or . . . crossing the bedroom, I got a look at myself in the mirror. The red raised bump in the middle of my forehead made me appear to be trying to grow a third eye.

Note to self: Don't go jumping off any more boats. Cautiously, I began descending the hall stairs.

Walking down, the interesting sensation of being smacked by a bag of hammers returned, along with the suspicion that maybe that bump on my head was actually a hatchet wound: ouch. The pain went right into my brain, it felt like.

Wade followed me, collecting dropped toys and toddler clothing as he went: a stuffed frog, a small red shoe, a sweater—

An adult-sized sweater, emerald green. I plucked Ephraim's new stuffed parrot from its perch on the bannister, then took the sweater from Wade and put it on with a shiver.

"I doubt Bob Arnold was supposed to tell me anything," I went on in the kitchen as I poured coffee; yes, it was on the don't-drink-it list and, no, I didn't care.

The first sip was heaven; the brain cells that still worked came to life and the rest quit hurting. So much for medical advice.

"But he felt terrible, he said, like it was all his fault that I nearly drowned." Which I nearly had; that last leap I'd taken off the half-sunk *Jenny* hadn't worked quite the way I'd hoped.

For one thing, the boat had chosen that moment to turn over in a death roll, coming down almost on top of me.

Bella stood at the stove. Frizzy-haired and hatchet-faced in a pink chenille bathrobe, a pink hairnet, and pink fuzzy slippers, she was like someone's nightmare version of a kitchen goddess.

But she was *our* goddess, and in that moment I could have kissed her, I was so glad to see her. Just then my father came in, seized her by her bony shoulders, and did kiss her.

"Oh, you," she exhaled, escaping his try at dancing her around the kitchen but looking pleased nevertheless. She carried a platter of hot pancakes to the table, where it was at once pounced upon by Sam, coming out from behind his newspaper.

"Hi, Mom," he said, sliding a short stack from the platter onto his plate. Then he got a good look at me—bumped, bruised, et cetera—and his eyes widened.

"Never mind," I told him quietly, and he went back to his plate and newspaper obediently, not much to my surprise. We'd been together a long time, Sam and I; he'd seen me worse, and vice versa.

Bella clucked worriedly at me, but she also played it reasonably cool. Only her eyes threatened ice packs, poultices, and who knew what other old-timey home remedies, any and all of which I meant to put up with, no complaining, right after breakfast.

"Owie," said Ephraim, pointing at my forehead.

That's for sure. "Hey, buddy," I greeted my grandson, resisting the urge to sweep him from his high chair and dance *him* around the kitchen. Just being here with him at all was such a . . .

Well. A gift was what it was. But lifting him would've hurt too much—along the way I'd pulled my shoulder, probably as I was trying not to drown—and anyway, he was already busy again, hurling toast crusts and chortling each time Bella snatched one up off the floor.

"Good morning!" said Mika as she came in, shimmering through the prism of my sudden tears; it was good to be here.

Mika was wearing black slacks, another of those impossibly crisp white blouses of hers, and makeup that made her look even more like a blooming rose than she did without it. At seven a.m. she already had her glossy black hair swept up into a sleek twist and her satchel over her shoulder.

"You look great," Sam said appreciatively.

Smiling in return, she plucked a toast crust off her little boy's high chair tray, the way she did every morning, and ate it while making a lot of exaggerated yum-yum sounds as he watched, astonished.

The way he did every morning. Bella handed Mika a cup of coffee, light and sweet, the way *she* did every morning.

Then she delivered my father's pills with a glass of juice and supervised his swallowing them before starting on his pancakes.

The way *he* did . . . oh, you get the idea. "Now you eat every bit of that, old man," said Bella affectionately, and he bent to comply. On his own he'd have had a delicious breakfast of black coffee, a shot of brandy, and a cigar, and never mind any of the pills.

But like I've said, those two loved each other a lot. "And you," Bella told Sam unnecessarily, "drink that juice. And remember to take a sweatshirt to work with you. It's not the middle of summer anymore, you know."

I had no idea what any of us would do without Bella, or without my dad puttering around the house, either—if, for example, they moved into senior housing or got a place on their own.

But that didn't change the fact that we were so crowded here, we could barely move, and it was about to get worse.

"Okay, I'm out of here," said Mika. "See you at the Moose."

It seemed her morning sickness had passed, maybe even for good this time. She'd volunteered to open the shop this morning so Ellie and I could catch our breaths.

Which reminded me that I also didn't see how we'd manage without Mika. Or Sam. For one thing, I wasn't about to start mowing that big yard, and Wade wasn't, either.

At the door Mika paused. "Sam's got some more news for you, by the way," she told me with mischief in her eyes. "Bella and your dad have, too, if I'm not mistaken."

I must've looked puzzled.

"The four of us had a family conference about everything that's going on." Her expansive gesture took in the whole house. "Last night, after you and Wade went up to bed," she said before heading out the door with a jaunty wave.

By then Sam had forked up more pancakes and was covering them with maple syrup. Wade poured what was left of the coffee into his thermos and started a new pot; my dad pried a few blueberries out of his own pancakes and popped them into his great-grandson's mouth.

Really, I didn't see how I could do without any of it, and this time the tears really did threaten to fall. I turned to Bella.

"What did Mika mean just now?" I demanded. "And how come you guys had a family conference without me?"

But then, I hadn't been exactly available for consultation lately, had I? So they'd come to a decision without my input.

"Jake. Mika's right, there's something you need to know," Wade said, turning from putting his lunch pail together: bread, cheese, an apple, a chunk of chocolate. The same things he took every day.

"That's right," said Bella, while Sam beamed brightly at me and my father looked smug.

"Your stepmother and I have come to a decision," my father said. "We've told Wade about it already."

My heart sank. "Go on, just get it over with," I said, looking from his face to Bella's and back again. "If you two are going to go live somewhere else, you might as well just tell me so I can—"

Cry my eyes out. Wander around this big old house alone. Try and try again to get used to living life without—

"Go?" Bella looked shocked. "Why, don't be silly, child. What in the world ever gave you the foolish notion that we're going anywhere?"

Relief touched me briefly. But then I realized that must mean—

Sam. I peered questioningly at him. "I've been so busy, I didn't know you were even looking for your own place, but I guess that you and Mika must've found a—"

New home, I'd been about to finish, but he interrupted. "What? Ma, no, calm down. You've gotten the wrong idea."

"Idea!" shouted Ephraim, flinging away his spoon. Sam retrieved it, gave it back with a blueberry on it, then went on.

"Ma, I'm moving all the lawn equipment that's in the yard to one of the warehouses out at the boatyard."

"Oh," I said weakly as he continued.

"They're giving me the space in return for keeping the grass cut and the snow plowed out there, and so on."

I blinked. This wasn't at all what I'd been expecting. "But, Sam, that's only going to get rid of all the machinery you've got stashed here in the yard, so I don't see what good . . ."

"Also," said Wade, "we're going to be moving some things around a little in here. And," he added, "we'll be moving people."

My dad and Bella nodded together. "That's right, we're moving downstairs to Sam and Mika's room," Bella said, looking pleased.

From their large suite on the third floor, she meant; a bathroom, two bedrooms, and—

"And the kids are moving upstairs," she finished. "Your father and I decided they need the space more than we do."

But, but . . . "What about your painting studio?" I asked my dad. "Canvases and easels, brushes and turpentine and those big windows—"

The south-facing ones, full of all that great light. But he just patted my hand reassuringly with his gnarled, mottled one.

"Don't you worry about that any, my girl. I've been wishing for a man-cave . . ."

Once upon a time, his idea of a man-cave had had bomb-making stuff in it; now he gave the phrase an obligatory ironic twist, but I could tell that the idea of a place all his own had really captured his imagination.

"And Wade says he'll build me one out in the yard once all the machines are gone," he said.

It was a big yard. There'd be plenty of room. "With," he added, "a woodstove, big windows, even some skylights, maybe, and lots of storage."

"Don't forget the cutting table for canvas," said Wade. "And overhead racks for frame pieces, stretchers . . ."

My dad sighed happily at the prospect. "Well, all right, then," I said, still feeling a little stunned.

"Sounds like you've got it all pretty well arranged. You're sure, though," I pressed Bella, "that you're okay with . . ."

Less living space, smaller bathroom. She nodded emphatically as my dad eyed me more closely than before.

"That green sweater looks good on you," he remarked.

Something about his tone alerted me. "So?"

"So, go look in the mirror." He smiled enigmatically at me. I went into the hall and looked at myself in the oval mirror on the wall by the front door.

Dark wavy hair, pale skin, full lips . . . "Oh," I said softly, recognizing myself.

From my dad's painting, I mean. I don't know why I hadn't seen it before, that the woman whose likeness he'd captured from the old photograph was me. In a certain light, from a certain angle . . .

Through loving eyes. Just then Bob Arnold came in. Still blinking from my discovery, I went back out to the kitchen to hear what he had to say.

"So," he said, clasping his hands on the table as Bella poured him coffee, "it seems our buddy Lionel woke up this morning feeling chatty. Want to know what he had to say?"

Oh, I did. But: "Are you supposed to tell me?"

In all the upset of the night before, I understood his blabbing a few things. I didn't want him to get in trouble, though.

"*Pfft!*" remarked Ephraim, and Bob seemed to agree.

"Jake, if anybody from Augusta wants to come up here and yell at me about anything, they are free to do so."

He sipped coffee, savoring it. "*Entirely* free," he emphasized. "But meanwhile, our little friend Lionel's been thinking about his options."

More coffee. Then: "I mean the ones that consist of either telling the whole truth and nothing but or going to prison for a long time. And the way he explains it, the situation was pretty simple."

Huh. You could've fooled me. Bob put his cup down. "Lionel says Amity Jones hated Hadlyme ever since she got sent away to a state-run children's home after her mother and grandmother died, here in Eastport."

Yeesh, that didn't sound like fun. Bob went on: "Over the years she'd watched Hadlyme get successful, stewed over it, then read about him coming to Eastport with his new podcast crew."

Bella refilled his cup. "She decided that this was her chance to get the revenge she'd been ruminating on for so long," he continued.

"Because he'd abandoned them all," I said. "Her mother, Amity herself, and her younger brother—"

Bob nodded. "Right, her baby half brother, Lionel. Hadlyme was the reason behind her mom's suicide, too. Or murder. Whichever, she blamed Hadlyme for all of it."

He took a breath. "He hatched a plan, got in touch with Lionel, who had his own reasons for despising Hadlyme, and recruited him."

"But how?" Wade wanted to know. He'd been standing at the counter listening. "Why would Lionel believe she could make such a wild plan fly?"

Bob shrugged. "She's a fast talker, in case you hadn't noticed. Very convincing, and she told him a lot of things he wanted to hear, I guess. She's a real cop, by the way. She wasn't faking that."

Oh, of course she was; had to be. If she hadn't been, real ones would've showed up, wouldn't they? And Bob was right about her being convincing when she wanted to be.

"None of the others could've lifted that antique cannon," Wade pointed out. "Lionel or Tim probably grabbed it off the porch."

I'd have snorted, but it hurt too much; my headache was back, and the rest of me didn't feel so peppy, either.

"Like the *Jenny* didn't have enough guns already," I said. Also, I was pretty sure Amity Jones could've lifted the cannon. Before I could say so, though . . .

"And Lionel admitted to me that he took the sword," added Bob. "From that weapons demonstration you put on, just like you thought. As for Amity, once she had Lionel on board, she recruited Karen Carrolton and Willetta Beck. Only not by persuading them."

I recalled Willetta Beck's voice the night before: tremulous, reluctant. Not having fun at all, and even the sturdy Karen Carrolton hadn't seemed enthusiastic. "She threatened them, didn't she?"

Bob nodded. "Sure did. And she got Tim to drive that white car around for her, scare you and Ellie, and run Willetta off the road, too, to let her know Amity's threats were serious. Turns out it's a rental that Amity paid Tim to drive over here from Bangor."

"Just the way Hadlyme must've paid Tim to bring the *Jenny* up here for him, from wherever he'd kept her?" Wade guessed aloud.

Although it wasn't really a guess. I'd told Wade the night before about the fancy galley kitchen in the vessel.

"Yeah." Bob sounded disgusted. "The boat's Hadlyme's. Some rich guy's toy, it was. Big-time weapons collector on Long Island, he put all those guns in it and rejiggered the helm, then got tired of it, sold it. Hadlyme redid the galley. And Tim Franco . . . man, don't even get me going about *him*."

He finished his coffee. "Yeah, I know, speak no ill of the dead. But for him I'll make an exception. Although . . ."

"What, Bob?" Bella asked. Tim's grandmother had been talking to her, and if there was any fact that might make Tim sound not quite so much like a monster, she'd want to know it, I gathered.

Bob shrugged. "Tim had money troubles. I mean." He held up his hands. "Big ones, not just his usual."

I must've looked skeptical. "Seems he owed money to the IRS. Always got paid cash, hasn't ever paid income taxes, it turns out."

That kind of stuff had been my job, long ago in the city. So I understood. "They've been hassling him for a while, and now they want all the money or else." I summed up the way it usually went.

Bob nodded. "Ayuh. They'd brought out the big knives. If he didn't pay up, he was on his way to the hoosegow. The *federal* hoosegow. But then Hadlyme found him. Seems he'd called the Chamber of Commerce looking for somebody like Tim who could run a boat."

"And Hadlyme offered Tim a way out? Paid him to run the *Jenny*. Then Amity Jones, once she got wind of Timmy, offered him even more?"

Bob nodded sadly. "But at the end, there, it was just that he'd . . . I don't know. Shooting at us all, people he'd known all his life, then practically committing suicide. Might as well have shot himself, the way he wouldn't get off that boat until too late."

At the mention of suicide, I thought again of poor Anna Benoit. We'd never know for sure, of course, but in my opinion she hadn't been murdered.

From what Willetta Beck had said, it seemed all but certain that the desperate young woman had simply leapt to her death from the Deer Island ferry, leaving her two children to people she must've believed—wrongly, of course, and so sadly that I could hardly bear thinking of it—would be able to care for them better.

Bob got up. "I'd say Tim Franco broke under a lot of different pressures, if I believed in that kind of thing," he said, echoing what I was thinking about Anna. Then, looking around at us:

"Anyway, there were a thousand ways it all could've gone wrong for the whole bunch of them," he said, "and considering how it ended, I guess a few of those things did. Luckily for us."

"Crazy," said Sam, folding his newspaper. "None of them could have done the whole thing alone, but together . . ."

Right. Teamwork. Like here in our house. Wade's eyes met mine, and I knew he thought the same.

"But the parrot," Bella objected, "how'd they get the stuffed parrot?"

Ephraim's face scrunched up ominously. Wade stuck a bit of chocolate into the boy's downturned mouth, which curved up again.

"Ephraim and I were down there that day, weren't we?" Sam looked at Bella for confirmation.

"On the breakwater for the weapons demo, I mean, and Ephraim might've had the parrot then."

Sure, now he tells me. "None of that explains how Hadlyme got into The Chocolate Moose's cellar," said Ellie from the hall. I hadn't heard her come in.

"Oh, that's easy," Bob answered. "Amity had checked out the Moose and picked Jake for the scapegoat after she visited a week earlier."

He got up from the table, ruffling Ephraim's hair affectionately as he went by. "She already knew from Lionel that Henry Hadlyme picked fights wherever he went," he added.

"And she figured we'd butt heads eventually?"

Bob nodded. "Which you did, exactly like she expected, so you'd look like you had a motive. But if you hadn't argued with him, well, there was no reason there couldn't be a change of plan."

"If she'd had to, she could've *made* me argue with him," I said. Then added acidly, "By just putting me within fifty feet of him."

My father had left the room while Wade was rinsing his breakfast things. Now Sam was gathering himself to go off to work and Ephraim was falling asleep, his little head sagged sweetly to one side.

"Your leaving that cellar door unlocked was just the cherry on the cake," Bob finished. I grimaced guiltily, then winced as my whole face protested this careless movement of banged-up body tissues.

"Lionel lured him down the alley under the awnings, where Amity was waiting. I don't know what they told him, so don't ask me. But they got the door open and muscled him inside. We know she'd meant to crowbar it if it was locked, because we found the bar in her cruiser's trunk."

He put his cup in the sink. "According to Lionel, Amity was the one who ran Hadlyme through the heart, then perched the parrot on his corpse."

"So *Lionel* says," Bella remarked skeptically, but before Bob could answer, his phone chimed.

"Damn, the little bastard's escaped," he said, and moments later he was outside in his squad car, zooming off down the street.

"But where would he go?" Ellie wondered aloud.

She'd brought along some crispy bacon strips that she'd dipped into dark melted chocolate, and I recommend that you sit down before biting into one of these. They're so good, you'll fall down, otherwise.

"I mean," she said, "we're not like the big city here. It's not as if he could just call a cab and—"

I thought about it: a young, not very emotionally sturdy guy like Lionel, the father who'd abandoned Lionel's mother and then Lionel himself . . . and now Lionel was in trouble. So what would the traumatized son of the murdered man want most right now, I wondered.

And then I had it: what deep down he'd probably wanted all along. Ephraim woke up, reaching fretfully for his dad as I spoke.

"Somebody call Bob," I said. "I think I might know where Lionel is."

* * *

We drove to the campgrounds in Wade's pickup truck and pulled over where he'd parked the last time we were here, under the big pines. The podcast crew members' cars were gone, but the big RV that Henry Hadlyme had lived in was still here.

Crossing the gravel driveway to where it bulked in the bright morning sunshine, I hoped we weren't too late. "Lionel? Are you here?"

I rattled the door handle. It was locked, but the hatch on the empty cargo area at the massive vehicle's rear was still open, just as it had been when we last saw it.

"I don't think knocking will work, do you?" Ellie said quietly.

Shaking my head, I climbed up behind her into the dim, cavernous cargo space. The low sliding door into the living area moved easily; inside, we crawled through a closet and out onto the bedroom floor.

Sunshine slanted hazily in through the window onto the room's high-end fixtures: king-sized bed, real wood trim, marble in the bath. The living area was the same as I recalled, also: leather upholstery, polished brass, massive wall-mount TV.

"Lionel?" I ventured into the stillness.

"Over here," said Ellie. Between the bathroom and the living area was a walk-in closet, still holding the same drawers, hangers, a full-length mirror on the wall . . .

And Lionel, crouched in a corner with his face in his hands. Wrapped in his arms he had the red leather jacket I'd seen that day on his father.

I crouched by him. "Lionel? Lionel, come on, now. You'll have to do it eventually, right? So get up and we'll help you."

Wearing a plaid flannel shirt, brown corduroys, and Hush Puppies on his feet, he let out a bitter chuckle of skepticism and buried his face farther into his arms.

"Come on, now," I repeated. "It's okay. It's all going to be all right."

Maybe, I added silently. If he hadn't done the actual deed, he might manage to plead guilty to some lesser involvement, testify against his half sister, and get off with a lesser punishment.

"Lionel," I persisted, and finally, after many more platitudes and half truths that he was too upset to recognize for what they were, he struggled to his feet.

Slowly, almost tottering, he let me guide him out to the living area, where he sat shakily on the edge of one of his dad's leather chairs.

"Did you kill him?" Ellie cut to the chase.

"No!" He looked shocked. "They'll see, Amity did it. I saw her do it and there'll be her fingerprints on the—"

He stopped, realizing what he'd just said: that he'd been there and hadn't stopped it.

A heavy sigh rushed out of him. "Yeah, I was there," he added dully. "I was supposed to do it myself, that's what we'd agreed on, but when I couldn't, she—"

"Okay, never mind that," I cut in. "What about the aunts, Karen and Willetta? How'd they get hooked into this?"

I already knew, but I wanted to hear it from him.

He shook his head. "Short answer is, she bullied them into it. See, Aunt Karen's got a criminal history, an old assault case that kind of went dormant somehow."

I glanced at Ellie, who shrugged: *I don't know.* But Karen was no pushover; running that half-wild homestead of hers took guts. So I could imagine it happening.

"Karen said she'd been defending herself and never should've been charged," Lionel went on. He seemed relieved to be talking; I thought again that, really, he was just a kid.

"I don't know details," he added, "but Amity said that because she's a cop she could get the authorities interested in Karen again."

Which I guessed maybe she could have. "And Karen hated Hadlyme, anyway," said Ellie, to which Lionel nodded emphatically.

"Willetta did, too," he agreed. "But what Amity told her to make sure she stayed in line was scary. She said bad things could happen to her horses, maybe a fire in the barn or something, unless she helped with all this."

I let out a deep breath. "And what about you, Lionel? When Amity told you her plan, did you really think that somehow it would help you two reconcile?"

Him and his father, I meant. Lionel looked surprised that I'd figured this out, seeming not to have realized how obvious it was, what he'd really wanted all along.

"No," he said finally. Tremulously. "I didn't think holding him at sword-point would make him like me better, okay? I'm not quite that stupid."

His voice strengthened. "All I wanted . . . all I ever *wanted*," he repeated urgently, "was for him to *listen*. I wanted to know he'd heard me, that for once that son of a bitch understood what he'd done."

But then he put his face back down in his hands. "But when I hesitated, Amity grabbed the sword from me and . . . and . . ."

Yeah. I could imagine the rest of it. Just one more thing:

"She was a cop, Lionel. Why would she leave behind a murder weapon with her fingerprints on it?"

Could she have thought that because she was on the job, she wouldn't be suspected? But that didn't make sense, and the answer when Lionel finally produced it was something else entirely.

"She couldn't get the sword out. Of his body, I mean. It was stuck in his ribs. Then we heard someone upstairs, so we had to get out of there fast, back down the alley into the crowd, and . . ."

He was getting his wind back. I could tell by the way he kept glancing at the door. "So she wiped it, but probably not well enough."

Suddenly I didn't like the feeling in the room, and it didn't help when he began eyeing the big knife rack over the RV's marble-topped kitchen counter.

Luckily just then Bob Arnold pulled in. The siren whooped once just to let us know he was there; he must've seen our vehicle.

Lionel bit his lip, straightened his shoulders, and prepared to run. I could see it in his whole body. But:

"Lionel," I said, "you're alone, feeling lousy, and I'm guessing close to penniless by now, too." That hit home. "Also that flannel shirt you're wearing won't do you much good later tonight when it gets cold."

All of which was true, and I could see in his defeated eyes that he knew it. So he didn't run.

Not yet.

Twelve

What was left of the fireworks got augmented by donations from the Fourth of July Committee, their celebration having been rained out the summer before. So a week later, we all trooped down to the waterfront to see the show.

Boom! Ephraim's eyes widened as a pink-petaled peony flared on the sky, dripping sparks. Right behind it came another explosion, this time from a white flashbang; luckily the baby wore ear protectors.

I wished I had some. "What?" I called back to Bob Arnold.

Water Street was jammed with wide-eyed people wearing jackets and hats, many with little kids perched on their shoulders. Bob gestured and mouthed something at me from where he stood by his squad car.

"What?" I said again when I'd reached him.

Older children ran in excited packs, sparklers and Silly String cans clutched in their hands. Bob leaned against his car, chewing a toothpick and watching the crowd.

"Thought you might want to hear some news," he said.

His gaze kept roving from one little group of fireworks

watchers to the next, but casually; his deputies were on duty tonight, and so far nothing was exploding, no one was shooting guns or firing cannon ammunition in the wrong direction, and nobody was getting stabbed.

So he could relax; well, as much as he ever did.

"Lionel escaped again," he said, his toothpick-chewing stilling as he waited for a toddler fleeing toward the fish pier to be caught and returned to his parents.

Whoosh, the dad snatched the kid up just in time for a pinwheel of flame to go rolling across the night sky. A spattering of applause rose from the crowd.

"Deputies were transferring him from county jail to Augusta this afternoon. He was so calm and polite, and I guess persuasive about it, that they uncuffed him so he could use the restroom on the way."

Bob didn't say what he thought about that, but I knew. Those deputies did, too, by now; their supervisors would have explained it.

Still: "But I thought—"

Boom! A dozen white stars exploded into a fan pattern overhead. Then Ellie appeared at my side. "Jake, did you hear . . ."

"Yes," I said, still puzzled by what Lionel had done. Escaping was silly if he'd been coaxed and/or bullied into the whole let's-kill-Hadlyme idea and hadn't ever really wanted to do it himself.

And, more important, that he hadn't done it himself, as the fingerprint evidence would show if his story was true. So why lie, and more to the point right now, why try to escape?

Especially since it was cold out at night already here in Maine. I hunched into my jacket, wishing I'd put on a light jacket and maybe even long underwear.

"I don't get it. A decent defense attorney could get a lot of mileage out of him just being an accessory."

But then I stopped. "Oh," I breathed, "you mean he—"

Bob nodded, watching a teenager on a bike thread through the crowd, then turned back to me.

"They let him out at the snack bar on Route 9 to answer the call of nature."

He lit one of the little cigars he occasionally allowed himself and puffed on it, then went on.

"Got back near the squad car. Ready to get in, Lionel elbowed one guy in the face, grabbed the gun off the other one, and hightailed it into the woods."

The place he'd picked to try making a run for it didn't bode well for Lionel, either; in Maine, the forests that line the sides of the highways aren't the scrubby back lots of nearby subdivisions. They're the edges of million-acre forests.

Strings of *pop-pop-pop!* flashes erupted over the dark water. Out on the barge, Wade and Sam and the other men lit the fuses and kept the fireworks aimed safely away from shore.

"Still, though, maybe he was just—"

Scared, I was about to finish, but Bob interrupted. "They located him as he was circling back around to the snack bar parking lot."

To grab the car, I guessed. He nodded, seeing me get it.

"And when they spotted him," Bob went on, "he fired the weapon at them several times. *Several* times. Pretty fine shot he turned out to be, too."

I rolled my neck around, wincing at the twinges of head pain each creaky movement still produced. The events of last week were going to take a while to wear off, and not just from my body.

"Darn," I said. "Those fingerprints on the cutlass that killed Henry Hadlyme are going to turn out to be Lionel's after all, aren't they?"

Bob nodded, eyeing the cigar, which had gone out. Shrugging, he dropped it into his shirt pocket. "Yeah, you know, I'll just bet they will."

He got into his car. "Anyway. You two just try to stay out of trouble tonight, okay?"

Ellie and me, he meant. He dropped the car into reverse. "As for me, now that the bing-bang-boom portion of tonight's program is almost over, I'm going home to get some sleep."

A barrage of multicolored lights turned the night sky fiery, accompanied by artillery blasts so concussive that I felt as if I were being punched repeatedly in the chest.

But that was the finale, and when the last sparks fell spitting and flickering to the dark water, the show was over. Murmuring, the crowd began drifting away, quite a few of them toward The Chocolate Moose.

So Ellie and I went there, too, to sell the dream bars, milk chocolate spinwheel cookies, and chocolate-cream-filled éclairs that Mika had been making all day just for this evening.

Inside, the air was warm and heavy with the aroma of baking. "Oh, this is so much fun!" beamed Mika from behind the counter. She really was feeling better, and I hoped the phase of expectant motherhood would last.

Smiling, she handed over a little boy's purchase; biting into his éclair, he marched out with his face full of the simple pleasure of running around outside with his friends after dark on a school night, eating chocolate.

Then Wade and Sam came in, with Ephraim grinning and babbling in Sam's backpack carrier. Behind them were Bella and my dad, and George Valentine brought up the rear.

Wade dropped his arm around me. "Gang's all here," he observed.

With Sam's help, Mika brought out another tray of éclairs. They were selling like . . .

Well, like chocolate éclairs, actually; the pirate festival had been over for a week, but the bell over the door jingled steadily with local customers going in and out.

"Mom," said Sam once he and Ephraim were settled, "I saw

Karen Carrolton and Willetta Beck watching the fireworks just now."

Both their pictures had been in the paper, even though they'd been released without charges.

"I still don't get why this Amity Jones person wanted the old ladies involved in her plot in the first place," Sam added. "I mean, they didn't do anything, did they? Not really."

Which is why they'd been let go. "No, they didn't. They were for backup, in case blaming me went wrong. A pair of spare scapegoats so Amity could *say* they had done things, maybe even the murder itself."

Because alone they couldn't have done it, but together the two older ladies might have managed the deed.

"And Amity stayed with them, used their houses for . . . well, for her hideouts, I guess you'd call it," I added. If she'd stayed at the Motel East in town, her every move would've been under observation.

"So all she really had to manage was not being seen in town the morning of the murder."

Although if she had been seen, she'd have had a lie to cover that as well, I imagined; she could just say she was here for the festival, for instance, if anyone asked.

My dad sat at one of our cast-iron café tables, munching a brownie while across from him Bella sipped the Moose's newest offering in the drinks department, a double-chocolate ice-cream soda.

"Tomorrow we'll start redistributing them," said Wade. People, he meant; our family members, into their new rooms in our big old house.

"I'm really glad," he added, "that nobody's going to leave."

Me too. Together we stepped outside, where the faint scent of gunpowder was being replaced by the familiar smells of the coming autumn in downeast Maine: wet leaves, chilly salt water, and a hint of woodsmoke.

Across the bay, tiny lights twinkled on Campobello. Wade wrapped his old denim jacket around my shoulders, then bit into the chocolate macaroon Mika had tossed to him on our way out.

"Oh, that's good," he said happily, looping his arm around my waist and offering me a bite.

I took it and let the taste linger on my tongue: sweet.

Double-Chocolate Ginger Cookies

Sometimes you just want a dozen fabulous chocolate cookies! Here you go:

Ingredients

¼ stick of butter (⅛ cup)
1 cup plus ⅓ cup chocolate chips
1 egg
¼ cup light brown sugar
1 teaspoon vanilla
¼ cup chopped crystallized ginger
⅜ cup self-rising flour
About 2 ounces white chocolate, coarsely chopped

Preheat the oven to 350°F. Melt the butter and 1 cup of the chocolate chips together, stirring constantly, over low heat. While the butter and chocolate cools, combine the egg and sugar in a mixing bowl, beating until completely blended. Add the vanilla to the butter and chocolate mixture, then add this mixture to the mixing bowl. Stir in the chopped ginger, then add the flour. Finally stir in that last ⅓ cup of chocolate chips.

Place 12 equal-sized spoonfuls of batter onto an ungreased baking sheet, spacing them out equally. (This should use up the batter.) Press pieces of white chocolate into the top of each unbaked cookie. Bake for 12 to 13 minutes.